SUMMER OF '58

SUMMER OF '58

JANICE GILBERTSON

P
Pen-L Publishing
Fayetteville, Arkansas
Pen-L.com

DEDICATION

My Parents

Those who thought I could

Brave girls

CHAPTER ONE

$\mathcal{A}$t twenty minutes until six on the first Friday morning of June, Angela Garrett sat on the edge of the chair nearest the front door, waiting. Two cars had passed by on the street in front of the wood frame house with the big porch, and both times Angela had shot up from her perch with the flutter of a nervous bird. She tilted her head toward the screen door and listened as their engine noise faded away to silence and then sat back down again. He had promised her he would be there by six.

"You be ready, now. This big old car won't wait." He had flashed his boyish grin and gently shaken her shoulder when he warned her, but she knew he meant what he said.

Odd, then, that as she waited she would be so filled with the anticipation of what was to come when she had no realistic notions of what that might be. Being so unworldly, so naive about what kinds of places and types of people existed beyond the countryside that bound her small hometown, did not keep Angela's heart from hammering inside her chest. When a girl is just twelve and has known only the beauty of the land and the kindness of nearly every human who has touched her life, why would she, or could she, think it to be different anywhere else?

Her mother's shabby suitcase, packed tight with jeans, shirts, and every undergarment and pair of socks without holes she could scrape up, sat out on the porch. Next to it, a cardboard carton printed with the words "CONTENTS: ONE DOZEN TOILET TISSUE" in blue letters on all four sides held a few comic books, a pink plastic container with some personal items she had snatched up, including the tube of Revlon Rosebud lipstick from her mother's dresser, her warm coat, and then her pillow stuffed on top. From her place in the living room, Angela could hear her mother moving about in the kitchen—the thunk of cupboard doors, the clink of the coffee canister lid, and the slipping-slide and metallic rattle of the silverware drawer. She knew the routine by the sounds, but she tried to ignore them so she could concentrate on the arrival of Lanny Ray's big car. The squeak of the faucet handle and the wet, hollow sound of water filling the metal coffeepot annoyed her for a moment, and then she felt guilty—and sad. She and her mother had hardly spoken since Arlene had come out of her room and discovered Angela already up and dressed.

"Well, you're looking ready to go this morning, sweetie," Arlene had said, trying to keep the glumness out of her voice. She had smiled a nice smile at Angela, but her eyes were red rimmed and puffy, and they didn't smile with her mouth. She had nearly made herself crazy during the night, second-guessing her rash decision to let Angela go away with her father. It was too long. She should have spoken up, said to him, "No, it's just too long." But she hadn't, and now it was too late. It wouldn't be fair to her daughter to change her mind now, and it was only she who mattered.

Angela watched the clock on the wall tick the minutes away, counting the seconds of them inside her head. Ten minutes until . . . five minutes until . . . and at six o'clock exactly, she heard his car pull up. Her stomach quivered, and her mind played a startling trick on her—maybe she shouldn't go with him after all. She didn't want to hurt her mother's feelings, and she knew her mom was worried. So worried. But then, there he came, clomping up the porch steps and peeking through the screen door like a boy coming to play.

"Hey, kid!" his voice filled up the living room. "You ready? Where's your ma?"

"I'm right here, Lanny Ray. You don't need to wake the whole neighborhood."

"This here's all you got, Ang? This ain't much for a long trip." He saw the questioning look on Angela's face and quickly shrugged his own comment away. "Ah, don't matter. We have to do our washin' along the way, anyhow." He picked up Angela's suitcase and the box and headed out to the car, carrying them effortlessly, as if they weighed nothing. Angela followed, and Arlene came behind, tightening the belt of her robe and twisting the soft sash in her fingers. Lanny Ray unlocked the vast cave of a trunk and put Angela's things beside his own large suitcase, his chaps neatly laid on top, and, back in the corner, his saddle bronc rig.

Suddenly, Arlene felt as though she had so much to say to her girl. Too much. Words came spewing out.

"Call me. Promise. Anytime. Well, not midday but, you know, after work. After five. Unless, of course, it's an emergency, then call anytime, okay? Promise me."

"I promise." Angela tried to look past her mother's face so she wouldn't see the concern.

"And try to eat decent, and go easy on sodas and junk. And I want that head of hair washed. It's so pretty when it's nice and clean." She ran her fingers through the dark, soft curls. "Don't let it get oily. Brush your teeth twice a day, same as you do here at home. Oh, Ang, what have I done?" Her face crumpled, and her fingers fluttered around her mouth, and Angela thought her mom was going to cry hard.

"Arlene, she'll be fine. She will. I'll take good care of her." Lanny Ray headed around to the driver's side of his Olds.

"Wait! Just one minute. Don't go. I'll be right back." Arlene ran up the steps, slippers slapping at her heels, letting the screen slam behind her. Angela glanced at her father and stood there, feeling awkward. Arlene came hurrying back with a bundle in her arms and thrust it at

Angela. "Here, hon. Take this with you. Your great-grandma gave it to me, and she'd be tickled for you to have it along while you're travelin'. I just know she would."

"Come on, Ang. Get in here so we can get goin'." He sat behind the wheel and leaned across the wide seat so he could see his ex-wife and daughter try for another hug with the quilt between them.

It was exquisite, the quilt. All put together with tiny hand stitches, as fine and perfect as any could be. The fabric, mostly floral, showed soft little flowers in blues and purples and gold. It felt cool and as smooth as silk where it lay against Angela's bare arms. Tears came to her eyes, and as soon as she put her face into the quilt to hide them from her mother, she smelled the pure cedar scent of the chest it had been stored in.

Angela turned away to open the back door, and she laid the quilt gently on the seat before swinging the door closed. She used both hands to tug the heavy front car door open and slid onto the seat.

"I'll be fine, and I'll call all the time. Don't worry." With those words, she pulled the big door closed with a thud. Lanny Ray stepped on the gas and waved a hand without looking back, and Angela watched her mother grow smaller in the rearview mirror.

At the corner, Lanny Ray made a left-hand turn toward Main Street. The big car swooped smooth as a breeze onto River Street and glided to a stop at Main. Angela's insides went giddy when she looked down Main Street. Everything—absolutely everything—about this morning had strangeness to it. Main Street was near empty and, in the faint light of dawn, had the eerie feel of a ghost town. One lonely car sat at the curb in front of the Blue Moon Café. In the opposite direction, the Burger Palace appeared dark and gloomy, and the faded pink milkshake glass, cut from plywood, looked tacky atop the building. The froth of the whipped cream painted on the picture, dirty-white and peeling, had a cherry on top that was so faded, without its red neon light one would hardly notice it. The big car with its hydroglide steering and suspension floated them past the Blue Moon, where Angela could see the warm lights glowing inside and the empty counter and booths. The sign on the door said "Open."

When they drove past the Five and Dime Store, Angela felt a lump form in her throat. The store had been her mother's place of work for the past few years, and it seemed odd to Angela that Arlene would be going there, just as she always did, on this morning. She had a vague feeling everything here in Jewel should stop and wait for her while she was away.

Angela felt relieved to see that the two old men who sat daily on the bench in front of the Mercantile weren't there at this hour. They would know soon enough that she had left town with her father, and they would spread the news like hawkers. Then, just before the big car rolled out of town past the city limit sign, they passed Jake's Place. The old bar looked shabby without the colorful beer signs and the one light over the door. Angela looked away so an old impression wouldn't linger on her mind.

Neither she nor Lanny Ray spoke for a long time. She'd watched the edge of town roll by in the morning dimness, but soon clean, clear light pushed up from behind the mountains in the east, and long shadows threw themselves across the narrow, paved road in front of the fence posts and telephone poles. The two-lane road ran for miles through the pastures and barbed wire fences stretching into the distance.

Lanny Ray rolled his window down a few inches and let the breeze flutter in, and they breathed in the perfume of morning. Angela stole sneaky glances at her father and came to the conclusion he looked happy enough about having her along. He caught her in a glance and smiled kindly.

"We'll stop for breakfast in a couple of hours. A place I always stop. They have pretty good food there. Maybe you can get ya some hotcakes."

"Okay," Angela said.

"Warm enough, are ya?" Lanny asked her.

"I'm okay," she said when, actually, she was a bit chilly. She'd rather die there in the car's seat than complain about something so trivial.

"Boy, I hope you don't talk this much the whole time we're gone." He flashed her a smile.

Angela relaxed, leaning her head back and watching the green pastures dotted with cattle and hay fields go by. She hoped her mother wouldn't stay too sad about her leaving. They had never been apart like this before. In fact, Angela had not left Jewel since she'd been too young to remember. Her parents had divorced the year she turned eight, and, eventually, Arlene had gone to work to make ends meet. Lanny Ray's life revolved around the rodeo circuit, which ran through the summer months, and he worked on local ranches the rest of the year. If he rode his broncs and made some good money, he gave plenty to Arlene, but winning a lot of money wasn't something to be counted on. They never had extra money for travel vacations, and Arlene couldn't miss work.

Angela never felt as if she were missing out on anything by not going away somewhere. She knew most of her schoolmates took vacations to faraway places like California or over into Arizona. One family had driven all the way to New York when their kids were only ten and twelve years old. But that had been back before Angela knew anything about New York.

Angela didn't realize she had dozed until Lanny Ray steered the car off the pavement, and the rattle of gravel under the car startled her awake. She looked to see if he noticed her sleeping, but he didn't let on. Lanny pulled into a line of cars on the side of a ramshackle building with broad windows displaying neon beer signs, shut the engine off, and stretched his arms up with a soft groan. They left the car and made their way around to the front where a flyspecked sign beckoned them—"Do come in. We're always open." Lanny told Angela where the restrooms were on the back of the building and said he would go on in and get them a place to sit.

Angela smelled the oily odor of diesel and exhaust and felt the rumble of the engines from the trucks out in the big lot. Once she finished in the restroom, she walked back around the building and stepped inside where the odors of coffee and fried bacon greeted her.

She saw her father sitting at the horseshoe-shaped counter, talking with the waitress. They were laughing about something when Angela slipped into the chair next to Lanny Ray's. She saw the waitress give Lanny a big wink with heavy black eyelashes before moving off to refill coffee mugs. They both decided on what to eat and were ready to order when she came back.

"Who's this little gal ya got with ya, Lanny Ray? She sure must be related to you. She's got those big, beautiful brown eyes of yours." She flashed a big smile full of pretty white teeth.

"Mickey," Lanny Ray said, "This here is my daughter, Angela. Ang, this is Mickey. She's been a friend of mine for quite a long time."

"Hello," Angela said in the polite manner she been taught to use. She thought Mickey looked pretty in a way. Her makeup was heavy, and her brown eyes had a thick, black line drawn around them. Her lips wore a heavy coat of pale-pink lipstick. She wore her platinum hair pulled into a neat French roll. Angela thought she looked like a movie star.

Mickey only glanced at Angela. "Friend? I guess you could say that, Lanny Ray. Close friends, I would say." And she winked at him again. An awkward moment of silence hung in the air until Lanny told Angela to go ahead and order her breakfast. He did the same while Mickey scribbled on her ticket book and, with a toss of her head, left to turn their order in to the cook.

Angela sat quietly and looked around the room. The dingy walls were yellowed with nicotine and cooking grease. A sign above the cook's window said "Western Omelets, $1.99" in loopy handwriting. What caught Angela's eye was the jukebox over in one corner. She asked Lanny if she could go look at the songs. He fished a dime out of his pocket and gave it to her. She ran a finger up and down the lists of song titles, recognizing most of them. They were all country songs, her favorite. She finally pushed F1 and waited until the record dropped onto the turntable. "How Much Is That Doggie in the Window" played.

As Angela returned to her seat, Mickey hovered over her father again and spoke to him in a soft voice. Their intimacy made Angela feel uncomfortable. She was relieved when she and Lanny Ray finished eating and went to the register to pay. Angela stepped out of the door, but through the plate glass window, she saw Mickey reach out to hold Lanny Ray's hand. They were saying something to each other with their faces close. Lanny turned to leave, and Mickey stood still and watched him go. Angela pretended she didn't see.

Back in the car, Lanny Ray said, "That Mickey, she's a real nice gal. I think you would like her a lot if you got to know her."

"She likes you a lot, doesn't she?" Angela said. She wondered if she sounded snippy, one of her mother's words.

"Oh, she's just a friendly gal, that's all. She likes to talk and kid around with her customers."

After a pause, Angela said, "She wasn't talking to any of her other customers much. I can tell she likes you." There was no fooling Angela.

Lanny Ray said no more about it, but Angela wondered if Mickey might be one of the women Lanny Ray had been rumored to be seeing.

Angela had seen and heard a lot of strife between her parents over the years, and she had an awareness of adult emotions most girls her age wouldn't possess—one more thing setting her apart from the other kids at school and making her feel different from them. Sometimes they seemed so much younger than she was.

During the entire first day on the road, Angela's emotions rose and fell with the passing scenery. She was both frightened about leaving Jewel and thrilled to be going with her father, and these two things kept her thoughts reeling for a time. When they pulled into a gas station, Lanny Ray bought them cold sodas out of a Coca-Cola case while the attendant checked under the hood and made small talk. Lanny went inside to pay for the gas, and he came back with an atlas and handed it to Angela.

"Now you can follow along on these maps and know right where we are. We have a long way to go. If I make the whole loop, we will be in six, seven states. You'll see how it turns out to be a big ol' lopsided circle with twists and turns in it. Some of it's real pretty country, Ang. Some of it's boring as heck and scorching hot, but the best is in the mountains. It's always better in the mountains. We'll have us a real nice time. You'll see."

Angela opened her atlas, flipped the pages to New Mexico, and put her finger on the road leading out of Jewel.

"We sure haven't gone very far, have we?"

"Nope. Sure haven't." He reached to open the book to the front where the United States map stretched across two pages. "Look here. This here is the way we'll be headed." He traced a path with his finger. "When we get up here to Cheyenne," he tapped the town with enthusiasm, "we'll head back south over this-a-way."

Angela looked at him carefully, trying to determine whether he might be teasing her.

"Really?" She doubted if what he'd said could be true. "Isn't that an awful long ways?"

"It is, for sure. Turn back to the New Mexico map and aim for Amarillo, Texas. You can follow along for the whole trip that way."

After they were back on the road, Lanny Ray said, "I guess I should tell you some about how this rodeo trip works. You know what I do and all, the bronc ridin', I mean. But this sure ain't a normal trip. Tonight we'll find us a motel up the road here. I usually stop at the same ol' places. But some nights, I don't even get a motel. It's costly, and I can get some sleep right here in the car. If I ride somewhere late in the afternoon, it's easier to pile in here, put my feet up, and take a little nap. Then I can drive the rest of the night to the next rodeo town. That's about the only way I can get around the circuit and hit all the places I need to get to. There's a few places that leave more time in between, and then we can get our washin' done and get a nicer place to stay. Get all scrubbed up again." Lanny Ray laughed a little.

"Is that how all the cowboys do it?" she asked.

"Yep. Most do. And the more you want to ride, the harder you try to get down the road." Angela could hear the excitement in his voice as he talked about it.

"Now, if there's anything you need, anything at all, you be sure to speak up. And if at any time—don't matter when—you get tired, you just crawl right back there," he motioned over his shoulder to the wide backseat with his thumb, "with your mama's quilt, and you'll sleep like a baby."

"Okay." Angela was nodding to show her understanding.

"Just don't talk so dang much." Lanny Ray flashed his smile.

"I am kind of hungry." She smiled back.

"Well, you're in luck," Lanny Ray said as they pulled into the parking lot of another café that looked much the same as the one where they'd had breakfast. When they went inside, the place smelled about the same, too, except maybe more like hamburgers than bacon. This time they sat in a red leather booth, and Lanny Ray didn't seem to recognize the waitress. They ate hamburgers and then wedges of thick, sweet apple pie, and Lanny Ray talked with knowledge and building excitement about rodeos and riding and how the money gets paid out. Angela listened intently and asked him a few questions.

"How many riders are there?" she wanted to know.

"Well, it depends," Lanny said. "Sometimes there are maybe twenty or more at the bigger rodeos. If that happens, they divide us up and run two separate bronc ridin's.

"Rodeo producers are in the business to make money, too, so they have to be sure the crowds get the entertainment they come for. If they have enough contestants, they can split up the rough stock ridin.'"

"How do you know which horse to ride? Do you get to pick your own?"

Lanny Ray smiled at this. "I wish we could," he said. "No, we draw for the horses, so we never know till then what one we'll get."

"Well, then, I hope you get nice ones."

"Don't hope such a thing, Ang. We don't want any nice ones. We want the best darn bucker there is. If we have a good ride on a real good buckin' horse, then we get a higher score."

"And when you get a higher score, you win more money, right?" She was getting it then.

"Right," Lanny said.

Angela relaxed more and, for a bit of time, forgot to wonder or worry how her mother was doing at home. She flipped through the choices of songs on the jukebox player at their table, and she sang the first few lines of the songs under her breath. She saw how Lanny Ray smiled at her, and she suddenly felt shy about her singing. The thought had crossed her mind more than a few times that she should grow up to be a country singer. She surely loved those songs. She didn't mention her idea to her father right then for fear he would laugh at her.

Over pie, Lanny told her about some of the friends he'd made and always looked forward to seeing at the rodeos. He said once in a while some of them had their kids with them, too. Or at least part of the time. He said casually that maybe she could make some new friends on the trip. He knew what a loner his daughter could be.

His idea didn't sound appealing to Angela. She didn't make new friends easily. It was so hard to talk to them about much of anything meaningful. It wasn't because of shyness really, not anymore. She was keen on keeping to herself.

After they left the café, they didn't drive far at all before Lanny Ray turned into a motel parking lot under a sign that said "Dew Stop Inn" in neon lights. Another brightly lit sign declared "Vacancy." Lanny left the car to go inside the tiny lobby to pay for a room. Angela had never stayed in a motel before. She found the cramped room to be stuffy and dim, even when all the lamps were on. There were two beds with a night table in between. The bathroom was so small a person could hardly turn around. The mirror on the wall had corroded around the edges where the finish had eroded with years of steamy moisture, and it made Angela's face look dark and wavy.

With no fuss, she and her father reached an agreement on how they would do things so they could each have their privacy. Angela took her turn in the bathroom first. She tried to hurry, just to please her father, but she couldn't make the faucets work right for a good hot shower, and she thought there might only be cold water. While she stood beneath the spray, though, the chill made her wince, and she refused to believe there could be no hot water. She fiddled with the handle some more until she finally felt some warmth from the high showerhead. Angela hoped to goodness that showers weren't always going to be so difficult. Finally clean and in her pajamas, she came out of the bathroom and climbed into her bed. She thought about her mother being home all alone and turned to the wall, concentrating on trying not to cry. She fell sound asleep before Lanny Ray finished his turn in the bathroom and turned out the lamp.

CHAPTER TWO

$\mathcal{A}$ngela's hometown, Jewel, New Mexico, sat at the edge of an eighty-mile-long fertile and productive valley. The gem of the valley was the river, hugged up against the base of the modest mountain range to the west. The Little Sweetwater supplied the land with the water needed to produce quality beef and supreme hay and grain crops. In spite of a low average rainfall in the valley, the mountain storms served the river well. Even in the driest years, the river had yet to fail the people of Jewel.

For the townspeople, the river was also the highlight of summer recreation. It was a beauty that ran high and raging during the rainy period, when the streams out of the mountain canyons flowed down to meet the channel, and then it grew lazy in the long, hot days of late summer. Fat catfish lay beyond the muddy banks, and bass hung in the willow-shaded depths of jade-green water. The languid pool of the swimming hole close to Jewel boasted the best diving rock on the river. Inner tubes, rope swings, and the squeals of happy kids were all part of an ideal summer afternoon.

In 1958, the Sweetwater Valley thrived. People were working, crops were good, cattle were fat, and the economy was on an upswing. Downtown Jewel ran three blocks long, lined on both sides with businesses. The old Mercantile sold everything from work clothes and boots to candy and baby blankets and remained the busiest store in town. It was a long, narrow, cavernous building that grew shadowy as one left the light of the big front windows. The high shelves were stocked with little thought given to organization—pet food next to the work socks and canned foods across from the motor oil—but with determination, customers could always find what they needed.

The Jewel Rexall Pharmacy supplied the town's medical needs and catered to the ladies' cosmetics boom. Revlon lipsticks stood lined up in all of their shades of reds and pinks inside scratched glass cases. The pharmacy owner's wife did her best to keep the modern fashions alive in Jewel by ordering the latest makeup fads. Pancake face powder and black mascara flew off the shelves until the supply met the demand, and then the leftover items collected dust. The store emitted a perfumed scent that wafted out of the double glass doors when they stood open on warm days. This summer, the heavy scent of Taboo hung over the sidewalk.

A dress shop went into and out of business regularly. It was usually a young, ambitious newcomer, trying to bring "good" clothes and femininity to Jewel's women, who jumped into the business with enthusiasm and both feet, only to find the customer base extremely small. The women of Jewel, like women anywhere, were fashion-conscious to a point, but practicality ruled the dress code. Besides, a Sears and Roebuck catalog could be found in every home in Jewel. The pages of the toy section and women's clothing and shoes would be dog-eared and ragged by the time the new edition came, which could be found stacked on the post office floor, free for the taking.

Probably the most infamous business in Jewel was the grocery store. It belonged to an elderly widow named Maude Stillwell and had been in her deceased husband's family since the beginning of Jewel. The first building in town to sport two-way automatic doors for convenience, and also to keep flies from the meat counter, the store was a moneymaker with no competition, other than home gardens and ranch butchered beef. The business had at one time nearly been lost to fire. By 1958, it had the distinction of being both one of the oldest buildings on main and one of the newest.

For the first thirty-six hours after the fire, the rumors of its cause ran through the town like the wind, the most interesting yarn telling the story about the building being haunted by Mr. Stillwell's long-gone family who hated Maude, and one of them took it upon his or her ghostly self to burn Maude out of business. But there were not enough people around town who believed in ghosts to perpetuate the rumor. Another short-lived rumor suggested that Maude herself lit the fire for insurance money, which seemed ludicrous because she was so old and had money coming out of her ears. Come to find out, after it was over and done with, two employees admitted to smoking in the storeroom and had most likely dropped a hot ash into a carton of Kleenex tissues, where it smoldered until the wee hours of night and then burst into flame.

When the store was rebuilt, which Maude had done lickety-split, she had painters come from out of town with a ladder truck and paint "Maude's Grocery" in giant, curly, red script, outlined in gaudy gold, across the high front of the new building. The town's people hated it and thought it ugly and inappropriate, but they knew that, as long as Maude lived, it would remain. She'd been heard to say that if the town fathers didn't like it they could change it once she died. A special committee had a list of new names in waiting.

There were two gas stations, one at each end of town, run by the Gonzales brothers. One had the Flying A, and the other had the Texaco. Jewel's kitchen cabinets were stocked with giveaway glasses from the Texaco, and everyone who had a car carried a key ring from Lorenzo's Flying A.

South of town, where there had once been a grain field, stood the drive-in movie screen. Aptly named the Grain Hill Drive-In, it had only three short rows of parking spaces and still never filled on movie nights. In warm weather, people would bring chairs and ground blankets and sit outside to watch a movie on the big screen. For blustery winter weather, an old school bus had been gutted and placed behind the last car row for kids to sit in out of the weather. The bus's scarred and cracked seats had been turned to face the side windows. The kids loved the old bus that allowed them to see a movie without car, pickup, or parent.

Angela's town was safe and friendly, for the most part. There were no truly evil people living in town, no murderers or rapists—at least none anyone knew about. Other than a few old men or ladies with Maude's cantankerous personality, who would chase little kids away from their yards and scat them with a broom like alley cats, people were polite and liked to chat and gossip with anyone who would listen.

Anytime the weather allowed, people spent time outdoors. They tended their yards or fiddled with car engines or lawnmowers in their driveways. When they needed a break, they sat on front porches where they could see out into their world. What they never ever wanted to do was miss a chance for a conversation with a neighbor or passerby. Like anyone anywhere, they talked about their kids, their day, their illnesses, their job, and what they would have for dinner, but what they loved most was gossip—and the juicier the better. Affairs—real or imagined, which ninety-nine percent were—topped the list of interest, followed by the bad, dangerous, or obnoxious things other people's kids did and how the city council was running the town's business.

So they gossiped, yes, but even if something they said was a little hurtful to someone else or made someone quake with anger, their intentions were never evil. Not truly evil.

Gossip central had come to be the bench in front of the Mercantile. Two old men carried out their self-appointed duties daily by showing up and taking in and spewing out every bit of information they could glean from any man, woman, or child willing to own up to what *they* knew or had heard. Fuzzy Jones and Lincoln were a Mutt and Jeff pair of guys. Linc, a bit of a mystery man, had come to live in Jewel several years before. Retired from the military, alone, and unwilling to talk about his own past, he had settled himself into Jewel, befriended Fuzzy, if you could call it that, and fit in as if his spot in Jewel had been saved for him. He was the epitome of retired military—tall, thin, still square-shouldered, and sporting an iron-gray crew cut. What he lacked most was a sense of humor.

Fuzzy Jones had been in town as long as anyone remembered. Fuzzy, a short, soft, little man with no neck and no shoulders, wore thick-lensed glasses, making his eyes appear to be bulgy blue marbles. He was chatty and funny, in a corny kind of way, and he had narcolepsy. He would often fall asleep in mid-sentence, and his bristly chin would fall to his chest until he woke up again. His naps could last a couple of minutes to a half an hour. If you were the one chatting with him while he dozed off, it could be a hard call to know if you should wait or go on with your business.

"Here comes the old Missing Linc," Fuzzy said over and over again and then would laugh and slap his leg with self-made glee.

"I told you not to say that anymore," Lincoln would bristle. "By God, Fuzzy, that isn't even funny."

It was right there, outside of the Mercantile door, that Angela experienced something that would change her life dramatically. Innocence was lost, and a pain she would never get over was inflicted in the name of gossip. She was eight years old when Arlene sent her one afternoon to the Mercantile to purchase two packages of daisy seed for the front flower bed. After Angela made her purchase and left the store, she heard Fuzzy, over on the bench, mention her father's name. She slowed to hear what he was talking about. Mr. and Mrs. Bowler were listening intently and nodding their silver heads while Fuzzy talked.

"The boy is runnin' off the track," he said.

"He isn't no boy," Lincoln interrupted, "He's a grown man, for gawd's sake."

Fuzzy continued, "Well, you know, I heard he has hisself a gal in every one of them rodeo towns. That's why his Mrs. put her little foot down and made him stay at home."

"She didn't *make* him stay home, Fuzzy," Linc said.

"Well, anyhow, that's why he ain't been on the road for a couple of summers. So now they're sayin' he has hisself a girlfriend from up north who he sees over at Jake's Place. Too bad," Fuzzy shook his head, "B'cuz he's got hisself a pretty little wife and all."

Angela quickly turned away, hoping no one had noticed her coming out of the Mercantile's door. She felt peculiar. Her heart pounded hard, and she had a difficult time getting a good, deep breath of air. Did she really just hear what she thought she heard? Did Fuzzy say her own daddy was seeing a girlfriend at Jake's? It sounded real bad when Fuzzy said it. It sounded naughty. She ran along the sidewalks until she got home and entered the house out of breath.

"You didn't have to run the whole way, Angela," Arlene said. "There was no big hurry for those seeds."

Angela, who looked pale, handed her mother the daisy seeds, but she avoided looking at Arlene. She mumbled an answer and headed for her room. Her mother followed right behind her.

"Are you all right? Are you coming down with something? Angela, you're acting all funny. What in the devil is wrong with you?"

Angela burst into tears. It scared the bejesus out of her mother.

"Did somebody do something to you? Answer me, Angela Jean."

"No, ma'am, nobody did anything, but I heard something bad."

"What in the world did you hear that could get you so worked up? Somebody hurt your feelings?"

Angela shook her head no.

"Well, what then?" Arlene softened her voice, hoping to calm her daughter.

Angela looked at the floor. She concentrated on the yellow-and-gray flower pattern on the linoleum. She didn't want to say what she'd heard. She sensed that, if she did, she would hurt her mama's feelings real bad.

"Angela," Arlene nearly shouted this time, "you are making me worry. What the heck is going on here?" She gave Angela's shoulder a firm shake.

Through choking sobs, Angela finally told her mother everything, exactly what she had heard Fuzzy say at the bench. Her voice got smaller until it came as a whisper. When she'd finished the telling, she flopped back on her bed and stared up at the ceiling. She fell silent in her misery.

Arlene's face felt stiff, and she wasn't able to speak right away. She struggled to find the right words for her daughter and not let her own confusion show.

"Oh, sweetie," she said. "You know those old men are just gossipy old buggers. Why, everybody knows they just make stuff up to get attention. By tomorrow, they'll be telling stories about some other poor soul."

Arlene pulled her daughter up to her and wrapped her arms around her real tight.

"You have to forget about this nonsense, and you mustn't worry about me and your daddy. It'll be all right. You'll see."

CHAPTER THREE

Things did not get all right after Angela overheard the gossip about her father. If only she hadn't stopped and listened to Fuzzy's words, hadn't told her mother, surely her parents would still be together. But instead, here she was in Lanny Ray's big car, headed out for God knew where, and leaving her mother home all alone. Once again, she began to question her decision to take the trip.

She recalled the unbelievable, fantastic feeling she had the day her father had come by the house the previous Easter and asked her mother for permission to take Angela with him on the circuit. She still remembered the look of incredulity on her mother's face, as if he had asked her for a million dollars. He may as well have.

"No," Arlene had said. "No, you cannot take her on a trip. Lanny Ray, you can barely take care of yourself these days. How in the world do you think you can take care of a twelve-year-old girl all summer while you're running all over the country? No."

"Come on, Arlene. Think about how happy she'll be. Some of the other guys take their kids along. Angela and me can get to know each other better. I don't want to miss out on a whole summer, being without her."

"No," but she could hear the hesitation in her own voice.

"Oh, come on. You know she would go in a fast minute if you let her. She wants to be with me, too, you know. At least say you'll think about it."

It sure wasn't Lanny Ray's feelings that Arlene worried about. She only wanted to make the right choice for Angela. This would give her a whole new opportunity to get out of Jewel and see something. She would see places and things that most people in Jewel would never see. It seemed almost too hard to think about. Lord, how she would miss Angela. They had never been apart for any time at all.

"You just let me talk to her. I want to know exactly how she feels about it. Leave us alone now. Go on." Arlene had shooed Lanny Ray away, closed the door, and put her hands over her face.

"Mama, are you okay?" Angela had been standing right there, listening to the entire conversation, and neither parent had spoken a word to her.

"I'm sorry, sweetie. I'm fine. He just always gets me going."

"I really want to go with him. I can, can't I?" Angela's eyes were big and questioning.

"I don't know. I have to think. And you need to understand some things. It's a long time to be away from home. A long time. You won't know anybody else, and what will you do when he's got other fish to fry?"

Angela didn't have any idea what that meant—and didn't care. She only knew how bad she wanted to go. She could picture herself riding along in the big car with the window down, laughing at something Lanny Ray said. She pictured herself happy. Ecstatically happy. She knew she still had some time to convince her mother to let her go. So her endeavor began. She became the perfect daughter, rushing to do chores without being told, starting dinner before her mother came home from work, and doing anything else she could think of to stay in Arlene's good graces. Angela was a responsible girl, so those things came easy for her.

Except for school. School did not come easy. She was a window gazer, losing herself in the light of the outdoors, fidgeting in her desk chair, and tugging at her disliked school dress, wishing for jeans and a walk to the river. That's where her mind wandered—to the places she loved—and so she often missed the lessons in the classroom. Her teachers adored her for her unusual and extremely bright personality, but they grew weary of having to call her back to reality. She daydreamed scenes of being down at the river park where, in reality, she spent hours alone. Though she didn't have a word for what she felt, there existed a sort of kinship to the river, making it a comfortable place for her to be. The familiar smell of the mossy shaded coves and the white noise of the river flow were soothing to Angela.

By the time she was nine years old, Angela knew every alleyway, backyard, flowerbed and climbing tree in Jewel. She knew who lived in almost every house on her side of town, their names, where they worked, or if they didn't. When she rode her old, blue bike or roller skated by, she would wave a friendly wave to everyone she saw. Occasionally, she would stop and chat to be polite, but not for long. Now, she could walk all the way to the river, but she had been forbidden to get near the water's edge while there alone—but being there alone was the whole idea.

A towering metal slide with steep steps and a lopsided merry-go-round stood on the park lawn. The top of the slide had become the perfect place for Angela to sit alone. She could see the entire park and watch the ripple and flow of the river. The only other person on earth she considered sharing her favorite places with was her friend Joseph.

Joseph, a boy in Angela's class and the son of a local lawyer and a phobic mother who rarely left their home, was quiet, extremely smart, and a good friend who sat at the desk in front of Angela's. On more than one occasion, Joseph had slid a test paper over just slightly so Angela could see his answers because he worried that her lack of classroom attention would cause her to fail.

Like Angela, Joseph had little interest in the same things the other kids his age did. He would rather read a book than play kickball, and he never got less than an A on a report card. He and Angela had had a tug-of-war over the desk they chose on the first day of school, and he had relented, letting her have it. They had been friends ever since.

Angela did her very best to get through the last weeks of the school year on her best behavior to help convince Arlene to allow her to go with Lanny Ray. By the last week, the weather had turned hot, and the classroom felt stuffy and claustrophobic. She wiggled in her chair, her scratchy slip sticking to the backs of her legs and her shoes feeling too heavy on her feet. The big hand on the clock, high up on the wall behind the teacher's desk, seemed to click the minutes so slowly it became exasperating. When the final bell of the day rang, she would gather her things quickly and call to Joseph to hurry up. They walked partway home together every day, Joseph leaving her at the corner of her street.

Angela tried not to talk about the trip with Lanny Ray too much, but every few days she would find a subtle way to remind her mother how much she wanted to go. Eventually, she wore Arlene's reservation down. As long as she wasn't saying flat out no, a chance remained. And then Lanny Ray stopped by again.

"So what do you think, Arlene? You going to let Ang go with me? I'm not gettin' any younger. I won't be doin' this trip forever. Guys younger than me are already hangin' it up. I really want her to have this chance."

Between the two of them, they finally convinced Arlene that allowing Angela to go was the right thing. Lanny planned to leave the week after school let out. That way, Angela would have a few days to get ready to go, and Lanny Ray would be on the road in due time.

On the next to the last day of school, Angela and Joseph walked in companionable silence for a few blocks, and when they came to Angela's street, they both saw the car in front of her house halfway down the block.

"Who's there?" Joseph asked.

"My father," Angela said, not taking her eyes from the car.

"Why is he here?" Joseph knew her father seldom came by her house.

"I don't know. We aren't leaving until next week." Angela spoke without taking her eyes off the car. She remembered then that she had not even told Joseph about going away. She had wanted to, but coveting her secret had kept her from telling anyone. "He's taking me to the rodeos. I'll get to watch him ride the broncs, and we'll stay in motels and eat at cafés all the time. He's a real good bronc rider, you know. He wins lots of money."

Joseph looked at Angela intently and decided she must be telling the truth.

"Well, I guess I'll see you when you get back then."

Angela didn't notice the disappointment in Joseph's voice. "See you then," was all she said, then left him standing at the corner.

Angela's heart thudded in her chest. At first, she hurried along the sidewalk. *Oh no*, she thought. *Oh no, please, please don't be here to say I can't go with you.* She felt a stinging behind her eyes.

As she drew nearer to the corner of her yard, she slowed her steps to hardly more than a shuffle. She didn't want to know why her father was at her house. He knew well enough that he wasn't supposed to be there if Arlene wasn't at home. She didn't think she could stand it if he had come to say she couldn't go with him.

When she reached the edge of the front yard, she could see Lanny Ray standing on her front porch, leaning casually against a pillar. She stared, trying to read his face. The minute he saw her, he grinned a slow grin.

"About time, Sissy. Where've you been?"

In her serious frame of mind, she took him literally. "At school," she said. Good grief, didn't he know that? "Where's Mom? Is she here?"

"Nope. She said I could come by and tell you the news."

Angela felt her insides cringe, her stomach knot. *Here it goes*, she thought, *I'm not going*.

"We'll be headed out of here tomorrow morning, so you better get packed," Lanny Ray said. "I'll be by at six. You be ready now, okay?" His hands were in his pockets, and he shifted a toothpick from one side of his mouth to the other. "We'll climb in the big, old car there and head out." He motioned to his car with the raise of his chin.

He stepped off the porch and cut across the lawn to the street in his long-legged stride. Angela stood and watched him go. "Okay," was all she could think of to say, and by then he couldn't hear her anyway. Lanny got in and drove off without looking back. She watched him until he'd driven out of sight.

Inside her house, Angela went straight into the kitchen. She took the metal ice trays from the Frigidaire's freezer and dropped ice cubes in a glass. She poured herself some tea and added two heaping spoons of sugar. Standing at the drain board, she stirred her tea for a long time, watching the sparkle of the sugar crystals swirl, then finally drank half of it down in thirsty gulps and poured a little more. She pulled a chair away from the small table and sat stiffly. Tomorrow. She would be leaving with him tomorrow. She had to get ready.

She stood and went into her little bedroom and sat on the edge of her bed. Packing for a trip was something she had never done, so she had to give it a lot of thought. Going to her dresser, she pulled open the top drawer and stood there looking into it. *Well*, she thought, *I'll need underwear that's for sure. And my jeans and some shirts.* She hurried into her mother's room and opened her closet, looking for the suitcase she remembered seeing somewhere. Pushing clothes aside, she peered into the dark corners. Not there. She felt a tiny stab of panic in her chest. What if they didn't even have a suitcase?

Angela was not to call her mother at work unless an emergency transpired. She went to the living room and stood with her hand on the phone, telling herself that this was indeed important. She took a deep, shaky breath, dialed the store, and listened to the ring on the other end. A man answered and told her to wait while he got her mother.

"Lanny says I'm leaving with him tomorrow?" It came out as a question, as if she still wasn't sure. "Do we have a suitcase?"

"Oh, Ang. I'll help you get things together when I get home, sweetie. There's time. Start putting the things you want to take with you out on your bed, and we'll go through them together after I get home. Are you okay? You sound a little funny."

"Is it okay? Me leaving tomorrow, is it okay with you?"

"I guess it has to be. Lanny Ray dances to his own tune, and you never know what the song's going to be. Don't worry about that. We'll get you ready. I have to go. See you pretty soon."

Angela prowled the house, room to room. How strange she felt. How unreal it seemed to her to know she would be leaving for a while—leaving the only place she had ever known. On a small, cherry table beneath a window in the living room stood several photographs in silver frames. She was so used to them being there she hardly paid attention to them anymore. She picked up the one of her and her mother and studied it. Even in shades of gray, it was easy to see the light in Arlene's clear blue eyes. Angela had been five or six years old. Her mother had trapped her wild curls in a ribbon high on the crown of her head. Angela remembered fussing about that, and, in reality, it probably hadn't lasted ten minutes. There was one photograph of the three of them—Lanny Ray with a huge smile, showing his straight white teeth, and Arlene, holding Angela in her arms and looking so happy. Arlene had put away the ones of only herself and Lanny Ray together a long time ago, but there were still a few of Angela with her father. She stood and gazed for a moment at the happy faces and remembered the one picture of her parents together on her own dresser. She would take it with her so she would have the picture of her mom with her all the time.

While she pulled clothing from her dresser drawers and closet, she thought again how different things would be if her parents were still together. No one else she knew had divorced parents. It was one more thing separating her from her peers.

She tucked the picture of Arlene and Lanny Ray under a stack of clothes so it could go into the suitcase. No one else needed to know it was there.

CHAPTER FOUR

Landon Ray Garrett was a hometown boy. Born and raised in Jewel, he had always been just Lanny. Born in the mid-twenties, he and the town of Jewel had, in a way, grown up together. His father had eked out a living on a few acres and then, later in life, had worked at one of the grain elevators over on the east side of the valley. He was a kind, God-loving man who took good care of his family. Lanny's mother had passed to heaven at a young age and left his father to raise him and his sister, Rose. There were some hard times without a wife and mother in their home, but with the help of community and church friends, the little Garrett family survived their loss and carried on as normal as possible.

When Lanny Ray was still a youngster, a family friend had taken him, along with his own son, to a place near Santa Fe to see a rodeo. After that very day, Lanny wanted to be nothing but a bronc rider. He dreamed about it and talked about it until he nearly drove his father crazy. He begged to go to rodeos—any rodeos, anywhere—and once in a while his father would take the time to go, if it wasn't too far to drive.

Lanny was headstrong and stubborn, but not a bad boy. His desire to become a rodeo star, as farfetched as the idea seemed at the time, gave his father the advantage he needed to keep his strong-willed son in school and out of trouble. No school, no rodeo.

As he grew to be a teenager, his dream hung on, and it became apparent to all who knew him that he would give rodeo a try, come hell or high water. Through the summers, he took any job he could find on any ranch close enough to town for him to ride his rusty Sears bike to work. Employees were desperately needed up and down the valley while the war was on because so many young men had left to fight for their country. Also, Lanny would do jobs the cowboys didn't want to do. He built fences, whitewashed entire barns, and hauled manure for crop fertilizer, all for the opportunity to be around the cowboys and livestock. Some of the older men took a crack at talking Lanny Ray out of his dream.

"Boy, I really wish you would think about doin' somethin' else for a livin'," one old cowboy told him. "It's a hard damn life, rodeo. I've seen things happen in the arena I won't ever forget. I've seen the best of the best get trampled or drug near to death. I've lost two good friends tryin' to get down the road for their next ride. Horse wrecks, car wrecks . . . it's a hard way to live."

But Lanny Ray was young and perceived himself as invincible; therefore, that kind of talk had little effect on him.

"Ah, I'll be okay. Didn't stop you, did it? Seein' all those things happen? It's in my blood same as yours."

The younger men liked to tease Lanny about women. They spent a good amount of time talking about the rodeo and offering Lanny Ray tips on living the life. They'd been down the road themselves, and they warned Lanny about the toll it had taken on their own personal lives.

"Oh, hell yeah," a cowboy told Lanny Ray. "It was nothin' but women and fun in the beginnin'. Ohhh, them gals were keen on cowboys and rough stock riders. They were excited to know us personally, sometimes real personally." The subject always brought sly winks and knowing smirks.

"Shoot, some women are more willin' than ever to show a cowboy a good time. Or you're gone so damn long your own woman has a good time for herself," another hand said.

Lanny listened, but he didn't hold much thought to what they said.

"Well, I ain't plannin' on gettin' married until I'm pretty old, so I ain't worried about all that."

"How old might that be, Lanny Ray?"

"Well, at least thirty. Maybe more." He didn't know why the age of thirty struck the older cowboys so funny. What they would give to be thirty again?

He had lots of girlfriends through his teen years. Maybe not real girlfriends, but girls who liked him. A handsome boy with a quick smile and a subtle sense of humor, he had charm, and the ladies around town had always said he would have every gal in town after him, that they'd be lined up at his door. It was almost true, but he didn't seem to notice. Lanny treated everyone nice, though he kept to himself a lot and worked most of the time. He got by in school, so he made his father proud by graduating from Jewel High. He had worked enough by then to save up to buy his first car. It wasn't much, but he could keep it going for a while.

As the war wound down and Lanny Ray was turning eighteen, he packed a few things in his jalopy and headed north to get his start in rodeo, riding saddle broncs. Those early postwar days were a hard time for rodeo. It was an entertainment event, but some people couldn't yet afford to spend money on extra things. Competition was still slim, though, proving to be an advantage for first-timers like Lanny. A lot of rough stock riders were soldiers then. Some never came back, and some who did couldn't ride anymore.

By fall, Lanny had ridden in five rodeos and earned enough to break even on his expenses. This wasn't much, considering he slept most nights in his old Ford and ate one or two cheap meals a day. Gas for his car was the biggest expense, and he found himself home sooner than he had expected to be. He remained damn happy with how he did his first summer out of the chute, and he'd heard some of the old boys were talking about him being a natural. His dream hung on as strong as ever.

Lanny Ray had never been away from home for such a lengthy time. His summer away on the circuit seemed much longer than it actually was. He had endured a heap of loneliness out on the road, and it felt good to be home. He rose early on his second morning back in town, feeling at ease and happy to be home. For the time being, he would stay at his father's house on Fourth Street, but he hoped for a ranch job that would supply a place to live, even if it happened to be a bunkhouse. He decided to venture up to Main Street and the Blue Moon Café for a good cup of morning coffee.

As he stepped through the glass-paned door of the Blue Moon, a tiny bell gave a familiar jingle above his head. He had come here all of his life, and the place had not changed since he could remember. It still had the same smooth, pale-green walls and the gray Formica countertop. The stools may have been reupholstered over the years, but they were the same shade of green as they had always been. There were only three people in the café when Lanny Ray entered. One man sat at the counter, and two ranchers were at a small window table. No one bothered to look up. It was always easy to recognize ranchers for who they were. Their clothes were usually neat and clean, they wore hats with no sweat ring around the crown, and they looked clean-shaven. They were the kind of men who were Lanny's bosses during the fall and winter months.

Lanny slid onto a stool at the counter and waited for the waitress to come out through the swinging door leading from the kitchen. After a few minutes ticked by, the big man at the other end of the counter turned and spoke to Lanny.

"Arlene'll be out in a minute," he said. "She had to fetch supplies from the storage room." Lanny nodded thanks. He fiddled with the salt and pepper shakers. He glanced over the menu. He contemplated getting up and pouring his own coffee when the door swung open with a bang. A young woman with her arms full of coffee filters, paper napkins, and loaves of bread piled high rushed into the room. Just as she started to set the items on the counter, they slipped and slid from her grasp. Once the calamity had ended, she stood holding one package of napkins in her left hand. Everything else lay on the floor.

"Oh, dammit," she swore under her breath. "Where the heck is Maggie? I can't do everything around here."

When she finally turned and saw Lanny Ray sitting at the counter, her face reddened.

"Oh Lord," she said with an apologetic smile, "I hope you haven't been here too long. What can I get for you this morning? How about coffee to get you started?"

"Just coffee will be fine, thanks. Blue."

"Blue? Blue what?" she asked.

"What?" Lanny said. "Did I say blue? I meant black. Black coffee would be fine."

Arlene started to giggle at the silliness of the conversation, but it turned into a full-blown, braying laugh, and she snorted through her nose so loudly the ranchers by the window stopped talking and looked across the room at her. Embarrassed and out of breath, she finally stooped and wiped her teary eyes with the hem of her apron.

"I am so sorry. I'm such a mess." She blushed a bright red. "I don't know what got into me. I just couldn't stop. Laughing, I mean. I hear people just break down and do that sometimes when life gets to be too much. You know, when things just don't go right for a long time, and finally they crack under all the pressure and go hysterical." Her eyes were swimming in tears again, only this time they weren't tears of laughter.

Lanny sat there looking at her and could not think of a single thing to say. Her blue eyes had struck him in the heart full force the instant she had looked at him. He was embarrassing himself by gawking at her, and now with her thick, wet, coal-black lashes blinking back her tears, he was left momentarily speechless. Finally, after an awkward silence, Arlene came to pour coffee into a heavy mug in front of Lanny Ray.

"Thanks," he said with a straight face. "I don't believe I've ever heard anybody snort so loud before."

The man down the counter had undoubtedly heard the conversation, but he had never cracked a smile. He cleared his throat to get Arlene's attention. She stepped over the pile of supplies on the floor and moved in his direction, coffeepot in hand.

"Can I get you anything else, Roger? More coffee?"

"No, thanks, Arlene. I've had plenty. Did you give any more thought to . . . you know . . . what we talked about yesterday?" He leaned toward her across the counter.

"Well, you know, Roger, I really don't want to date anyone right now." Arlene smiled but took a step back.

"You been awfully friendly toward me lately, Arlene, and it seems to me like maybe you been leadin' me on a little. You been askin' me all about my life and if I was a married man and all. I think you been leadin' me on." He hunched his shoulders forward and stared into her face.

Arlene's hand trembled slightly as she sat the coffeepot on the counter. She felt unnerved by the man's narrow-eyed stare.

"Well, Roger, I'm real sorry you got that idea because it wasn't how I meant anything I said. I was only making conversation. That's all, really."

Lanny Ray sat close enough to hear what the man had said and wasn't comfortable with the tone he'd heard in his voice. Not being one to mind other people's business, he'd always made a point of not getting involved in personal conversations, but this one wasn't going well for Arlene, and Lanny had been paying attention.

"So is this here your new guy?" Roger slung a hand in Lanny Ray's direction without looking at him. "You were laughin' up a storm there. Did you ask him if he's married?" His voice became lower, and his tone nastier.

"Okay, Roger. I think you need to go now." Arlene picked up Roger's tab from the counter and said, "Don't worry about this. Breakfast is on the Blue Moon this morning. I hope you think this over and come back more friendly like."

"Oh, I'll be back. But you better watch yourself. I know your type, and I know where you live, too. Keep that thought in mind." The flesh of Roger's cheeks trembled as he spoke, and his eyes were the meanest eyes Arlene had ever seen.

Lanny Ray rose from his stool. He ambled toward the end of the counter where Roger was standing, moved up real close to Roger's shoulder, and very quietly said, "I think it's time for you to leave now, Roger. I can see you are upsetting this girl here, and it isn't necessary. I believe I heard a threat in those things you were sayin' to her. Least it sure sounded that way. You need to be on your way."

Roger hardly glanced in Lanny Ray's direction, choosing to ignore him. He pulled his wallet from his back pocket, thumbed out some bills, and threw them on the counter top.

"Be seein' you," he said to Angela and went out the door.

Lanny Ray was the first to finally speak. "So," he said with a grin, "that fella a friend of yours?"

"Oh, my gosh! That man is scary, isn't he? I knew he was an odd one the first time he came through the door, but I thought he was harmless." She pressed the fingers of one hand against her pale forehead. "Now I have to worry about him on top of everything else." She moved away and started picking up the supplies she had dropped.

"I'm sorry," she talked as she worked, "I don't even know your name, but thank you so much for stepping in there. No telling where the situation might have gone if you hadn't helped me out. Course, I was the one with the coffeepot in my hand." Arlene tried to keep a smile.

"I'm Landon Garrett. I just had a hankerin' for a cup of Blue Moon coffee this morning. Actually, everyone around here calls me Lanny. Lanny Ray, mostly. I grew up here. You must have started working here while I was gone all summer."

"Nice to meet you, Landon Lanny Ray Garrett. I've heard your name around town. You're the bronc rider."

"Well, I'm trying to be," Lanny said modestly, but he liked the sound of what she'd said. "I'm back here to work a while. I'll have another shot of coffee."

Lanny Ray sat at the counter for two hours that morning while Arlene spilled her heart to him. She told him she had left her own hometown and her fiancé clear up in Salina, Utah, to come to Jewel to care for a grandmother she hardly knew. Grandma Ellie was her father's mother, who had taken sick and ended up with pneumonia.

"Arlene will do it," her family had said. "She won't mind dropping her entire life to go south to some Podunk town and take care of a grandmother she doesn't even know." She mimicked her family. "So here I came, dumb as can be, left my man and my home, 'because nobody else can go, Arlene, honey,' so you know what happens?" Lanny watched her pretty mouth sip from her coffee mug. "I'll tell you what happened. I get here, I move in with poor sick Ellie, I take care of her like a baby—feed her, bathe her, even kind of get to love her—and she ups and dies. So then, I'm thinking what should I do with her little house over on Opal? Sell it, rent it? And guess what happens next?" Lanny Ray shrugged. "I get a 'Dear Jane' letter. My fiancé calls it off, well, us off. He says he's so sorry, but seein' as how I chose to leave him alone and come down here, he's found somebody else. Kick me while I'm down, why don't he?"

"I'm real sorry to hear that." Lanny said it, but he didn't mean it.

"Ah, just as well. If he gave up on us so easy, we had no business being married anyway. My heart's mending. It's my pride that's suffering, I suppose."

She went on about the house and working at the Blue Moon and how the town really was a nice little town. Lanny Ray listened and drank so much coffee his vision blurred. By the time he left the café that day, he had been lassoed like a calf. From then on, he hung around the café as often as he could, mostly on the pretense of protecting Arlene from crazy Roger. He needn't have bothered because by then Roger had moved on to bothering some gal down at the Burger Palace.

At first, the couple pretended to themselves—and anybody else who noticed—that theirs was just a mutual friendship. Arlene had appreciated Lanny Ray's concern about crazy Roger. But it wasn't long until seeing Lanny come through the café door made her heart jump in her chest. Lanny's strong, quiet way and dry sense of humor overcame any defenses she might've had.

Lanny fooled himself for a week or two and then just gave in to his feelings. He felt like the luckiest man on earth. With eyes like Elizabeth Taylor's, a pretty smile, and all her spunk, there would be no reason to ever want anybody else.

By Thanksgiving, they were talking marriage, and on Christmas Eve, they became man and wife. Lanny moved his few belongings into the little Opal Street house. From the beginning of their relationship, Lanny Ray tried to make sure his new love understood how much he still had the fiery desire to follow the rodeo and ride those horses.

He talked about it almost daily. He would work on the ranches and make a home with her, but come time, he would leave to make the circuit. He would hold Arlene tight and tell her that, even though he would have to be away, when he got real good, he would make real good money and bring it home to her. He promised he would take care of her, and she believed every word he said. She knew he meant it.

In fact, Arlene was agreeable to most anything Lanny Ray said in those days. She even took it in stride when he convinced her to move into an old ranch house so he could work there. They put the little house in town up for rent. The ranch house was a cold, leaky, ancient place, but Lanny could go to work right from the front door and be home early every night. It made financial sense because they could save the rent they made off of the house in town.

It became a lonely existence for Arlene way out in the middle of nowhere. She could only busy herself so much, trying to fix the place up. The first thing the house required was a good scrubbing. Arlene tackled every surface with hot soapy water and a horse brush she found in the saddle shed. She scoured sinks and toilets, but the rusty, red stains wouldn't budge. She hand stitched, to the best of her ability, new curtains for all the windows. All four of them.

The kitchen floor was so rough and slanted that sometimes Arlene would nearly lose her balance in there. At first, it seemed funny. They would tipsy around and then laugh at themselves. Even though springtime neared, the temperatures hovered around freezing, and the loose window panes rattled in the night wind. They snuggled under a pile of blankets and slept in each other's arms. A dozen times, Arlene filled the house with thick wood smoke while she tried to keep the fire stoked in the stove. Too often the pipes would spit out a stream of rusty water and ruin the clothes in the washer. The thing she did best was cook, and in spite of the cantankerous kitchen range, she could fix a good supper for Lanny. It wasn't that she minded doing the work—it was that every day presented some new challenge. Some days, she felt too worn-out to deal with the problems. She had afternoon headaches and lost her appetite. But she tried to do right by Lanny Ray. Always.

The first time or two Lanny showed up late to eat, she listened to his reason and decided not to make a big thing of it. She knew his job sure wasn't a nine-to-five. She understood how he had things to finish up sometimes.

Then one night as she waited up extra late, Arlene could feel herself growing extraordinarily angry. She had made Lanny Ray's favorite chicken-fried steak and potatoes. As the evening passed, the potatoes turned gluey in the pot, and the once crispy steak lay limp and greasy on the plate. Resentment built in her until she thought she would explode. Suddenly, she stood up from the chair at the rickety kitchen table and grabbed the pot of mashed potatoes and the platter of meat from the stove. She moved quickly to the front door and fumbled it open. She stepped out into the dirt yard and flung the pot and the platter as far into the dark as she could. It was then that she saw Lanny move into the light. She stood her ground, fists clenched.

"Lord, Arlene, what's got into you?"

"What do you think, Landon? I'm sick and tired of sitting here by myself in this crappy house. And then you don't even come home to eat the damn supper I made for you. What are you doing that can't wait until morning?"

"Well, me and the boys have a lot to discuss with calvin' time comin' and all."

"Like what Lanny Ray? Cow obstetrics?"

"We do talk a little bit about that . . . and other things." He could hear how ridiculous he sounded.

"What? What other things?"

"Like rodeoin'. It's interestin', and I learn a lot from those old bronc riders. They just wanta help me out, is all."

"Landon Ray, you are full of crap past them brown eyes. You sit around with those guys and get all worked up about taking off to rodeo. Then, when you finally get home, you don't have anything to say to me. I think you feel guilty, that's what I think. You're chomping at the bit to get going, and you don't think I get it. Well, I do. You warned me enough times about how it would be, but, meantime, I didn't know I would be stuck out here in this crappy house in the middle of nowhere. Like a creaky old barn, for God's sake. And then, I don't even have you for company."

Arlene started to turn back into the house. "I know you'll be leaving soon. I think I should go ahead and get our house in town back and get some things moved. I'm not staying out here by myself all summer. Let the next hired man have it. "

Not another word was spoken while they got ready for bed. When the room had grown dark and the quilts were pulled up to their chins in the cold room, Arlene spoke again.

"Lanny," she whispered. "I think I might be pregnant."

Lanny Ray stayed silent too long for Arlene.

"Well, say something."

"You think you are? I mean, if you are, that's great, Arlene. I mean, isn't it great? Us havin' a baby?"

"You ready to be a daddy? If I am pregnant, you got no choice, you know."

"I'll be a good daddy, Arlene. We'll be good parents, don't you think? It'll all work out, baby." Neither of them moved. They both lay perfectly still without touching.

CHAPTER FIVE

$\mathcal{B}$lindsided by domestic life and responsibility, Lanny Ray felt the tug of the rodeo road stronger than ever. He did a good job of lying to himself about it, though. He told himself and anyone who would listen how he was just anxious to get out there and have his best season yet. He'd ride those horses like nobody's business and bring home enough winnings to care for his wife and the baby coming in the fall. His fans slapped him on the back and congratulated him on his attitude and his coming fatherhood. But people who knew him the best, including his father and his sister, Rose, thought that at times they saw a trapped animal look in his eyes. Rose, especially, had caught glimpses of him staring out across the valley or toward the mountains, as if he could see things a thousand miles away.

When Doc Blaine had confirmed that Arlene was pregnant, things changed for the Garretts. Lanny Ray tried to be around more for Arlene and worked at being more attentive. He moved her back to the Opal Street house and settled her in. She got busy making it home again and seemed more at ease, but sometimes she felt a coolness come off Lanny Ray like a winter chill, even though he was trying to do better by her. He lived like a man acting a part for a play that his heart wasn't in.

Being in town got her out and about and closer to people. She wanted to go back to work at the Blue Moon until the baby came, but while she and Lanny Ray had lived out in the ranch house, another waitress had been hired. The new gal's name was Norma, and it didn't take long for Arlene and Norma to become good friends. Arlene would walk uptown to have a soda in the mid-afternoons, and the two women would talk up a storm and laugh like school girls. Norma, a few years older than Arlene, had two kids of her own to raise. She was outspoken, and a life which would have broken many women had made her strong and feisty.

"My old man used to hang out at Jake's every night," she told Arlene. "He got him a job driving a long-haul truck, and the next thing I know, he's driving out of town with some little bar whore. I don't really care much now. He was always a lousy husband and father anyway. He hardly paid any attention to his own kids. Long as I can work and take care of them, we'll be okay."

On a morning that made Jewel sparkle under the rising sun, Lanny Ray left town, just as planned. He made a ton of promises about keeping in touch. He declared his love to Arlene every day leading up to his leaving. He talked incessantly about how well-off they would be by the time the baby came. He would be coming home with a wad of cash too big for his pocket. He promised to be home well before the baby came.

"Don't worry," he said.

Arlene listened quietly and willed herself to believe him. They would be a family by fall. Maybe Lanny would be more willing to settle down by then.

Baby Angela arrived right on time. Lanny Ray did not. Norma was the one who sat by Arlene while she wailed and swore and squeezed Norma's hand so hard she dislocated Norma's little finger. Doc Blain yanked it straight again and warned her not to hold on to Arlene's hand anymore until her labor was finished. The baby girl slipped into the world showing off a head of dark, downy hair. She arrived into the world beautiful.

Lanny Ray came home four days later. He arrived at the tiny community hospital just in time to take his wife and baby home. He did nearly everything wrong from their new beginning.

"What are we going to name her?" he asked after they were home.

"I named her already," said Arlene. "Her name is Angela because she looks like a little angel."

Lanny felt a little hurt. "Golly, Arlene, don't you think we coulda talked about what her name was going to be? Maybe we could name her after my mother. You know, with her being gone all these years. Would be a real nice thing to do."

"No." Arlene was blunt. "I don't think we could have talked about it, Lanny Ray. You have never once even talked about your mother, and I'm not naming my child after somebody I don't know anything about. Her name is Angela. Angela Jean Garrett. It's on her birth certificate, so there's no changing it now anyway."

Arlene avoided Lanny's eyes as tears came to her own. "You should have been here. It should have been you there with me instead of poor Norma. And we should have talked about her name a long time ago instead of acting like she wasn't coming. That's what parents do, Lanny Ray."

"I know, I should have, Arlene. I know, and I'm real sorry, honey. But guess what, baby? I rode in Payson, and I won the big money there. If I'd come on home, I would have missed out on the money." He put his arms around her and hugged her to him gently. "I'm sorry, sweetheart. I really wish I woulda been here."

Arlene felt herself backsliding. She needed someone to talk nice to her and make her feel loved. She felt so vulnerable. All it took was his smile and strong arms around her to melt her resolve to stay tough with him. And she felt too exhausted to fight.

Lanny would have been well off if he would have just hushed up right then and there.

"Sweetheart, I been thinkin' maybe next month we could move on back out to the ranch house, if I can get on as a cowboy there again. You know how good they pay, and we can rent this place out again. The rent money really helped us out, remember, baby?"

Arlene moved away from him and stood across the room for distance so she could look right at him.

"Is there something just plain wrong with you? Do you think I would take this baby to that freezing cold dump of a place? The kitchen floor has probably fell through by now. She can't be breathing nasty stove smoke into her pure, clean, little lungs. You want to live that way, well, then you go on out there, but don't expect we will." Tears poured down her pale cheeks.

"Naw," Lanny said. "It'll be okay. We'll just stay here, and I'll find a job closer to town."

Lanny Ray did that. He took a job on a poorly run ranch and worked for a boss he had no respect for. Since he was the newest hire, he didn't do much real cowboy work, and it wouldn't be too long until he was looking elsewhere for work. Work—that's what Lanny Ray did best. He might have been irresponsible in a lot of ways, but he knew how to work and was proud of his reputation for being a good hand. He'd become known for his work ethic throughout the Little Sweetwater Valley.

Lanny Ray did his best to be a good family man for the next few years. He worked nearer to home so he could be there more. But in late spring, he still left to rodeo. The economy surged, and people welcomed the opportunity to get out and live a little. Country fairs and rodeos drew people in again, and there was good money to be made. He did well on the circuit, but he paid a different kind of price when he returned home. His daughter would change so much in those few months he would hardly know her. Angela grew from an infant into a girl while Lanny followed his dream. Arlene was a remarkable mama and took fine care of her little girl. Each time Lanny Ray came back home again, life for Arlene and Angela carried on as usual, and he often felt like a visitor in his own home.

Angela went through the stages children normally do. She either completely ignored Lanny Ray or clung to him and cried when he left. Lanny's heart would ache, and his paternal love grew, but he had little to do with her upbringing. It was Arlene who disciplined Angela, taught her manners, and encouraged her independence.

She was tomboy through and through, hating ribbons and ruffles by the time she went to school. She would come home from a school day with the hem out of her dress and her bows torn off. The minute she hit home, she donned her jeans and scruffy boots. Angela seemed to have been born an animal lover, and she attracted them like a magnet. When she sat in her yard, neighborhood cats sought her lap and gentle hands. If she explored town on her own, dogs came wagging their tails, happy to see their friend. She desperately wanted her own dog, but Arlene said no. Maybe when she was older, she said.

When Lanny Ray came home again, he sometimes took Angela with him to his ranch job and let her ride the horses. Riding came as natural as could be for Angela. By the time she turned six years old, she rode well. She adored the horses and had no qualms about climbing on their warm, smooth backs. Sometimes she got to ride out with Lanny to check the cattle or the fences. They would leave the valley floor and ride into the Gallo Mountains where she learned about tracking and manipulating steep trails on horseback. She was at ease out there with Lanny, no matter what their job entailed.

Arlene had mixed feelings about the closeness that was developing between the two of them. She wanted Angela to know and love her daddy, but she worried because Lanny Ray's reputation around town wasn't so good in those days. Small-town gossip was hard enough for Arlene to hear, but it could be devastating for little Angela.

Lanny Ray had been hanging out at Jake's Place way too much for a married man and father. In spite of his normally easy going spirit, he had a couple of run-ins with some out-of-town cowboys looking for work. Arlene had learned about two fistfights through town gossip and wondered exactly how much she had not yet heard. Oftentimes, she would remember Norma's words about her ex-husband leaving town with another woman. When Arlene and Lanny Ray fought about his late nights out, she would say, "Lanny Ray Garrett, I swear, if I ever hear of you cheating on me right here under my nose, they will find you buried in the backyard, and don't you think I'm kidding."

He wouldn't doubt she meant it, but at the same time he knew she would think he was a little too friendly with some of the women he met out on the road. There were a couple of them he saw regularly during the rodeo season, and he looked a little too forward to seeing them again. He had a way about him that attracted all kinds of gals. He didn't go looking for them on purpose, but then he didn't have to. He seemed like such a loner, and he appeared to have no responsibility to anyone else. He didn't talk about his family. In Lanny Ray's mind, there was a line separating his rodeo life from his home life, and he didn't like for either side to step over it.

So by the time Angela had run home with Fuzzy's words playing over and over in her head, things had already turned sour between Arlene and Lanny. Arlene gave him one more chance to do right.

"This is it Lanny, the last time I will go through this kind of thing. Be a husband and father, or I will go to the courthouse and file for divorce."

He tried, and it lasted maybe a week. Another late night at Jake's, and their marriage ended. Arlene did just what she said she would do, and he couldn't even blame her. He loved her as much as he always had, but he couldn't be depended on to be a family man. Like a disease, rodeo was in his blood and his heart, and he craved the life that went with it.

For three years, he withdrew from his wife and daughter almost entirely. He would stop by the Opal Street house on occasion, usually unannounced, and most of the time he and Arlene would be in an argument about something by the time he left. He still took Angela with him to work once in a while, but not often enough to know what was really going on in her life. She adored him and prayed at night that she would get to spend time with him, but she was careful not to say such things to her mother. She learned quickly what not to say to keep peace in their little home.

Chapter Six

It was the beginning of a day right out of one of Angela's classroom daydreams when Lanny Ray drove the big car through the back gates of the arena on the second morning of their trip. Before they got out of the car, they could hear the rodeo announcer over the loudspeaker telling the audience about the men galloping down the arena, swinging their loops at fast-running steers. There was activity everywhere Angela looked. Cowboys and horses were coming and going all around the lot. The atmosphere had an excitement that made Angela want to jump out of the car before Lanny could get it parked in the shade of a big tree at the back of the parking area.

"I have to go over and check in, pay up at the office," he said. "You can come on with me, or you can go look around if you want. I'll be back over behind the chutes in just a bit. Just stay out of the way of the rigs pullin' in and out, and don't get in front of the horses. If you want to watch the rodeo, you can park yourself on the fence to the left side of the chute area." As he talked, he pulled his wallet from his back pocket, thumbed out a dollar bill, and handed it to Angela. "You can get a soda pop over at the snack shed." Lanny Ray nodded his hat brim in the direction of a squat wooden building. He turned and took his spurs out of the trunk. Placing one boot at a time on the bumper, he strapped them on. He slung his chaps over his shoulder and hefted his saddle out, settling it on his hip. He slammed the trunk lid down, turned, and headed across the parking lot in long, fast strides. Angela watched him go, sure that all he had on his mind now was his ride.

Angela fairly buzzed with excitement. After many hours exploring Jewel by herself, it didn't bother her to take on the rodeo grounds alone. In fact, she liked seeing this new place on her own. She could take her time, poke her nose in here and there, and not miss anything. The exciting smell of the place—horse and cow manure, dust and sweat, and leather—she breathed it all in as she neared the area behind the arena.

There was a maze of pens and alleyways. Two of the biggest pens held the bucking horses. They were big-boned and wild-looking, with stringy manes and tails and the biggest hooves Angela had even seen, except on workhorses. They stood huddled together, heavy heads hanging over the broad backs of their pen mates. There were all colors, and as Angela looked them over, she picked her favorite, a palomino with a dirty-white mane and forelock. Just maybe, her father would ride that one.

There were cattle in several other pens, the roping steers and bulldogging steers next to each other, and across the alley, the bulls. Smaller calves were bawling so loud Angela could hardly hear herself think. Men on horseback rode up and down the alleys, opening and closing gates with loud clangs and hollering or whistling at cattle to move them from place to place. As she walked around to get closer to the bulls, she had to stop and stare. They stood staring back, flat-eyed and menacing. They didn't move much, a shuffle here and there within the herd. She'd seen plenty of bulls before, but never so many in one place.

She found her way to the arena fence and watched the roping for a while, but as the sun rose higher, she already felt sticky and thirsty. She decided she needed a shady spot and a soda pop. She stood in line with a few cowboys and a couple of little kids, waiting her turn at the order window.

"Howdy, hon, what can I get for ya?" A big woman whose face glowed bright red from the heat inside the shack peered down at Angela from the high window. "Ain't ya on the wrong side a' the arena, sugar, or are you one of the contestant's kids?"

"My dad's a bronc rider," she said and felt proud to tell it.

"Is he good? I bet he is. You're needin' a cold drink, aren't ya?"

"Yes, ma'am." Angela asked for an orange soda pop and took a long, sweet, icy swallow as soon as she'd paid her money and had the bottle in her hand. She had decided to head back to the horse pens when she heard the announcer say to "get ready for the bronc riders" in his booming voice. She wove her way through a crowd of men to reach the back fence where she found a place to perch on the top rail. Horses were kicking up a dust cloud in the alleyways, making their way to the chutes, cowboys whistling and talking to them to move them out. Cowboys were everywhere—gathered in close groups behind the arena, sitting along the fence, and inside the arena, waiting for the nod to open the gate. Angela's heart beat fast with expectation. She watched as riders settled themselves down on their broncs, sitting just right and pulling their hats down snug, and she was swept up in the excitement.

The rider out of chute number one was announced, but before the fast talking announcer could finish his words, the cowboy had already been thrown. He plowed through the loose dirt on elbows and knees, picked himself up, and limped to the out gate through the dust. The riders from chutes two and three rode to the buzzer, and the crowd whistled and clapped like thunder.

When Lanny Ray's name came over the speakers, Angela could feel her heart beat like a drum in her ears. She watched him sit down on his bronc and saw his hat brim duck with his nod to go. The second the gate swung wide, the palomino bronc busted into the arena, and every time he struck the ground, he twisted his body back up into the air. Over and over, he jumped and twisted with his head between his front legs. Lanny Ray sat back and held his seat, long legs swung in rhythm from the horses flanks to high up on his shoulders with each jump and dive. His chaps flapped with his motion, and his spurs glinted in the hard sunlight. The crowd was hollering, and many stood to watch the ride. In less than a split second after the buzzer went off, Lanny Ray flew through the air and landed solid in the arena dirt. He lay still long enough to catch a breath and scare the wits out of Angela, and then he stood, tipped his hat toward the bleachers, and walked toward the back fence. Angela had held her own breath for so long she felt lightheaded when she clambered down from her fence rail seat and ran to meet Lanny Ray, yelling "That's my dad!" to the people around her.

When she caught up with him, he wore the biggest grin she had ever seen on his face, and he had already started shaking hands with another man. She overheard someone say no one would beat that ride today. That turned out to be exactly right. In the end, Lanny Ray scored the highest by far—an amazing 87!

CHAPTER SEVEN

*A*s the celebration of Lanny Ray's ride eventually quieted down, some of the rough stock riders found a shady spot to have a few cold beers and talk about rodeo. Angela sat on the ground with her back against a fence post, watching the men interact and listening to the cowboys' stories. Her father gave his account of his ride several times over, each telling bringing howling and laughter like it was the first time he'd told his story. The cowboys slapped each other on the back to show their approval of their peers.

While Angela watched the men and listened to the banter, she figured out who was who. Red was the most obvious, of course, with his red hair, rusty-colored mustache, and light blue eyes. He seemed to be the nicest of the men. He wasn't as loud and rowdy as some. Toby was the short, muscular one and probably the youngest. He hardly spoke a word. Angela thought maybe he stayed quiet because of being bucked off. She also noticed he kept rubbing his shoulder and occasionally winced when he moved.

Then there was the one named Olin. Though she felt ashamed for thinking so, Olin had to be the homeliest man Angela had ever seen. He stood taller than her father and was thin as a rail. His face was stretched extraordinarily long and thin, as was his very prominent, bony nose. His dark eyes were small in his face and hooded by heavy brows. His smile wasn't a friendly one. It crossed his face like a crooked sneer. At least two teeth were gone, and most of the ones showing were badly stained and rotted or broken away. Angela felt compelled to either stare or look away. She had been brought up with her mother telling her not to judge people by how they looked, so judgment was something she seldom thought about—but that had been before she met Olin. She didn't like the way he talked with the other men. He used a lot of cuss words, and he didn't laugh good-naturedly like the others did. Something about his demeanor seemed angry. Angela's instincts turned out to be correct.

Olin was, in a way, a tormented man. Ever since he had been a boy, he had been different and difficult. Different in that he didn't look or dress like his peers. Different in his poorness and in the things he did. Difficult was a mild way to explain his defiance of any authority figures in his life. His mother would say he seemed to have the devil in him. Trouble followed him like a lost puppy. He spent time in jail as a teenager for destroying private property, didn't finish school, and wasn't willing to work a regular day-to-day job.

His father had cowboyed all throughout his own life and had been a hard living, hard drinking man. A disagreeable sort, he had spent his share of time in jail. He came and went as his selfish lifestyle dictated. Olin grew up idolizing a man he knew little about.

After Olin's first time out of jail, when he was still a kid, he married a woman he didn't really even know. They met in a bar, married soon after, and she was back sitting on a barstool within a week of their wedding. She turned out to be as irresponsible a human as her husband. They soon had a baby girl, and neither of them could claim the sense or gumption to rear a child with any caring. Divorce came before long.

Eventually, Olin fancied himself a bull rider. Not a great bull rider, but it was a place he managed to fit in. A place where nobody seemed to care about his disreputable past. Plus, it meant he wasn't hanging out around his ex-wife and daughter, causing trouble. The divorced couple fought regularly, more over who had to care for the little girl than over who wanted her. The little girl had to learn early on to take care of herself.

Finally, after the excitement had died down and everyone finally cleared out that evening after Lanny Ray's excellent ride, it had grown well past time to get something to eat. As they walked to the big car across the lot, a cowboy yelled out to Lanny, "See ya over at The Rodeo?"

"Don't know about that," Lanny Ray hollered back. "Got my girl here with me."

Lanny Ray drove to a café on the main street of town, and he and Angela had a good meal of Lanny Ray's favorite chicken-fried steak and mashed potatoes. Angela was so excited about Lanny's ride that she chattered away about it. It would have been easy for anyone who knew him at all to see how happy that made Lanny. He smiled and laughed easily at Angela's enthusiasm. They had only been on the road a couple days, and already they were getting along just grand. He felt like maybe this would all work out as he hoped it would.

After they ate and headed out to get in the car, Angela said, "Where we staying tonight?"

"Well, I was thinkin', if you don't mind, I'd like to go to The Rodeo and visit with the boys a bit. They'll be celebratin' a little, I imagine. Least some of them will. Maybe you can settle in with your funny books and get some sleep in the car. I won't stay too long."

Angela was confused. "But we already went to the rodeo."

Her father laughed a little. "I mean the saloon called The Rodeo," he said. "It's where we all go here. What do you think about me doing that?"

Angela shrugged. "I don't know. I guess it's okay if you think so."

Taking her answer as a yes, Lanny Ray drove the short distance to The Rodeo Bar and parked as near the front door as he could. There were several other cars and pickups parked along the street. Angela could see the glowing colors of neon beer signs in the high windows on the front of the building. The door sat deep back from the sidewalk between the high, dark-tinted windows. With the car's engine shut off and the window down, she could hear the jukebox music, men's voices, and a lot of laughter.

She watched Lanny disappear through the door and then looked around to see what else was nearby. The rest of the buildings on the block were businesses, all looking closed up tight for the night. Lanny Ray didn't say she had to stay in the car, but there didn't seem to be anything around to explore anyway. Crawling into the backseat and lying on her soft quilt, she propped her head up, pulled her knees up, and looked through her collection of funny books. She had read them so many times she knew the words and pictures by heart. She could still laugh at Beetle Bailey and Blondie, and she liked the stories of Billy Buckskin and Red Ryder. But she'd grown tired of them and wished she had something else to read.

In a short time, Angela became bored with her books and stacked them on the floorboard. She pushed herself up and leaned back into the corner of the backseat. She could hear Patsy Cline singing on the jukebox, and she sang along in a low, soft voice. "I go out walkin' after midnight, out in the moonlight . . ." Then, for some reason, she got to thinking about home. Not about being homesick, but about Jewel and some of the things she had experienced in her young life. When she couldn't control the direction of her thoughts, she would find herself thinking about her parents being together again. She never got over wishing for it to happen. If they tried again now, maybe they wouldn't fight anymore. And if they did still fight, maybe she could just plug her ears or go outside until it was over. And, as she did so often, she wished she had never, ever told her mother what Fuzzy had said that one awful day, about her father "seein' some gal at Jake's." She still felt sure it had been her fault her parents decided to split up.

When Lanny came out of the bar that night, Angela had fallen sound asleep in the backseat. He eased the big car out onto the street and headed out of town. After a few miles on the quiet, empty highway, he pulled over into a wide dirt lot beside the road and put his seat back. He kicked his boots off, leaned his head back, and instantly fell asleep. He'd had a big day. Lanny Ray Garrett was a winner.

CHAPTER EIGHT

Jewel was afire with gossip. Lanny Ray had taken his daughter away. Poor, poor Arlene, some said. How in the world would she manage to get through this suffering? That rumor was only one version of Angela's leaving town. It came from the minds and mouths of Arlene's friends and supporters.

Sure, they said, Lanny Ray could be an okay guy, but he was no kind of father to be caring for a teenager by himself. His morals had certainly been questionable lately. And what would he do with her on the road? Leave her in the car while he partied with the other cowboys and who knew who else? And poor little Angela. Even if she happened to be a bit of an odd child, she was sweet as could be, and she loved her mom no end.

And, they said, anybody with a lick of sense should know rodeo life was a man's world. Children, especially girls, had no business around all those hard men. The language and the lifestyle were touched by the devil. Some folks were more than willing to believe it.

But, on the other hand, guy's got a right to spend a summer with his daughter, the pro-Lanny side declared. Just because Arlene and him can't see eye to eye don't mean the girl can't have a dad. It would be a wonderful experience for any youngster. Good heavens . . . she would get to stay in motels around the country, see places most folks would never see. She'd be with her own father, who thought the world of her. She would be the envy of all the rest of the kids in Jewel.

Eventually, the rumors got around to Arlene. She heard it all, the good and the obnoxious. By the end of the first week of Angela's trip, Arlene was exhausted from explaining the situation over and over again. Her effort seemed to make no difference in the extent of the gossip anyway. The people in Jewel were determined to squeeze every single drop of enjoyment out of this major occurrence.

Fuzzy and Linc confirmed both sides on a daily basis from their perch on the Mercantile bench. Fuzzy hung in with Arlene. Linc took up for Lanny Ray. They greedily gnawed both ends of the bone of contention.

As for Arlene, she found solace in conversations with Norma.

"No time ago, I sat right here taking up for this town. Goin' on about what a wonderful place it was. Now look. Good Lord, Norma. What could I have been thinking, allowing Lanny Ray to take Angela away?"

"Don't exaggerate, sweetie. He didn't take her away. He just borrowed her for a while. What did she have to say when she called?" Norma asked.

"She told me about some places she's seen. She does like that part of her trip for sure. She said Lanny Ray is ridin' real good. She seems okay. Truth is, she sounds worried about me. She asked me a million questions about what I've been doin.'"

"She'll be okay, Arlene. You know how she worships her daddy. I know he can be a real horse's patootie, but he loves her."

"I asked if she's met with any of her daddy's friends. I was meaning any women friends, but she told me about some of the cowboys. She says they're nice to her," Arlene said.

"Now, don't you be askin' her about other women. You'll put her in a spot she can't get out of," Norma warned.

"Well, wouldn't you ask if you were me?"

"Nope. I wouldn't want to know. Try to relax, hon. Angela will be just fine. As far as this town goes, well, you know how these folks are. Some of these old buzzards can pick and prod somebody to pieces, but if something truly bad happens to somebody, they'll be right there to help."

CHAPTER NINE

$\mathcal{T}$heir first week on the road went by as fast as the scenery. Angela loved watching the world go by through the big car's window. Throughout the desert, there were small shops beside the road where Indians sold everything from pretty handmade jewelry to plastic toys and tobacco. Once in a while, in a deserted spot beside the road, they would come upon an old Indian woman selling her wares on a colorful woven blanket. They stopped to look so many times Lanny Ray finally had to tell Angela that they just couldn't stop at all of those places. They would never get to where they were headed in time for the next ride.

The motel rooms all looked about the same—two beds with faded floral print bedspreads and a tiny bathroom. Fans were a bonus for the sweltering nights. At least they could prop a fan against the screen of the open window and feel the night air.

The truck stops and cafés were so alike they started to seem familiar. The food tasted the same from one kitchen to the next. Some maybe a little greasier or saltier. The smells and sounds were the same. Same men's voices. Same songs on the jukeboxes.

Her father introduced her to people he had come to know as he traveled the rodeo road. It was plain to Angela that the ladies she met all liked her father. They went out of their way to talk with him, and they laughed and teased with him a lot. Most of them seemed nice enough and treated Angela friendly like. They almost all told her what a pretty girl she was and how much she looked like Lanny Ray. She had heard it a million times, but it still made her uncomfortable when someone said she was pretty. One time, when one of the waitresses told her how pretty she looked, Angela had glanced down and said "thanks" barely audibly.

The waitress laughed a big laugh and said, "Don't you be shy about being pretty, girl. One day you're going to be real happy that the boys are all telling you how pretty you are. Yes, you will."

Angela felt her face flush and wished the waitress would go away. In fact, Angela had just begun to look at some boys in a different light than she used to, but she would die of embarrassment if anyone knew about her secret thoughts. She had one good boy friend in school—smart, quiet Joseph. He helped her get her work done and keep her grades up to passing. They had spent a lot of comfortable time together. Once in a while, in the summer, Joseph would even walk to the river with her. They didn't always talk much, both being the quiet type, but when they did, it tended to be about the river or a movie out at the drive-in or something like that. But he was just a friend. It was other boys she didn't really know that she had a curiosity about. Still, she was shy. Angela had come to feel that too much attention from anyone, especially boys, could make her feel real self-conscious.

Although Lanny's and Angela's traveling had no real routine to it, Angela started understanding how things usually worked out. It all seemed to depend on the time or distance between rodeos. Some nights they stayed at motels, and some nights they drifted off to sleep in the car and drove on when Lanny Ray awoke. She also learned that, if time permitted, Lanny would spend the late evening in a bar somewhere. She wasn't keen on the evenings he stayed late. She knew he was drinking and carrying on inside, and she would wonder if he was spending the time with a lady. Besides the uncomfortable thought of that idea, she also would get bored and anxious to travel on.

One day, Lanny Ray went into a long speech about how stressful it was to follow the rodeo and ride those horses. The anticipation and worry about the next draw and ride could wear a guy down, he'd said, not to mention how hard it could be on a man's body, especially since he was getting older. He'd called the time he spent in the bar his "resting-up time." It helped him relax and feel better, and he learned a lot talking with the other cowboys.

Angela thought some of his talk sounded like a bunch of baloney, but she was just a kid and couldn't say for sure. She couldn't grasp the idea that her father was getting older. He seemed the same as ever to her. He didn't look any older. Not to her anyway.

If Angela woke up when her father came out of the bar and got behind the wheel, he would tune the radio knob until he found a country western station for them to listen to. Much to her amazement, Angela learned that her father knew the words to most of the songs just like she did, and he would sing along with the radio, too. It wasn't long until they were comfortable with belting out the words as they glided out across the open land. The radio would crackle with static, especially if there was a lightning storm somewhere nearby. The stations would fade in and out as they traveled away from the broadcast, and they would have to tune in to another one.

Angela treasured the nights he skipped the bar and drove longer. She could snuggle in her quilt and watch the stars in the sky through the back window. She felt protected there, somehow. Wrapped up in her soft quilt in the back of the big car seemed a safe place to be.

CHAPTER TEN

Charlotte turned out to be an extraordinarily special girl. She was fifteen years old when Angela met her. Charlotte and her brother Billy were the children of Red and Katie Bingham. Red had not spoken of his family any of the times Angela had been around him, so she was surprised when they all met up at the same café one morning. Lanny Ray and Angela were sitting in a booth against a far wall finishing breakfast when Red came through the door with his kids following close behind him. The men spotted each other across the room, so Red brought his family around the horseshoe counter to their booth to say good morning.

"Lanny Ray, Angela, these are my kids." He put his hand on his daughter's shoulder. "This here is Charlotte, and this handsome boy over here is Billy." Billy shot his dad a pained look, and his ears turned bright red.

"Charlotte, Billy, this is my good friend and fine bronc rider Lanny Ray and his daughter Angela."

Billy nodded toward them shyly and reached to shake Lanny's hand, but Charlotte smiled big and said, "Hello. It's nice to meet you. You have a pretty name, Angela." Her voice filled the room when she spoke, and Angela saw a few heads turn in their direction.

Angela and Lanny Ray both said hello, and Lanny rose and invited them to sit down. Red said no thanks, they would sit at the counter and just get a quick bite. Charlotte listened to her father speak and then repeated, "No thanks. We're sitting at the counter to get a quick bite."

After Red's family left them to sit at the counter, Angela looked across the table at her father with a question in her eyes. Lanny Ray gave his head a little shake. They finished eating in silence. Lanny gave Red and his family a wave on his way out the door.

"Is there something wrong with Charlotte?" Angela said when they were in the car.

"Well, it seems like it. Red never mentioned it before, but maybe she's just a little slow," Lanny said.

Charlotte was, indeed, a little different from anyone Angela had known before. Eventually, she and Lanny Ray would learn more about Red's family. The story came one day when only the three of them— Red, Lanny, and Angela—were sitting in the shade at a rodeo. Lanny Ray had asked Red how his wife was doing. Red looked a little sad, and then he spoke about his family.

"Wish y'all could meet my Katie," he said. "She is the most beautiful little gal in the world. She's soft, ya know? All blonde hair and pink skin. She has the clearest blue eyes a person's ever seen. I fell in love with my Katie the second I laid eyes on her." He grew silent, and Angela could tell he was looking back in time. His gaze was seeing things much further away than just the rodeo grounds.

"When Charlotte was born, Katie was the happiest mother you ever knew. She doted on that baby. But once we saw how Charlotte wasn't learning like she should be, we got scared, ya know? Started going to doctors, a bunch of 'em, but they all said the same thing. That's when Katie started having spells. She'd get so sad she couldn't get up outta bed sometimes. Christ, I was so worried. I thought maybe she was dyin'. But then, after a while, she'd get to feeling a little better, and then she'd get back to her old sweet self again. She's a wonderful mother when she feels okay. And she never complains about me being gone."

It was true that Katie had some affliction no doctor had really diagnosed. She would be fine for a while, and then she would start sliding into a state of depression and despair. She would be struck nearly dumb and would take to her bed.

"The good church folks stepped right in to help us out when Katie couldn't manage. Charlotte and Billy sure never lacked for love. Made us all close, ya know? We've all learned how to take care of each other. It isn't bad that Charlotte is like she is—in fact, I would say it's made us all better."

When the silence fell again, Angela asked, "Does Charlotte go to school?"

"She did. Went to the eighth grade in some special classes. Afterwards, there wasn't any place for her to go. She wouldn't ever fit in at a high school. She does good, though. She can read and write as good as I can." He smiled for the first time since he had started talking. "Maybe it isn't sayin' much, but yeah, she does okay."

He went on to tell them how she was so crazy about her little brother, Billy, who was just a little over a year younger than she was. Charlotte had her own ideas about people she met in life, he told them.

"She'll watch and listen carefully before she decides who will be her friend and who most likely won't. She has a habit of speaking her mind, even if it isn't always appropriate. Tact sure isn't her main attribute." Red smiled again. "Sometimes she's really funny, and boy does she love to laugh. She's a teaser like me. And like her brother."

Billy had his father's red hair and blue eyes and was a smart young man. He seemed shy, as most boys his age were. He loved his sister unconditionally and had taken on the responsibility of being her protector. Lord help anyone who was rude to Charlotte in Billy's presence.

The next day, after meeting Red's family at breakfast, Angela met up with Charlotte and Billy at the rodeo. They sat side by side on a stack of hay bales and watched the rodeo for a while. Charlotte clapped and laughed good-naturedly, whether the stock riders made the buzzer or were thrown to kingdom come. She was delighted by all of it. When it was Red's turn out of the gate, she squealed with excitement and yelled as loud as she could for her dad to hang on.

When it came Lanny Ray's turn to ride, she said, "Angela, Angela, Angela, there's your father!" She clapped and squealed for Lanny, too.

Later, while they walked together to get a soda pop, Charlotte asked Angela a dozen questions about herself and Lanny Ray. She wanted to know where they came from, what grade Angela was in, where her mother was "right now," when did Angela have to go home, and on and on. It was her way of collecting information so she would have a basis to decide if Angela was friend or foe. Angela liked Charlotte. There was something honest and refreshing about her that made Angela smile. By the end of the day, Charlotte had decided Angela should be her friend.

"Angela, Angela. Can I call you Ang, Angela?" Charlotte asked.

"Well, you can if I can call you Char," Angela answered.

"Okay, Ang. Deal, okay?"

"Deal, Char," Angela said.

It was the beginning of a friendship that would mean much in the days and weeks still to come. They looked forward to seeing each other at rodeos and cafés, and sometimes they stayed at the same motel.

Angela liked Billy, too. He had a dry sense of humor and liked to tease like his dad. He and Angela were quickly becoming good friends when another girl made a grand entry into their lives. Her name was Marie, and Marie was like no one Angela had ever known before. Marie was brash, pushy, and arrogant beyond belief. She was fifteen and looked twenty-five. She was exceptionally developed already, as Billy would later be heard to say with a silly smile, and she was very aware of her effect on others, especially males. She also cussed. Marie was the daughter of Olin.

Marie had long, black hair, worn parted down the middle. She wore eye makeup drawn way up at the outer corners of her eyes and pale, almost white, lipstick. She only wore sandals on her feet, even to the rodeos. She made it clear from the beginning that she did not care a whit about Angela or Charlotte. The very first day they saw her, she came striding across the parking lot and walked right up to them where they stood.

"Are you guys rodeo brats?" she asked in a rough voice.

She had caught the girls so off guard they stood and looked at her without answering right away.

"What's the matter? Cat got your goddamn tongue? Or are you too good to speak?"

"You said a bad word," Charlotte was quick to condemn.

"So what? I'll say it again . . . damn, damn, damn. There, you like that?"

"I don't," Charlotte said.

"So, are you cowboys' kids?" She looked directly at Angela, already erasing Charlotte from sight and conversation. "Does your old man ride bulls?"

"No, he doesn't," Angela answered and then said nothing else. She could already feel her own anger flaring.

"So, maybe he don't ride nothin' then," Marie said.

"As a matter of fact, he rides saddle broncs."

Marie peered closer at Charlotte again. "What's the matter with you?" she said to her.

Angela felt herself bristle at Marie's rudeness and was about to speak in Charlotte's defense, but Charlotte spoke right up for herself.

"Nothing." She put on her best critical look. "You are not a nice girl," Charlotte said back.

This seemed to put Marie off for a second. Most people didn't just say things like that to her. She was the bully who could intimidate people into being careful how they spoke to her. Charlotte already had this mean girl's number.

"You are a bully. You don't even know me and Ang. What's your name?"

"My name is Marie. Olin is my father. He's the best bull rider there is."

Charlotte bristled. "No, he is not. Casey Tibbs is the best bull rider there is." Her voice had grown louder. Charlotte knew just about all there was to know about rodeos and rough stock riders, and no one was going to tell her anything different than the facts. She had been listening to her father and reading about rodeo since she had learned there were books about the life her father loved.

"Who the hell is he?" Marie snapped back.

Charlotte and Angela exchanged quick glances and laughed a little bit. It tickled them that this smart-aleck person didn't know Casey Tibbs, the most famous rough stock rider ever.

Marie looked furious, spun around, strode away at a brisk walk, and didn't look back. She was not used to being laughed at.

It became clear within just the first couple of days that Marie liked Billy and wanted nothing to do with Angela or Charlotte. She flirted with Billy so relentlessly he would become embarrassed as soon as he would see her. Embarrassed, but flattered. After all, he was a teenage boy. Charlotte tried to intervene when Marie's overly flirtatious behavior around Billy made her uncomfortable.

"She is not a nice girl, Billy," Charlotte admonished. "She says bad words, Billy."

"I can't help it if she likes me." Billy would wiggle his eyebrows up and down to tease Charlotte.

Then one day Angela and Charlotte came upon Marie smoking a cigarette by the horse barns. It was not unusual for the girls to wander the grounds when the rodeo took place along with a country fair. They liked to watch the hustle and bustle of the fairgoers and walk down the rows of stalls, looking at the horses and other livestock.

Marie became real put-out when the girls walked near her. She dropped her hand, holding the cigarette behind her back.

"What are you brats doing back here? Spying on me?" she said.

"No. We were just looking at the horses, like we always do. I don't care what you do. Why would we spy on you?" Angela said.

"You better not tell Olin you saw me smoking. I could beat you to a pulp real easy if I wanted to. Just remember that." Marie took a deep pull on her cigarette and blew the smoke toward Angela.

Angela took Charlotte by the arm. "Come on, Char, let's go back to the arena."

After they had walked a bit, Charlotte said, "Ang, she calls her dad Olin. Why does she do that, Ang?"

"I don't know why she does what she does, Char. She's a little crazy, I think. I want you to stay as far from her as you can, okay?"

"Okay, Ang. I will stay as far from that crazy Marie as I can."

Keeping their distance from the wrath of Marie turned out to be easier said than done since they so often traveled in the same direction and ended up in the same places. Angela noticed Olin's old, dented-up, green pickup at the same honky-tonks Lanny Ray frequented. She seldom saw him leaving the bar. Probably because he usually stayed until closing time.

Angela had heard the cowboys talk about how much Olin drank some nights. He was a beer drinker, for sure, but if he did imbibe the harder stuff, he turned mean as a badger and would invariably pick a fight with another bar patron. He was hard to get rid of. It was the barkeep's discretion to call the police or bring out a big stick. On the rare nights she did see him, Angela would sink down in her seat and hope he didn't notice her sitting in the car alone. She always wondered where Marie could be while Olin hung out in the bar. Angela thought maybe she just waited back at a motel where they stayed.

Truth was, Marie could be most anywhere. She had no qualms about roaming around town and seemed to be able to find trouble every-where she and Olin stayed over. She would find the local teenager's hangout or maybe just stand around with other kids on a town sidewalk. No doubt her brashness offended a lot of nice town kids, but girls like Marie seemed to have no problem finding people much like themselves. Smoking, cussing, and drinking were usually high on the evening's agenda. Sometimes her behavior was much worse and might even include shoplifting or breaking the windows of a building or maybe some innocent victim's car. Window breaking was high on Marie's list of fun things to do. She seemed to have Olin's wicked spirit, and she was game for anything the local hoodlums were up to.

She especially liked attention from older boys and would disappear with one for a while if the situation was right. Surprisingly, that didn't happen as often as one might imagine. Boys were intrigued but leery of a girl like Marie, who was a stranger in their town. Her aggressive manner could scare the devil himself.

It wasn't only the teenage boys who had a bit of fascination for Marie. Older men, who had no business doing so, noticed Marie, too. Of course, most knew better than to approach her. The consequences for an older man spending time with a fifteen-year-old girl could be costly in many ways.

CHAPTER ELEVEN

On one of the warmest summer nights they had endured, several of the rodeo men ended up at the same ragtag Prairie Sage Motel in a small Kansas town. They lay over there for two nights. There was a Laundry-Mat where they could wash their clothes, a general store, a post office, a gas station and, of course, a bar. A dilapidated structure connected to the bar held a small café. It had been added on as an afterthought. The floor slanted, and there were cracks between the window frames and the building's walls. One tired-looking woman was both waitress and cook, and having so many customers at one time was proving to be a chore for her. The air inside stayed comfortable through breakfast time, but after ten a.m., the café sweltered. Most customers who came over from the motel took their food in bags and boxes back to their rooms to eat.

The town was surrounded by a dusty expanse of land, and a hot, dry wind blew litter and tumbleweeds against the barbed wire fences. Each of the town's business places had a little shack of a house close behind it, and Angela guessed those must be where the business owners lived. There were no yards, no flowers. The dirt in the hot wind made Angela's eyes feel gritty.

With little to do after the clothes were all done up, the kids had to find ways to entertain themselves. Angela, Billy, and Charlotte played card games for a while and then walked to the gas station to get sodas from the Coca-Cola machine.

Marie did not join in. She sat in the shade in an old metal chair against the wall of the motel building. She read a funny book and polished her fingernails fire engine red. She watched a few cars come and go at the gas station across the street. An attendant would come out of the office and pump gas and check under the hood for each customer. As the evening shadows grew longer, the men left the motel and wandered off across the dirt parking lots to the bar.

Angela, Charlotte, and Billy sat outside at a splintery, old wooden table where it felt cooler. It wasn't long after the men had left for the bar that Marie walked across the road to the gas station. Angela watched her as she stepped through the door of the front office. The entire front of the station was a huge glass window. A young man wearing a blue gas station shirt stood from behind a battered, old desk and greeted Marie with a big smile. Angela noticed them talking for a bit, and then Marie slid up to sit on the edge of the desk and made herself at home. After a few minutes, she lit up a cigarette and offered it to the young gas station man. He took it from her, taking a deep drag. Angela quit watching.

As the evening light became too dim to play cards, the three kids decided to go inside. The motel room doors stayed open for a while to let some cooler air in, but when darkness settled, Angela closed hers to keep the moths and night fliers out of the lamplight so she could read her book. As she closed the door, she noticed the gas station office brightly lit, but no one could be seen inside. She wondered where Marie went. There wasn't much of any place to go.

Lanny came in a couple of hours later. The key in the door woke Angela briefly, and she said hello and went back to sleep. Sometime after that, a loud noise woke Angela so suddenly that she sat up in bed with a start. Her heart pounded, and she wasn't sure what she had heard in her sleep. She sat frozen with anxiety.

"Dad?" she said

"I know, Ang. It's okay. I'm awake," Lanny Ray said.

"What was that noise?"

"I'm not sure, but it came from Olin's room. Shhh, listen," he said.

They both sat still and silent. They could hear voices from next door. Or maybe they were coming from outside. It was hard to tell. Then they heard the room door slam hard, and the noises and voices came loud and clear through the flimsy motel room wall. First, they heard Olin.

"You tramp!" he hollered. "You're just no damn good, are you? You get more and more like your filthy mother every day." There were some muffled thumping noises, and then Marie's voice came to them through the walls.

"You don't scare me, you mean old man. You think you're real tough when you get enough liquor in you. No wonder my mother didn't want to be with you. She hates you!" Marie yelled.

"Shut up, Marie. She don't want you around, either. Why do you think she sends you to live with me?" Olin growled.

"Go ahead, Olin. Go ahead and hit me again. It ain't going to do any good, and tomorrow everybody will know how I got the bruises."

"No, they won't, 'cuz I'll tell them that your friend, the gas station attendant, did it to you. They'll believe it, too, because he came braggin' in the bar about the little gal he had just been with behind the station. All the boys heard him talkin' about you. They all know you're no damn good, Marie."

The next noises Angela and Lanny Ray could hear were obviously made by Olin hitting or pushing Marie around the small room. When one of them bumped into or fell against the wall separating the rooms, Angela feared they would come right through it.

Angela cried. It all seemed so horrible. Lanny Ray moved about the dark room, pulling on his pants and boots and finding the door.

"I want you to stay right here and do not move," he told Angela. "I'm going over there."

Angela heard her father rap on Olin's door. It took what seemed like forever for Olin to respond.

"Get the hell away from here!" Olin yelled. "This ain't none of your business!"

"Olin, it's me, Lanny. Come on and unlock this door. What the hell is going on in there?"

It grew silent for a couple of minutes, then Olin said, "We're fine here, Lanny. Go on now and mind your own business. This is family stuff."

Lanny heard more shuffling around inside, and suddenly the door flew open with a bang. It wasn't Olin in the doorway, but Marie, who stood there glassy-eyed and breathing hard. She slipped past Lanny Ray and out into the cool darkness. Olin walked slowly to the door and looked at Lanny. He didn't say a word, just stood and tried to focus his eyes on Lanny's face.

"Olin, what the hell are you doing, man? You can't be hitting a little girl like that . . . your little girl. What's wrong with you?"

"She ain't no little girl, Lanny. She's no good, just like her ma." Olin's speech came slower and slurred. His face shined with sweat, and his hooded eyes looked sunken into his long face.

"Get what you need out of there, and go bunk in your pickup. You're drunk and ought to get to sleep. Let Marie in here to wash up and get some rest. I mean it, Olin. I don't want to see or hear you till the sun comes up. Don't even think about coming to this door. Understand?"

Lanny turned to go find Marie. She sat alone out at the old wooden table, holding a towel to her face. She didn't acknowledge Lanny Ray when he sat across from her.

"You okay?" Lanny asked her. No answer. "Olin is going out to the pickup to sleep. He won't bother you now. Go on back in and lock the door," Lanny said.

Marie stood and walked to the door. She didn't even look back at Lanny Ray. She went in and locked the door behind her.

Back in their room, Lanny and Angela lowered their voices to a whisper.

"Is Marie going to be okay?" Angela asked

"I guess so. I think she had a bloody nose, but I didn't really see her face," Lanny Ray said.

"It's so awful. What makes people act that way?"

"I don't know, Angela. People just do real dumb stuff sometimes. This probably isn't the first time this has gone on between Olin and Marie. My guess is the gas station man caused Olin to feel embarrassed in front of the boys over at the bar, so he came back and took it all out on Marie."

"Maybe I should try harder to be her friend. Maybe it would help."

"You be careful, Angela. People as bitter and meanspirited as Marie can hurt you. Even though she don't act much like it, she's a kid, and she can't really help how she is. It's the way she's been treated that's made her the way she is."

As Lanny Ray and Angela both tried to get back to sleep, their own personal thoughts kept nagging at them. Lanny Ray thought a lot about all the fights he and Arlene had fought over the years, a lot of them in front of Angela or at least within hearing distance. Maybe one day he would try to talk to Angela about that. Tell her how sorry he felt for acting that way. One thing for sure, it wouldn't happen anymore. Seeing how Marie had been affected by her parents made him feel real bad. Yeah, one day he should talk to Angela about it.

Angela had heard every word of the fight next door. She felt a little sick to her stomach. Her own parents had fought, but never as bad as that. And it hadn't made her hate either one of them the way Marie hated Olin. Maybe she really would try again to make friends with Marie, but she was too tired now to think about it anymore.

The next morning, everybody was up stirring around and getting ready to get on the road. Red and his family and Lanny Ray and Angela walked to the café to get some breakfast. After a bit, Olin came in and ordered something from the same tired-looking waitress to take with him. He looked pale and shaky. He took two bags of food and went out the door without a word.

"What's wrong with old Olin this morning? Too much hooch and dice rollin' last night?" Red said with a grin.

"Reckon so," Lanny said. He wasn't willing to discuss what had gone on in the night. He and Angela had witnessed something awful, and now Lanny Ray couldn't help but wonder where the responsibility of his involvement ended. It seemed clear to him that Marie's safety couldn't be guaranteed as long as she traveled with Olin. It was also more obvious than ever that Olin could be big trouble.

Charlotte and Angela were talking with each other, but Billy stayed unusually quiet, even for him, and he watched after Olin for a long time. Red and Charlotte could sleep through a lightning storm, but Billy had heard everything that went on the night before. Marie was something else, for sure, but Olin, he was a dangerous man, Billy thought. He sure hoped something even worse than last night's fight didn't happen.

CHAPTER TWELVE

*R*odeo life—and the cowboys who traveled to live it—had an objectionable reputation in the late fifties. Of course, it wasn't about packing six-shooters and burning out homesteaders like it depicted in the movies, but it was a rough and rowdy period, a time lending itself to both camaraderie and competition. Strong-willed, self-confident men, who were physical by nature, were brought together over and over again. Add to that some whiskey and ego, and trouble was sure to ensue. The bigger the rodeo, or the rodeo town, the rougher things could get.

The men may not have pulled their pistols and shot up the barrooms, but a fistfight turned brawl could really wreak havoc at the local hangout. If the barkeep saw trouble brewing, he was seldom brave enough—or dumb enough—to try to break it up himself. Instead, he might holler down the bar to "take it outside." Bar owners didn't really want to call the local law unless they had to. Too many calls and next thing they knew the authorities would be hanging around watching for trouble all the time. And that could be real bad for business. No bar patron wanted the law looking over his shoulder. If it came to that, they would just take their business to another establishment down the street. After all, it wasn't the place that really mattered. What mattered was who was there.

And, of course, there were the women who loved the whole scene. Perfumed and hair sprayed, dressed in clothes most women wouldn't have been comfortable wearing—low here, high there—they were plumb giddy about rodeo nights at the local honky-tonk. Their booze usually flowed free, sent to them from down the bar by a cowboy looking for love. They could get just as rough as the men. Catfights were not unusual—the inebriated, green-eyed monster of jealousy usually being the instigator. Love and lust—mostly lust—flowed abundantly on Friday and Saturday nights.

Inevitably, Angela gradually grew more comfortable hanging out in the big car while Lanny Ray spent an evening in a peaceful small town bar with men she had come to know. On a warm night, she could roll the windows down and sing to the jukebox to her heart's content. Besides, she was guaranteed a few new funny books from time to time. The faces of the patrons coming and going became familiar, as most were rodeo contestants.

But the atmosphere and the bar crowd could often be different in the big towns. Those were the nights when Angela saw and heard more than a young girl should. Fistfights landed in parking lots, and foul language filled the hot night air. The women's fights frightened Angela the most. How could they act so mean and crazy? Why would they act like that? What could make them so angry they would actually try to beat each other up? If they could see themselves through Angela's eyes, with their hair-sprayed beehives sticking in all directions and their eye makeup smeared down their cheeks along with blood and dirt, then surely they wouldn't ever do that again. Or would they? There had never been any women in Angela's life to compare.

The men's fights were physically violent, ugly, and filled with unnatural groans and growls. If there were women involved—and there usually were—they cried and begged for the men to stop, which seemed to only make the men fight more. All of this was driven by irrational emotions Angela could not yet understand. It made her stomach hurt, and she carried the pictures in her mind for a long time. Sometimes she watched in horror, and sometimes she snuggled down in her quilt and covered her eyes and ears.

If Lanny Ray knew something like that was going on out on the sidewalk or in the parking lot, he would leave the bar and call it a night. He would tell Angela not to worry about what she had seen. It had nothing to do with them, he would say. Those were just people who had too much to drink and were acting crazy. His words didn't help to soothe her much. The awful things she saw and heard would stay with her anyway.

Angela never told her mother any of this kind of stuff when she called her. She knew, if she did, Arlene would insist Lanny Ray send her home immediately, and Angela would rather put up with a few bad nights than have to go home early. So, instead, she told her mother about her father's accomplishments at the rodeos, bragging on how good he'd been doing. She described the sights along their route, and she talked a lot about Charlotte and Billy. Arlene sensed Angela's genuine fondness for Charlotte and felt relieved to know her daughter had a friend. Even though Charlotte was different, it was clear she came from a nice family and that her father and brother had also befriended Angela. It comforted Arlene to know Angela had responsible people around her. Angela and Arlene would sometimes linger on the phone for a costly amount of time, and Angela would add coins to the slot after they finally hung up. After their talks, they would both feel a little sad. Arlene, especially, wished summer would hurry and be over and things brought back to normal. She wished a hundred times that she had not let Lanny Ray and Angela talk her into allowing this trip.

Even after weeks had gone by, Angela still loved the rodeos. The excitement of it never grew old. When she sat on the back fence to watch the rough stock riders, her heart would pound with anticipation. Even though she always wished for her father to be the best, she had her favorite riders she rooted for. Of course, Red was one of them, and Angela, Charlotte, and Billy had great fun clapping and hollering their support. Sometimes there were trick riders and ropers there to put on a show. Angela daydreamed she could be a trick rider, doing those incredible stunts on her own black-and-white pinto horse. She could follow the rodeo like her dad did.

Charlotte could make everything delightful. She would just about burst with enthusiasm when she became excited about something. She could and would delight over everything from lemon pie to rodeo events.

"Ang, Ang, did you see that lady, Ang?" she would say about the trick riders. "She stood up tall right on top of her horse, Ang!"

The bronc rider named Toby Abel gave Angela an old rope, and she carried it around behind the chutes and practiced throwing loops almost constantly. She had plenty of help, and tips from the best ropers came free and easy. It wasn't long until she had mastered the art of roping fence posts, imaginary calves, and Toby's boot when he would hold his leg out for her. She hoped that once she got back home her father would let her rope from one of the ranch horses.

It wasn't hard for the kids to find things to entertain them through the midday hours. They climbed haystacks, played cards, and prowled the area to see what they could see. Angela befriended every dog she came across, and it wasn't unusual to see more than one following her around the rodeo grounds. Her independent streak was growing deeper and deeper, but she knew to show up to meet her father after he rode, and she never missed seeing his ride. Lanny Ray gave her enough money to buy a soda pop and something to eat, and she had no other needs.

She didn't see Marie as often as she had before the dreadful night at the motel. Marie wore a blue-green bruise at the corner of her left eye for quite a while and tried in vain to cover it with face powder. When she and Angela did come across one another, Marie never spoke of that night and had little else to say. Angela steered a wide path around Olin. She was genuinely afraid of him.

Then one evening just before dark, Angela was sitting in the big car parked in front of a local bar, reading a book and lost in its pages, when she sensed someone watching her. She glanced up with a start. There stood Marie on the curb in front of the car, just looking at her.

"Hi," Angela said with surprise.

"Hi, yourself," Marie answered. "What are you doin'? Readin'?"

"Yeah, I am. Are you waiting for your father?" Angela said.

"There's nothin' to do in this hick town," Marie said with a shrug.

Angela put her book down and got out of the car. She was thinking about what she had said to Lanny Ray that night at the motel where Olin had abused Marie, about how she would try to make friends with Marie again. She sat down on the curb, and after a minute, Marie dropped down beside her.

"Don't you get sick of this crappy life?" Marie asked her, looking around the dirty parking lot.

"No. Not really, I don't. I kind of like it most of the time. I get to be with my dad and watch the rodeos and see him ride the broncs. Besides, it's only for the summer, and then I'll go back home to my mom's and go to school," Angela said.

"Where do you live?" Marie asked.

"Jewel. It's just a real little town. I was born there. What about you?"

"Well, I did live near Phoenix with my mom, but I couldn't stay there anymore. She couldn't take care of me, so she sent me to be with Olin."

"Is your mom sick?" Angela asked. "You know, Charlotte and Billy's mom is sick sometimes."

Marie laughed a little. "You could say that. She's a drunk. She falls off the wagon, and all she does is sit in the bar or sleep all day."

Angela didn't know what to say. They sat quiet for a minute, both looking away across the street.

Finally, Marie said, "Somebody turned her in for not takin' care of me, and a woman from the county came by the house. They were going to send me away to a foster home, so my mom said I had to stay with Olin until the county quit watchin' her. I think she just wanted to get rid of me. Olin says she don't want me, anyway."

Angela remembered the harsh words she overheard that night at the motel.

"Seems real bad, Marie. Is Olin always so mean to you?" Angela asked.

"He doesn't always hit me. Sometimes he tries to be nicer. There's just somethin' wrong with him. He's always been mean. It's just worse when he drinks too much whiskey."

"When will you be able to go back home where your mom is?" Angela said.

"Well, I been thinking about running away and just hitching rides. All I have to do is go to a truck stop and ask for a ride till somebody says yes."

"Can't you just ask Olin to send you home on the Greyhound or something?" Angela tried to picture Marie walking around asking strangers for a ride all the way to Phoenix.

"I ask him all the time. He just says no. I don't know why. He doesn't want me, either. I think he's afraid he'll get in trouble with the law or something if he just quits having me around sometimes." Marie was still looking away across the street.

"So what's it like in Phoenix?" Angela asked.

"It's real good," Marie said. "There's always parties and stuff. All my friends there listen to rock and roll, and we dance and stuff. I used to have a record player at my house. I had all of Elvis Presley's 45 records and a bunch of others. One time I came home and they were all gone. Record player and everything. I think one of my mom's friends took them."

"Well, didn't your mom get mad? I mean, didn't she even try to get them back?" Angela was having a hard time getting the picture.

"Naw, she don't care. She hates rock and roll. She likes all this hick music, like what's on the jukeboxes."

"I like country western music, too," Angela said.

"I bet you don't even know who Elvis is or who Ricky Nelson is." Now Marie was getting snarly again. Probably trying to pay Angela back for laughing at her because she didn't know who Casey Tibbs was.

77

"I've heard them, but in Jewel we mostly listen to country music," Angela defended.

"I'm goin' to try to find something to do." Marie stood up. "Do you want to come with me?"

"Oh, no thanks. If my dad came out and I wasn't here, he would be real worried," Angela said.

"Too bad," Marie said. "See ya later."

Angela watched Marie walk away down the street. She got back in the car and thought about Marie and her strange life for a long time. Her father had been right. What an awful way to grow up. Angela's life hadn't been great, but at least she had people who cared about her. Nobody really cared about Marie. As soon as Lanny Ray came out, Angela told him the whole conversation.

"Olin is inside, and he's a ornery man tonight. I'll be surprised if he doesn't pick a fight pretty soon. He gets meaner with every drink. Where do you think Marie might have gone off to?" Lanny Ray said.

"I don't know. Mostly she just walks around the main parts of town until she finds somebody to talk to. Or she finds a local café to hang out at for a while. You just never know about Marie. She might find some other town kids to be with," Angela said.

"We'll take a little drive around and see if we can spot her," Lanny Ray said. "I sure would hate to see her going through another night like that last one."

Again, he thought about his responsibility to Marie, now that he knew Olin abused her. Should he tell someone? Who would it be? Then what would happen to Marie? Would it be better for her to be put in a foster home somewhere? He had heard some bad stuff about foster homes, too. She probably wouldn't stay there, anyway. Sure as heck, she would run away. Then she would just be out on the street. Lanny Ray was at a loss of knowing what to do to help her.

CHAPTER THIRTEEN

$\mathscr{A}$rlene had a new friend. A man friend. And Jewel's gossip circle was spinning out of control. This was undoubtedly turning out to be the best summer for gossip the town had known in a long time.

A few anti-Arlene enthusiasts were practically in a frenzy, but at the same time they claimed it was really no surprise. After all, with Angela taken away by her father, a woman like Arlene would be out looking, right? There she was, a good-lookin' woman with no responsibility. Footloose and fancy-free, they said. A few pot-stirrers even insinuated that the married women better keep an eye on their husbands.

But most people knew it was hard not to like Arlene, and the forked tongues were growing fewer and fewer. Some had decided to sit on the fence and see what happened before they took sides.

Her friends and supporters were excited. They wanted to know everything there was to know about the new man in Arlene's life. The few who had seen him said they were not one bit surprised that he, in a way, resembled Lanny Ray. He had the same dark-eyed good looks. Not many of Jewel's folks had actually met him, but if they had, they crowed about it. He's real friendly, they said. Had a nice way about him.

Arlene, herself, had been thrown for a loop, for the two had first laid eyes on each other in front of the Mercantile. He, on his way out, and she, going in. They dodged one another's steps in the doorway—back and forth, back and forth, a slapstick dance—right next to the bench where Linc and Fuzzy sat and watched as the meeting unfolded like a big screen movie. They were so delighted, they could have applauded the scene.

The man pardoned himself for the awkwardness, and then he asked where he might get a cold drink and a sandwich. Where else but Norma's Blue Moon Café? And that is where they met again a few days later. It was all very casual. They chatted like new friends do, about work and family. Grady was a feed broker. Jewel and the Sweetwater Valley were on his new route.

"So did you tell Angela about your new man?" Norma asked Arlene.

"Lord no, why would I do that? Besides, he isn't my man," Arlene said.

They were sitting in their booth at the café on a hot afternoon, drinking sweet iced tea. Arlene had carefully polished her newly grown-out fingernails a frosty coral.

"Everybody knows you're sweet on him. You've always got your hair done up, and you bought yourself a couple of new blouses. May as well own up to it. You'll have to tell Angela eventually." Norma lit another cigarette. "Come on, Arlene. He likes you, too, and you know it."

Arlene capped the bottle and slapped both hands flat on the table.

"Norma," she said, "I don't want to discuss this anymore. Grady is a nice man, but I don't want another man. I don't even remember how to act. I get all goofy, actin' like a teenager when he's around, and it just gives me a stomachache. I'm not putting myself through all that foolishness for a man."

"Oh, baloney. You're not eighty years old. It would do you good to have a man around, if you know what I mean. You're still fairly young." Her words brought a quick glare from Arlene. "There's Grady—big, strong, handsome guy—wantin' your attention. There are a few women in this town who think you're plumb nuts."

"Look who's talkin'. When's the last time you ever gave a man a chance?" Arlene said.

"My kids ain't outta town, Arlene. And they're younger, and I don't have the luxury of having my own time. I'd really give this town something to talk about if my kids left with their rotten daddy for an entire summer." Norma actually looked pouty. "Besides, there aren't many Grady's around."

"I don't care. I'm not telling Angela anything about Grady." Arlene blew on her shiny, wet nails.

She didn't mention how Grady would be coming over to her house that evening for supper. She felt like she was keeping a secret from her best friend, but she couldn't stand hearing the remarks that were bound to be made. It would be the first time he had been in her little house, and she was nervous as a cat. She'd been in Maude's three times already because she couldn't decide what to fix for supper. That morning, she had tried on half the clothes in her closet, like a teenage girl going on a first date.

If Grady was still around when Angela came home, she would just tell him they couldn't see each other anymore. No big deal. Angela didn't need to be involved in Arlene's private life. Her father was the one who was known for that kind of lifestyle. Arlene was determined not to ever be like Lanny Ray.

CHAPTER FOURTEEN

$\mathcal{I}$t never crossed Lanny Ray's mind that the life he lived that summer with his own daughter might, in a way, be abusive to her. There was no structure in their daily life, and it never occurred to him there should be. Her nutrition lacked . . . everything. As far as he was concerned, a hamburger with everything on it and a milkshake covered the five food groups. And the very worst thing he did was leave her to sit in a car—in a honky-tonk parking lot—several times a week, all alone. Didn't he know she could be taken away from him for that one offense, just as Marie could be taken from Olin? He drank, though not usually to excess, and then drove his big car with his daughter in it. Angela had no bedtime. Hell, sometimes she didn't have a real bed.

Still, Lanny Ray thought for sure he was becoming a better father as each day passed. It was true they had developed a bond like there had never been before. They talked about all sorts of things. They laughed. They sang the honky-tonk songs they both loved. They shared their meals, no matter that they were usually awful meals. They spent more time together than any father and daughter he had ever known back in Jewel.

If he gave a thought to how Arlene would feel if she knew how comfortable he and Angela had become with each other, he would get a little tickle of guilt in his gut. After all, for twelve years Arlene had been the most important parent in Angela's life. Arlene had always been the stable one. The one who put Angela first, no matter what. She taught Angela the rights and wrongs of life and how to behave herself. Lanny Ray had not been an example setter, that's for damn sure.

When those thoughts crowded into his mind, he didn't let them hang around too long. He had a way of sending them away and thinking of something else—like his last ride, or his next ride.

His usual way of showing Angela how much he cared about her was to give her an extra dollar or two to spend, or he would buy her more books. She never failed to smile and say thank you to him. She just seemed to require so little to make her happy.

He had no idea that just being with him was what really made her happy. She was living a twelve-year-old tomboy's dream, traveling the rodeo circuit with her bronc-riding father. She wore scruffy boots and pants with holes in the knees and played around the stock pens. Thanks to Arlene, she had ingrained hygiene habits, keeping her washed up and in clean underwear. Nobody made her brush her unruly curls. She was a beautiful girl with wild hair and shining eyes and a big smile on her smooth, tanned face.

She got to help open gates, and sometimes she even got to sit on a cowboy's horse and watch the rodeo over the fence. She loved the smell of the big leather saddles and the horse sweat. No, Angela sure didn't feel abused. She knew that waiting in a car for your father to come out of a honky-tonk was probably not the best thing for a girl to be doing, but she was trying to get used to it. Besides, it wasn't hurting her any. Some nights she would feel a little lonesome maybe. Especially if she thought a lot about Arlene and home. But that was only natural.

One hot evening, as she sat on the fender of the big car a ways down the street from the bar Lanny Ray had gone into, three girls, around Angela's age, walked by on the sidewalk. They were chattering happily and laughing together. It was plain for Angela to see that they were good friends. One spoke to her as they walked by, and Angela smiled and said hello. To her surprise, as she watched them walk on down the street, she felt a longing to be part of their little group. She could see herself walking with them and laughing at something one of them said. She had always been so guarded about sharing herself with anyone—the longing to belong was an unfamiliar feeling for her.

She thought maybe she would ask Lanny Ray if Charlotte could ride with them in their car sometime. Maybe when they had a few days' travel between rodeos, Char could stay a night with her. It might be fun. She and Charlotte were friends, and Charlotte could sure make Angela laugh. She would have to think about it. Red might not even allow his daughter to go with Angela and Lanny Ray.

A couple of days later, the idea of Charlotte traveling with them in their car was still on her mind. Angela brought the subject up to Lanny Ray.

"I've been thinking it might be fun to ask Charlotte to ride with us for a while. Maybe stay one night at a motel with us. Do you think that would be okay? I mean, I know we have to ask her father and all. He might not let her, though. He probably wouldn't. No, he wouldn't, would he?" She looked defeated.

"Are you asking me if she can, or are you telling me she can't?" Lanny Ray teased. "I'll mention it to Red and see how he feels about it. Just don't be too disappointed if he says no. He worries about Charlotte."

True to his word, Lanny Ray did talk to Red about Angela's idea. At first, Red seemed reluctant to say yes.

"I don't know. She's never done that before. She's always with her mother or me at night. I'll talk to her . . . see what she says," Red said.

The next morning when they all pulled into a truck stop to eat, Charlotte bolted out of Red's car and ran as fast as she could to Angela. She was so excited she could hardly speak.

"Ang, Ang, Ang! I get to ride in your car, Ang. I get to stay all night with you and everything. I won't be scared, Ang. I promise I won't." Charlotte was the most excited any of them had ever seen her.

"I know you won't be scared, Char. We'll have fun. Bring your cards, and we'll play games, okay? And you can read all my funny books."

Red took a paper sack from the trunk of his car and handed it to Char.

"Here's some things you might want, Charlotte. You be a real good girl for Lanny Ray here, and we'll meet up tomorrow, okay?" He gave his daughter a gentle hug and a pat on top of her head.

After breakfast, they piled into their cars, and Charlotte's adventure began. For the first hour, she chattered nonstop. Angela caught her dad's smile and saw him roll his eyes as if to say, "Holy cow . . . this girl can talk."

Eventually, Charlotte calmed down, and the girls talked between themselves while Lanny Ray listened to the radio. They each made their comfortable spots in the corners of the big backseat. They shared Angela's quilt and played cards on the seat between them. After a gas station stop, they both dozed off to sleep. Angela was content. It felt nice to have someone to share the day with.

It was a long day of driving and almost dark when Lanny Ray pulled off the road into the dirt lot of an auto court. The place he rented had two tiny rooms with a double bed in each one. He would sleep in one, and the girls would share the other. Red and Billy had stopped in the town back along the road a ways to have something to eat and would be along even later. It ended up being a long night and not very restful for Lanny Ray. The girls giggled and talked half the night. Twice he tapped the door between the rooms and shushed them.

When Lanny Ray and the girls met up with Red and Billy, Charlotte pleaded with Red to let her stay again. Her first night away from her family had turned out to be a successful and fun adventure, and she wanted more.

"I had the best fun in my whole life," she told him. "Didn't I, Ang?"

Red looked to Lanny Ray and got a nod. She was so happy, he couldn't tell her no.

"I should tell you, Red, I'll be stopping by Josie's Place for a while tonight. I don't plan to be real long, but I've got friends to see there. I hope you don't mind, the girls will have to wait on me a bit," Lanny Ray said.

By this time, Red was well aware of Lanny Ray's traveling habits and how he often left Angela to wait for him when he went to a bar or a roadside honky-tonk. It wasn't something Red thought to be really right, but Angela sure didn't seem to mind. As long as the girls didn't go away from the car, he guessed it would be okay. And Charlotte wanted to go with Angela so badly.

"I guess that'll be all right, Lanny. As long as they stay in the car, I can't see no harm in it," Red said.

The girls happily tumbled into the big car and settled into their places. Charlotte chattered again like she had the day before, but she eventually calmed down, and they brought the playing cards out for a game.

It rained a bit off and on. Angela liked the times it rained. She felt cozy in Lanny Ray's big, smooth car, and it had a soothing effect on her. The long windshield wipers moved across the wet glass, making a rhythmic sound. Somewhere in the distance, lightning flashed and rumbles of thunder rolled over them. There was too much static to keep a good radio station tuned in.

When she rolled her window down just a crack, she could smell the dampness on the big, sagebrush-covered land that was rising and falling beside them. Something about that made her feel melancholy. For a couple of minutes, she had a strong heart-tug of homesickness. Maybe tonight or tomorrow she should call Arlene again. She had a lot to tell her about with Char traveling with them and all. She would ask Lanny Ray about calling later.

"What's this Josie's Place you're going to tonight?" she asked Lanny Ray. "Is this something special? I heard you tell Red you had friends there." Angela always thought that Lanny Ray was probably talking about women when he mentioned friends.

"I do," he answered. "I've been stopping there since my very first time out on the road. Before I even met your mother. I was feelin' pretty low when I came this way. I'd never been away from Jewel so long before, and boy, I felt so lonesome and sorry for myself. It was raining, just like this here, and I was hungry, so I pulled in to get a bite to eat. Josie and her husband Rafael welcomed me in, fed me homemade tamales, and served me up a couple of beers. They treated me real nice. We've been friends ever since. I always look forward to seein' them."

CHAPTER FIFTEEN

$\mathcal{I}$t had been another long but pleasant day on the road. The girls read, played games, and took two naps, dozing in their backseat corners like contented cats. They had stopped for a supper of sandwiches at a tiny café in the late afternoon and then continued on. It had just turned dark when Lanny Ray pulled into a large corner parking lot at a four-way stop, where the crossroads wandered off into the desert. The lot was graveled and deeply rutted, with huge puddles everywhere from the thunderstorms passing overhead, one behind another. The big car bounced smoothly across the deep dips toward a low-slung building that sat halfway back in the corner of the lot. Angela saw that it was a much bigger roadside honky-tonk than most of the places Lanny Ray stopped at, and there were a lot of cars and pickups there nosed in around the front of the building. A country western band played inside, and the bass of the guitars and drums drifted across the lot, thumping out their rhythm. Even with the windows up in the car, she could hear the music clearly and hoped it would stop raining for just a little while so she could roll a window down.

A tall pole light loomed near a front corner of the building, shining a bright circle of light that quickly grew dim around its edges, and there was a bright neon beer sign in each window along the side of the bar. Other than that, it was coal-dark to the outer reaches of the parking lot. Lanny pulled his car into a vacant space and shut the car off.

"I'm going to run in and get you girls a soda pop and some peanuts, and I'll be right back. Sit tight, okay?" Lanny Ray climbed out of the car and trotted his way around the puddles, shoulders hunched under the rain, until he disappeared through the front door. He came trotting back in no time, and to Angela's delight, he had a cellophane bag of salted peanuts, some candy, and two grape soda pops for her and Char.

"Thank you, Mr. Garrett. You're a nice man, Mr. Garrett," Char declared with her big smile.

"You're very welcome, Charlotte, but I think you should start calling me Lanny Ray. I'll just call you Char, how's that?"

"Deal, Lanny Ray," Charlotte said with a smile.

"Deal, Char." They grasped right hands and made a little playful handshake.

Lanny Ray assured them he would be back in a short while to check on them and asked again if they felt they would be okay for a while. Angela sensed he was being extra careful because Charlotte was with them that night. She knew he wouldn't leave them if he didn't think it safe.

After he had hurried away again, the girls settled back into the seat, eating their salty peanuts and enjoying their grape soda pops. Charlotte was quiet for so long that Angela asked if she was okay.

Char said, "I never sat in the car in the dark without my mother or my father. Do you get scared, Ang? Isn't it spooky, Ang?"

"No, I've never been afraid of the dark, Char. When I was little, my mother used to say the dark is our friend. She said God made the dark so we could dream and rest. She said things around us were just the same in the dark as in the daytime, except we just couldn't see them so good."

"That's nice, Ang. Real nice. You have a good mother. I have a good mother, too, Ang. She just gets sick sometimes."

"Maybe you and Billy will get to go see her soon," Angela said.

"Yeah, maybe me and Billy will, Ang."

Angela could hear sadness in Char's voice, so she changed the subject and talked about what good bronc riders their dads were. That got Charlotte on a whole new subject, and she became her animated self again. They giggled and laughed about everything and nothing for a long while.

The more they talked and laughed, the more the inside of the big car's windows fogged over, and they could just barely see the fine little raindrops on the outside of the glass. They watched them build and trickle down the glass. They made up a game of picking which one would reach the bottom first. The bright colored lights from the neon beer signs zigzagged down the windows in watery trails.

They were drawing comical faces on the inside of the steamed-up side windows when they heard someone angrily shouting nearby. A man's harsh voice startled them into silence. Something thumped against the back fender, causing the big car to dip and sway. Both girls spun around only to discover they couldn't see a single thing through the big back window. Because of the rain and the fogged glass, the window was only a gray slate. Charlotte spoke in a quick whisper.

"Ang, what is that? Who's talking outside, Ang? What hit Lanny Ray's car?"

"Shhh. We have to be quiet, okay, Char? Don't talk right now."

"Okay. I won't talk right now, Ang. But you say when I can, okay, Ang?"

"Shhh," Angela said again.

"You're a lying son-of-a-bitch," a man hollered out. "You know damn well I didn't cheat you." He sounded so close beside the big car.

"Yeah, you did. Everybody in there knows you're a cheatin' snake. I should have never played at the same table as you in the first place. That was my own mistake."

The other man said, "I've had it with you. You think you can just go around doin' whatever the hell you want."

"If I do what I want right now, you'll be layin' down there in the mud where you belong," the first man said.

There came a loud thud, then another and another. Angela knew it was fists hitting flesh. The car bounced a couple more times when the men fell or struggled against it. They had moved around to the back of the car by the trunk. The girls sat and stared into the blank back window, frozen in place with fear.

"Get down, Char," Angela finally said softly. "Get down as far as you can on the floor. We don't want them to see our shadows in here." She didn't even know if such a thing might be possible, but she didn't want to risk being seen.

Char did as she was told. "Ang, I got down like you said," she whispered.

"Good girl. We have to stay quiet," Angela said. For once, Charlotte didn't have anything to say.

The men continued to wrestle around. Angela knew because they were still making the car move. The noises they made were frightening—grunting and growling like mean dogs. The thuds of fist against flesh kept on. When they spoke, she could no longer understand them. They were out of breath, and the words were breathed out in gusts.

Finally, one of the men said more clearly, "Get up and fight, you lousy son-of-a-bitch. You can't call me a cheater and get away with it. I'll beat you to kingdom come. Get up, I said."

The girls, crouched down on the floorboard, stayed motionless, and then, suddenly, it grew eerily quiet. The men had stopped speaking, and the girls couldn't hear the sickening sounds of fighting anymore. They didn't want to move and were trying to hold themselves still, but they cringed and gasped again when they felt a slight movement of the car, so slight it could have been just a strong hand against it. The men were still there. Or at least one of them had to be.

Angela heard Charlotte sniff and realized she was crying.

"It's okay, Char. Don't cry. I think it's over. Maybe my dad will be out here to check on us soon." She spoke softly and put her arm across Char's shoulders.

"Okay, Ang," Charlotte said in a small wobbling voice.

Angela slowly, very slowly, pushed herself up and tried to peer out of the back window again. No . . . she still couldn't see out. She crawled on her hands and knees across the seat to the side window. She put one small finger against the glass and made a short swipe. A clear, watery slit appeared in the fog on the window, and she quickly peeked through it. What she saw shocked her so hard she shuddered. Several feet away from the car, the blurred figure of a man was bent low, his hands gripping the outstretched arms of another man lying on his back and being dragged through the mud and water. His body was coated in mud from his head to his boots, and his hair was matted to his head. The little peephole fogged over too fast, and she couldn't see the man's face.

"Ang . . . ?"

"Shhh . . . wait, Char. Don't talk yet."

Angela put her hand up and made her peephole bigger. She watched in horror as one man dragged the other one away from the car. He dropped one limp arm, had to bend lower to pick it up again, and kept tugging. His feet were slipping in the mud, and he fell backwards, sitting hard. Trying to move quickly, he kept losing his footing. He would glance around furtively, and one time, it seemed to Angela that he looked directly toward her. She quickly dropped down onto the seat, resting her forehead on her arms, and waited. When she built the courage to look again, the men were still moving away, out of the ring of yellow light from the tall pole and into the dense darkness of the lot.

Angela had begun to tremble so hard she could hardly remain sitting. She found Charlotte's hand and pulled her up onto the seat next to her.

"It's okay now, Char. They're gone. It's all over." She found her quilt and tugged it up close around both of them the best she could. They were both shivering as if they were in a snow bank. "My dad will be here pretty soon."

They sat huddled there in silence for several minutes, breathing easier and trying to make sense of what just happened as time seemed to drag in slow motion.

Angela had just started to speak when there came a loud cracking sound against the big car's side window. The car swayed from the brute force of it. Both girls screamed, short and shrill, and flung themselves to the other side of the car's seat.

"Roll this window down," a man's voice growled through the foggy glass.

"No," Angela tried to yell, but her words sounded weak to her own ears. "Go away."

The man hit the window with his big hand again, and the impact shook the car even harder. The girls cringed into themselves and mashed themselves against the opposite car door. Charlotte sobbed a long shaky sob. They could hear the man tugging on the door handle.

"Roll it down right now, or I'll break it out."

Angela stretched across the seat and reached as far as she could with the tips of her fingers and found the knob to crank the window down. She trembled so hard she couldn't control her hand, so it took several tries before she was able to give the knob a couple of turns. The window slid down only a few inches.

Angela was still struggling to turn the knob when the man put the lower part of his face right up to the opened window. She could only see his watery silhouette with the light from the pole shining down behind him. She could smell the sourness of him. Her stomach twisted with nausea and fear.

"I know who you are in there. You listen to me. If you tell one single person what you think you saw out here tonight, you will be a sad and sorry little girl, do you hear me?"

"Yes." Angela's voice cracked. "Yes," she said again, louder.

"Fact is, I'll tell you what. I hear that you told anybody anything about this, that daddy of yours that you love so much will disappear, and you won't ever see him again. You understand that? Nobody'll see him again. So you better get yourself straightened up right now, so when your daddy comes out to check on his little girl, you're going to act just like nothin's happened." The man's voice sounded low and throaty. His breathing was ragged, and some of his words were hard to understand. He stood there, breathing his sour breath into the car. Angela waited. She thought he was going to say more, but, finally, the man turned and walked away into the dark.

Angela couldn't move. She stared after the dark form through the window where the face had just been. She heard an engine start somewhere over on the dark side of the lot and saw headlights shining crazily across the rutted parking lot. In just minutes, she heard another pickup start. Then more headlight beams bounced across the lot.

She let herself slump onto the seat. Char . . . oh my God . . . how would she make Char understand that she must never tell anyone what happened? Charlotte sobbed with her face hidden in the quilt. Angela had to make her stop crying before Lanny Ray came out to the car.

"Char. Char, listen to me." Angela still whispered as if someone might hear her. "You have to stop crying now. The bad man really is gone. I saw him leave. Did you hear what he said about my dad, Char?"

"Yes, I did, Ang," Charlotte said into the quilt.

"Then you know how important it is to never tell about tonight, right? Right?"

Charlotte uncovered her face. "I know, Ang. I heard what that man said. I won't tell anybody, Ang. I promise."

"Do you really know what it means to promise something? This is very important, Charlotte." Angela gripped Charlotte's hand hard and leaned in to her to look her in the eyes.

"I know what promise means, Ang. I learned it a long time ago. You called me Charlotte, Ang." She looked hurt.

"I'm sorry. I'm worried. I'm scared. That man will hurt my father."

They sat quiet for a long time. Angela was sure that the poor man who was drug away through the mud must have been dead. She had never seen a dead person before, but he'd looked like he could have been. Besides, if it had only been a fistfight, why would that other man be so worried about anybody knowing?

Charlotte quit crying and sat, shrunken back into her corner of the big backseat. Angela had begun to relive the whole awful thing in her mind. She could hear the men's voices and recalled what they had said. Suddenly, it occurred to her that the man who had threatened her didn't know that Char was in the car with her.

What exactly had he said? "You'll be a sad and sorry little girl ..." He had only been speaking to her. He'd only threatened Lanny Ray. The man didn't say anything about Red because he didn't know Charlotte was there.

The girls sat without moving or speaking for what seemed like a very long time. Angela's instincts were urging her to get out of the car and run to get Lanny Ray, but she couldn't do that. What would she say if she found him?

"Char, did you see the man?" Angela said.

"No, I didn't see the man. I was too scared to look, Ang. I hid in your quilt. I was quiet though, wasn't I, Ang?"

"Yes, you were, Char. You were very quiet," Angela commended her friend. "Did you know the man's voice, Char? Do you think you ever heard him before?"

Charlotte didn't answer right away. "No, it was too mean," she finally said.

Angela tried to think hard about every word the man had said. She tried to hear again exactly what his voice sounded like. Was there something familiar about it? Maybe just the way he said some of the words he used? No, she guessed not. It was hard to concentrate right then. Pictures and voices kept flashing through her mind so fast they were getting mixed up. She tried closing her eyes against them, but then the pictures only became more vivid and frightening.

The girls were still and silent when they heard Lanny Ray slip the key into the door lock. The noise scared them, and they both jerked instinctively. Lanny Ray opened the door and climbed into the car. His hat was wet and dripping off the back of the brim. The girls had been so deep in thought they hadn't even noticed that it had begun to rain harder.

None of them knew that the dark-red smears of blood on the back fender and trunk of the big car were turning a pale pink in the raindrops and trickling down into the reddish-brown mud. A telltale clue, lost in the rain.

"Hey, girls," Lanny Ray said happily. "Sorry to be in there so darn long. It was real good to see Josie and old Rafael again. They are darn good people, that's for sure. You gals ready to go? I bet you are. Were you sleepin'?" He turned to really look at them.

"Almost," Angela said. Charlotte didn't speak. "I think Char's about out."

Angela had given Char the opportunity to stay quiet, and she had taken it. She'd pulled her end of the quilt up over her face.

"I just found something in the mud here by the car," Lanny Ray said. He turned the dome light knob and held something up to the light to see it better. "Oh. It's just an old shirt snap, I guess. It shined in the light, and I thought it was maybe a big sparkly diamond or something." He handed it back to Angela. "Here," he teased, "don't say I never gave you anything."

"Gee, thanks a lot." Angela kept her voice as light as she could. She wiped the mud from the white pearl snap with her fingers to get a better look. It was still attached to a tiny bit of blue cloth and had wet stringy threads hanging down. She guessed it was no good anymore. She held it and unconsciously rubbed it between her thumb and fingers. It felt smooth and soothing. With Lanny Ray there, she wasn't feeling so afraid, and her body lost its tension. She felt as if she was melting in the safety of her father's presence and her warm corner of the car. She held a corner of the quilt up to her cheek.

The big car bumped and swayed back out onto the main road. Lanny Ray sat back and got comfortable behind the wheel for the drive to the next motel. Lost in his own thoughts, he didn't notice the silence in the backseat.

CHAPTER SIXTEEN

$\mathcal{I}$n the clean sunlight of morning, the horror of the night before seemed surreal to Angela. The memories were already dim. The pictures in her mind were dark and seemed far away, both in time and place.

Char was her funny, chatty self all morning. Angela, who had worried so much about how Char would be, was bewildered but relieved to see her so upbeat. It seemed as if Charlotte had forgotten what had happened. Her mood was contagious, and it lightened Angela's outlook.

When they met up with Red and Billy, Charlotte was tickled to see them and hugged her father's neck tight.

"Did you miss me, Billy?" she said to her brother.

Her brother rolled his eyes. "Are you kidding, Charlotte? It's been the quietest two days I ever had." He put his arm around her shoulders and gave her a squeeze.

Charlotte poked his ribs. "You're a big kidder, Billy. You are."

She turned to Angela. "Billy taught me about promises, Ang. Billy knows I'm a good keeper, Ang," she said.

"Well, that's good Char," Angela said, "because promises are very important."

Angela stuck close to Lanny Ray for the next few days. She didn't wander the grounds like she usually did. At his next rodeo, she hung around in the chute area and sat on the back rail to watch. When the cowboys gathered around Red's truck for a few beers, she sat on the running board and listened to them talk among themselves. If Olin and Marie came along, Angela quietly left and made her way to Lanny Ray's big car. As she passed by them, she avoided looking at Olin and said a brief hello to Marie.

She hadn't seen Billy and Charlotte since morning, and she guessed they'd spent the day at the motel. She thought about how much they must miss their mother by now. Poor Char. She had a lot on her shoulders these days. So far, she had stuck to her promise.

Suddenly, Angela had a strong yearning to call her own mother, and the feeling stayed with her all day. Later that evening, she asked Lanny Ray for extra change and hunted up a phone booth near the motel office. It was hot and stuffy inside, so she left the door open and leaned against the coolness of the glass. She felt relief flood through her the moment she heard Arlene's voice in her ear.

Later, when Arlene shared the news of the call with Norma, her own voice was solemn with worry.

"She sure doesn't sound like herself. It's like she's keeping some secret, the way she picks around at her words."

"Don't get too worked up, sweetie. You know how teenage girls get to be." Norma rolled her eyes. "Moody. You say black, they say white. You aren't askin' about Lanny's women friends again, are you?"

"Well, I mighta mentioned something about friends in general." Arlene looked sheepish. "I don't press her about it. I just kind of provide an opening for her to talk about Lanny's friends."

"Provide an opening? You aren't foolin' her. She knows darn well what you're saying, and maybe she just doesn't want to talk about it. You need to quit that, hon."

"We talk about other things, too, Norma." Arlene's tone was defensive. "I tell her everything that's happened around here. Takes about five whole minutes. She tells me about all the places she's seen. I can just hear a difference in her, is all. Oh, never mind."

"I'm sorry, Arlene. Don't get huffy at me. I'm just tryin' to make you feel better."

Norma left the café booth they'd been sitting in and brought back a fresh glass of sweet tea for her friend. She lit another menthol with her new, slender, silver Zippo lighter and exhaled a blue cloud toward the ceiling. She squinched an eye to avoid the smoke and studied her friend across the table.

Norma said, "She'll be changin' a lot, you know. It can't be helped. She's almost a teenager. This trip will change her, too. You'll have to get used to just knowin' that's going to happen."

Arlene sat back in the booth with a big sigh. She ran her fingers through the curly hair at her temple.

"I know it. It's just hard, you know. She's all I have."

Angela herself had felt guilty after the phone conversation with her mother. She had answered all of Arlene's questions, although sometimes she couldn't bring herself to be perfectly honest about everything. She cleared her conscience by deciding that omitting wasn't the same as lying. It seemed like there were more and more things Angela couldn't tell her mother. The secrecy wasn't a good feeling, no matter how she justified it.

One evening after the parking lot incident, Angela didn't feel like eating, but she also didn't want to stay in the motel room alone while the others went out. When Lanny Ray asked if she wanted him to go get Charlotte, Angela said no. She had begun to avoid everybody but her father, and even when the other kids were nearby, she made excuses to be inside after dark.

"Well, Ang, you can't have it both ways, hon. You don't want to go, but you don't want to stay by yourself. Tell you what. If you'll just hang in here a bit by yourself, I'll go get us something to eat and bring it back. How's that?"

"Okay, I guess," she said. "You're coming right back though, right?" She could not keep the anxiety from her voice.

"I promise." Lanny Ray had no idea what this was about. This was new behavior for Angela.

At the next rodeo, she was sitting alone by the bronc pens, watching the horses, when Marie came by.

"What's the matter with you lately? Gettin' homesick for your mommy?" Marie chided. "You look like a sad ol' hound dog."

"I always miss my mother," Angela said. "I'm not sad. I just like to be alone sometimes. So do you, Marie."

Angela was so direct, Marie didn't always know what else to say. She couldn't get under Angela's skin with words like she did with other people. Angela acted more like a grown-up than most of the grown-ups Marie knew.

"Have you seen Toby around?" Marie said, looking toward the stock pens.

"Nope. I haven't seen Toby for a while. Didn't he go on north last week?"

"I sure hope not," Marie's eyebrows raised, and she batted her heavy black lashes. "He's pretty cute, don't you think?"

"I never really thought about it, Marie. Toby is just a nice guy, that's all. Besides, he's way too old for you. Why don't you find a nice boy your own age?"

"Well, I don't like nice boys much. They act like little kids. I like older, more mature guys. They're a lot more fun, if you know what I mean." Marie smiled a wicked smile.

"See you later, Marie. I have to go." Angela was not in the mood for Marie's nastiness. She stood and walked away to watch Lanny Ray come out of the chute.

When Lanny came out of the arena's back gate, he observed, once again, how Angela waited there alone. He'd noticed she had been quieter the last few days, and she spent her time alone. He hadn't seen her chatting and giggling with Charlotte. In fact, he had hardly seen Charlotte at all.

"Hey, Angela," he greeted her. "Want to get a soda pop with me? I sucked in a ton of dust out there today."

Angela smiled big. "Heck, yeah. Sure glad I showed up. You rode real good again today."

She felt better, calmer, just being there with him. Her insides quit churning around like they'd been since she'd seen Marie earlier.

"I been wondering about you, girl. You're awful quiet these days, and I never see you with your sidekick. What's that about?" Lanny Ray said.

Angela was caught off guard for a moment. She hadn't guessed it was so obvious that she was avoiding her friends.

"Oh, it's nothing. I think Charlotte is homesick for her mother, that's all. And you know how Billy watches over her. I think they mostly stay at their motel room."

"Are you homesick, Angela?" Lanny Ray asked. He was hoping she wasn't. He would understand if she said yes, but now he and Angela had grown closer, too. He sure wanted her to make the rest of the trip with him.

"You know, Angela, if you really wanted to go home, you could probably make the trip on the bus. I just want you to know I sure do like having you with me this summer. I guess this was kind of a big test for both of us, wasn't it?" Lanny Ray said.

"Sometimes I miss mom a lot," Angela said, "but I don't want to go home now. I'll be okay."

"Well, we're on our way to closin' the loop now. There's still some beautiful country to see. We'll be going over some real pretty mountain roads. It'll be a lot cooler up there, and I think you'll like it." He gave her shoulder a comforting squeeze.

They found a shady spot and sat to drink their soda pops. It was a comfortable silence. They were so familiar with each other's ways now, neither felt it necessary to fill in the quiet.

As they headed for the big car, Angela thought to ask about their friend.

"Did Toby go north last week?"

"I don't know. I guess he must have. I was wondering that very same thing. I didn't ever hear him say he wasn't going on with us, but he's a young'un," Lanny Ray grinned. "Boy's got a mind of his own."

"Marie was asking," Angela said. "Don't you think he's really old for Marie?"

"Oh Lord, yes. Don't tell me that girl is chasin' Toby now." Lanny shook his head.

"She just asked about where he was. Said he was cute," Angela said. "She doesn't like boys her age. She says they're too immature." Angela made a prissy face, tossing her head and peering down her nose, mocking Marie.

"I don't know what in the world will ever come of that girl. I think trouble is her middle name. Toby would have a conniption fit if he knew she was thinkin' of him in that way."

The subject of Marie made Angela think about Olin. She had become good at avoiding him, staying on opposite sides of the stock pens or heading the other way when she spotted him. Every time she saw him, she became more leery of him. She knew what he was capable of after seeing how he hurt Marie.

"I'm real afraid of Olin, you know," she blurted out like a confession, looking away from Lanny Ray.

"I don't blame you none, Angela. He's a real bad guy, it's for sure. But he won't bother you. He's too much of a coward to have to face me. He's the kind of guy who picks on people who have no way to defend themselves. He knows what I would do to him if he ever laid a hand on you. Try not to let him scare you, okay? But you be sure and tell me if he ever bothers you at all. At all."

"Okay." Angela nodded, but she was still afraid.

When they reached the little motel they were staying in, Red came out of his room to ask if they wanted to go get some supper with him and the kids. Lanny Ray looked at Angela, and she nodded yes. She knew she needed to try to be nicer to Charlotte and her father and brother. They had all been good friends to her. They were going to think she wasn't being very nice if she kept making excuses for not joining up with them.

They met up down the road at suppertime, and Angela was happy to see that Charlotte was acting like her old self, so she relaxed and followed suit. Billy was his usual funny self and kept the girls laughing all through supper.

When they started back to the motel, Charlotte climbed into Lanny Ray's big car with Angela for the ride back. Angela instantly became uneasy again—she was so worried about Charlotte forgetting and saying something about what had happened in the parking lot at Josie's Place. The man's words came back as clear as could be every single time she thought about that night. He had said she wouldn't see her father again if she told anybody what she'd seen, and she believed him.

After they pulled in at the motel, Charlotte stayed put while Lanny Ray got out of the car.

"Ang, are you mad, Ang?" she said.

"No, Char, I'm not mad at all. Why?" Angela said.

"I think you're mad or sad, Ang," Charlotte said.

"I guess I'm just worried, Char. I'm worried about that man at Josie's and what he said about my father," Angela told her.

"I'm keeping the promise, Ang," Charlotte said.

Angela gave Charlotte a smile, and they left Lanny's big car together. She would feel better for a few days. She wasn't as anxious about things. As long as no one ever said anything about the night in Josie's parking lot, it would eventually all go away.

CHAPTER SEVENTEEN

*T*he days passed comfortably for a week or so. Angela's fears had calmed down some, and she no longer thought about her secret almost constantly, like she had been. She still spent a lot of time alone, but that was Angela's way. She stayed close around Lanny Ray at the rodeo, and he hadn't made any social bar stops all week, so she had not been left alone to wait in the big car.

She still preferred to avoid Olin and Marie, and even that hadn't been a real problem for a time. Marie must have found someone to hang around with or stayed at the motel, and Olin wasn't showing up with the other cowboys as often. Maybe he was staying low because he had acted so hideous the last couple of times he drank too much. Angela thought perhaps Olin was like Marie's mother. Marie had told her how her mom would stay sober for a while and then "fall off the wagon." Angela knew what that meant, and she couldn't help but have pangs of sympathy for Marie.

Since the first morning of their trip when Lanny Ray had given her the atlas, Angela had traced their route every day. It was fun to see the names of all the places they had been. In hindsight, some of the days seemed to blend into each other, and it was hard to keep track of them all. She wished she would have kept a diary about all the things she had seen to help keep the days separate in her memory. She had known girls in school who chattered about their diaries and how they wrote in them every night. They had keys that opened a lock on the cover so no one could read the secret things they wrote. Angela wondered how they could have so many secrets needing to be locked away. She didn't have many secrets. In fact, she didn't have any she could remember until she witnessed what had happened that night in Josie's parking lot. She would never have written that secret down anyway. It was too awful for words.

One morning, she asked Lanny Ray how long it would be until they got back to Jewel. It was hard for her to determine by looking at the map. They went here and there in too many directions. Sometimes they had even backtracked for miles to return to the road that would move them on their way. Lanny Ray thought over her question a minute. Angela wasn't expecting the answer she got.

"Well," he said, "I'd say about three weeks or so. But I've been thinkin', if you get really bad homesick and missing your mother, well, I could maybe try to cut the trip a little shorter."

"Do you want me to go back sooner?" Angela said. This was the second time the subject of going home had come up.

"No. Now see, I knew you'd think that if I said it. That ain't what I mean at all. The next few weeks will be gone before we know it, Angela, and our summer will be over. I don't look forward to the end of it, you know." His voice was quieter than usual.

"I don't need to go home early. I'll be fine, I swear. But do you think I'll be home by my birthday? Mom would be sad if I wasn't."

"I guarantee it, kiddo," her father said. "I wouldn't let you miss out on a big birthday like that one. I can't believe you're gonna be a teenager. I sure hope you don't have a serious boyfriend," he teased.

Angela was embarrassed. "I don't want a boyfriend. I'm too young to have one. I don't want a boyfriend until I'm way older, like twenty-five. And I'm not getting married until I'm really old."

"How old?" Lanny Ray asked.

"Maybe thirty."

Lanny Ray let out a burst of laughter. "You know what? I said exactly the same thing, sissy. I sure did. And then I met your mother and fell in love, and I plumb forgot I ever said such a thing. Life has some funny ways, and we never know what's going to happen."

It was hot, dry, and dusty at the next rodeo town. Lanny Ray drew a good horse and had an outstanding ride—a big sorrel bucker, who had made a name for himself and the stock supplier. Lanny Ray rode him clean and scored high. The gelding's big hooves threw the dirt into the air every time he vaulted up from the arena floor. It was amazing how many moves a horse could make in eight seconds while trying to rid himself of his rider, but Lanny sat him admirably. It was a spectacular ride.

It was early afternoon when they were ready to pull out. He and Angela and Red were talking over the plans for the next couple of days in the shade behind a little snack building when an unexpected sight caught their attention. Rolling slowly through the back entrance gate to the rodeo grounds was a Randall County Sheriff's car and behind it, trailing in its dust, was what appeared to be a town police car. They drove straight over to the snack building, bouncing and swaying over the ruts in the dirt lot. The sheriff's car window was rolled all the way down, and the driver's elbow was resting there on the door. The big man inside wore dark glasses and a cowboy hat, and his bulk appeared to take up ample room in the front seat.

The police car pulled up and parked close beside the county car. Both drivers emerged at the same time. The policeman hurried around the back of the sheriff's car while the sheriff heaved himself from behind the wheel and hefted the weight of his gun belt to a more comfortable position, and then they both walked to where Lanny Ray, Angela, and Red were having their discussion. Angela turned away and waved the drift of parking lot dust away from her face with her hand. Red, always friendly, was the first to speak.

"Howdy-do, officers. Pretty hot to be out here today, ain't it?" He stuck his hand out for a shake.

It was the young-looking policeman who stepped forward, shook Red's hand, and said, "Hello, sir."

The deputy touched the brim of his silverbelly Stetson and said, "How you boys today?" He paid no attention to Angela or Red's offered handshake. Before Red or Lanny Ray could answer, the deputy asked where the rodeo office might be.

After Red pointed out the way to the office, the big man said, "You boys going to be around here a bit?"

"We were just gettin' ready to head out," Lanny Ray said. "Me and my daughter anyway. Don't know about Red here."

"I'd appreciate it if you'd stick around here a few minutes. We may need to talk to you and some of the others here," he gestured toward the arena with a big thick hand. "We'll be back when we finish up in the office." With that, the deputy wheeled on a boot heel and headed off in the direction of the rodeo office. The young police officer followed close behind him.

"Well, I reckon that was an order, don't you?" Red said to Lanny Ray. "Wonder what this is all about."

Every person in sight had stopped to watch as the lawmen got out of their cars and approached Red and Lanny Ray.

"Hey, Lanny," somebody hollered, "I told you not to rob that bank, didn't I?" There was some laughter, and Lanny Ray waved a go-away gesture without looking up.

The two men squatted on their haunches with their backs against the snack building's wall. Angela sat on the grass with her legs crossed Indian style. Everybody who walked by had a comment to make about the deputy and the policeman. The predictable comments were already getting tiresome when the lawmen returned from the rodeo office. Red and Lanny stood as they approached.

"Either of you fellas know a man by the name of Toby Abel?" the deputy asked.

"Yes, we sure do," Red said, and Lanny Ray nodded in agreement. "Has something happened to Toby?" Angela stood and moved next to her father.

"How well do you know him?" the deputy asked without answering Red's question.

"We all know him pretty good," Red said, looking to Lanny Ray. "'Least most of us do."

"He's made almost the whole rodeo circuit with us," Lanny Ray added, "and some of us knew him the last couple of years, I'd say. Is Toby in trouble?"

"When's the last time you two boys seen Toby Abel?" the deputy said.

"Well, let's see," Red said first. "Boy, I'd say more than a week ago since he headed off in another direction."

"Yeah, it's been about a week or maybe a little longer," Lanny Ray added.

"What exactly would you mean by 'in another direction'?" the deputy asked.

"We just figured he decided to head back north, maybe pick up a ride or two that way, and then go on home. You never know what those young boys are thinkin'. They can change their minds at the drop of their hat."

"So he never actually said that's what he was going to do?" the deputy asked.

"Maybe to somebody. Not to me," Lanny Ray said.

Lanny Ray was getting more than a little annoyed because the deputy wouldn't say why he was asking about Toby, or even say if Toby was okay. He was getting more worried by the minute that maybe he wasn't okay. He tried one more time.

"We think pretty highly of Toby and would feel real bad if he was in some kind of trouble. We'd sure like to know if we can help him out any."

"You could help out by knowin' where he is. Or knowin' somebody who does know where he is," the deputy said. There was a sarcasm creeping into his voice.

Lanny Ray felt a little prickle on the back of his neck. What was going on here? It was feeling wrong. He sure wished the deputy didn't have to act like he was knowin' some big secret.

"He has folks in Utah," Lanny Ray said. "Maybe he's there already. He has a mother there, and a sister, I think. I know he calls them pretty regular."

"His folks ain't heard from him for well over a week," the deputy said. "It was them that called us. Anybody else here we might need to talk to? Somebody who knows more than you fellas?"

"Well, like we said, most the rodeo cowboys know Toby, but I'd say we would be more apt to know the most about him," Red said.

"I need a specific day you last saw him. Can you remember?" the deputy asked.

Lanny Ray and Red looked at each other, trying to think back through the days. The young policeman took a little notebook and ballpoint pen from his shirt pocket and was poised to write any information the cowboys might give. He had yet to speak a word since he and the deputy had returned from the rodeo office. He looked like the deputy's secretary, ready to take shorthand.

"I reckon it would be the day we left Milton, so that would be, let's see, yeah, about nine days ago. Is that about right, Red?" Lanny Ray said.

Red nodded in agreement. "Yeah, and then I didn't see him at the next rodeo and figured he'd gone north."

"Do either of you recall what he mighta had on last time you saw him?" the deputy asked.

The cowboys both smiled a little. "We don't pay much attention to that kind of stuff. So long as a man's got his hat and boots on, that's about all anybody expects."

"Glad you boys can see some humor in this," the deputy said.

Angela touched her father's arm. "I think I know what he might have had on the day we saw him." She spoke directly to Lanny Ray, already leery of the deputy.

"Who are you?" he said, looking at Angela.

"She's my daughter. Her name is Angela." Lanny Ray's words were clipped with annoyance.

"How old are you?" the deputy asked without even looking at Lanny Ray.

"Almost thirteen," Angela replied.

"So you know Toby, too, do ya?" he said

"Yes, sir. He's a friend," Angela said.

The deputy studied Angela for a moment. She looked to her dad. A familiar uncomfortable feeling squeezed her stomach. This man was a grown-up bully.

"What do you remember about Toby on that day, Angela?" the deputy asked.

"Well, he was finished riding for the day when I saw him by the bronc pen. He looked happy, you know, smiling, because he had a real good ride. He had on a red plaid shirt, maybe with some blue, but not much."

"Do you usually remember what people you haven't seen for a week were wearin'?" The deputy looked doubtful of Angela's statement.

Angela looked to Lanny Ray again. His face was flushed, and his body stiffened. This deputy was a rude bastard, and Lanny Ray wasn't going to let him bully his daughter.

"No, sir," Angela said, "I don't usually remember what folks wear, but I noticed Toby's shirt was tore at the elbow. Like when the material wears thin and your elbow pokes through it. I just saw it, that's all."

The police officer was writing quickly in his notebook. When Angela looked at him, he gave her a nice smile, as if attempting to make her feel more comfortable.

"I'd like for you boys to stay around here for tonight. There might be some more questions in the morning. I'm Deputy Beale—MJ Beale— and this here is Robbie, the new boy from in town. He's just learnin' the ropes about missin' person cases. I'll look you boys up in the morning."

Deputy Beale turned and walked to his car. The police officer did the same, and they never spoke one word to each other. They climbed in their cars and drove out just the same as they had driven in.

Red, Angela, and Lanny Ray turned away to let the dust settle. A lot of curious folks stood some distance away, still watching. Red and Lanny Ray didn't want to talk to them right then. Their thoughts were reeling, and they were worried.

"The kids and me are at the White Bird Motel, if you want to stay there. I'm ready to get outta here," Red said.

Lanny Ray and Angela followed Red to the White Bird, another run-of-the-mill motel. At least it had several shade trees for relief from the heat of the afternoon. They all eventually settled at a picnic table in the shade of a tree, and the inevitable subject of Toby came up. Billy and Charlotte were both obviously worried as soon as they heard the story. But it was Billy who seemed almost angry. Billy had always thought Toby was probably one of the nicest people he'd met. He was quieter than the rest of the cowboys, like Billy himself, and he had always treated Billy like a good friend—like an equal instead of just a boy. He sure hoped something bad hadn't happened to Toby.

Red said, "Maybe if we went to the town police and asked them what was goin' on, they would tell us a little more. That poor policeman who was with Beale might still be around."

"Good idea. Let's go together, then we'll all get something to eat after that," Lanny Ray said.

When they parked at the police station, the kids waited in the car. Angela went over the entire rodeo grounds scene with Billy and Charlotte, repeating everything the deputy had said. She told them how she had pegged Beale for a bully, not unlike Olin or Marie.

Charlotte's eyes teared up. "I don't want something bad to happen to Toby, Ang. He is a real nice man. I don't want any *more* bad things to happen, Ang."

Angela was alarmed by Charlotte's words. She knew what Charlotte was referring to. *Don't say any more, Char. Don't say any more,* Angela begged silently. *Don't talk about it in front of Billy.* She avoided looking Billy's way in case his eyes had a question in them.

They stayed quiet then, lost in their own thoughts, but Angela's heart was beating fast. Would that night always come back to haunt her and make her worry? No, she was sure once she got back home and didn't see Charlotte or the rest of them all of the time, it would all be forgotten. Once they were home in Jewel, the monster of a man who had threatened to hurt Lanny Ray would be far away.

When the men came out of the police station and got in the car, all three kids asked questions at the same time. Their words tripped over each other.

"Hold on. Hold on a minute," Red said. "We're going to tell you."

"Officer Glenn told us a little bit more about what has gone on here. And by the way, his name isn't Robbie, it's Robert. I got the feeling he don't care much for Deputy Beale and his condescending ways. Officer Glenn says word was sent out to all the law enforcement agencies along the route where Toby's family thought he might be or at least traveling through. Toby's sister had a birthday a few days ago, and when Toby didn't even call home for it, the family knew something was wrong. So far, no one has seen or heard from Toby since we all saw him last. They've sent the law to check out every rodeo office to see if Toby has been there. So far, he has never entered a rodeo anywhere else."

"Shouldn't somebody go look for him where we saw him last?" Angela asked.

"Smart girl, Angela," Red said. "That's exactly what they're going to do. They'll start there, and if they don't come up with anything, they'll move in this direction and the routes north."

"This is bad, isn't it, Dad?" Billy said. "I mean, where could he be that somebody wouldn't know about?"

"I don't know, son. Maybe he met a pretty girl and couldn't tear hisself away. Pretty gals can make men do goofy things, you know," Red teased to lighten the moment. Charlotte wiggled her eyebrows up and down at her brother. She loved the chance to tease him. She liked to see his ears turn bright red. She received her dirty look with glee.

"Can we go look for Toby?" Angela asked. "All of us could look for him."

"Well, Ang, I don't know. I guess we'll wait and see what Deputy Beale has to say tomorrow and then figure out what we should do," Lanny Ray said.

They found a drive-in to get hamburgers and malts, and they all ate quietly. Worry dampened their appetites, and neither of the girls finished her meal. It was hard to think of anything to say that didn't have something to do with Toby. He was all they could think about right then, and none of their ideas about his disappearance made sense.

When they got back to their motel, Charlotte went to get her cards so they could sit and play a game outside. Card games could be a saving grace. Distracting. And thought-provoking if one wanted to win.

Lanny Ray was casually leaning against the door frame at the motel, looking out across a patch of scraggly grass, when he mentioned to Angela that he may take a walk and get a beer somewhere.

She lashed out so quickly she shocked herself and stunned Lanny Ray.

"No," she said. "You can't go off and leave me again tonight. I don't want you to go."

"Angela." Lanny Ray's voice was stern. "Where the hell'd that come from? I don't go off and leave you."

"Yes, you do. All the time. I'm alone in the car, or I'm alone in some crappy motel room." She was almost crying. She stood between the two lumpy beds with her hands on her hips.

"Well, I could see how maybe you feel a little bit lonesome in the car, but I'm always right there close by, and you never seemed to mind before. You've always got your books and everything. And as far as being alone in a motel—well, Angela, most times you know half the people staying in it. Now, that's not what I would call being alone. You ain't abandoned, Angela." Lanny Ray was on the defensive. He didn't like having to explain himself. Not to nobody. Not even to his daughter.

She was crying by then. She couldn't help it. Her chest and throat hurt with all the words she wanted to yell out. She wanted to tell Lanny Ray how scared she sometimes was of Olin after he beat his own daughter. She didn't want to be alone in the same motel Olin was staying at anymore. And even more, she wanted to tell him every single thing that had happened at Josie's Place. Let it all out. How terrified she and Charlotte were that night. How it made her sick to her stomach when she thought about what that man had said through the dark, wet window. She wanted him to know how constantly worried she was, that if she said the wrong thing or, God forbid, if Charlotte said the wrong thing, someone was going to make him, Lanny Ray, disappear. Those were the words that horrible, sour-smelling man had spoken. The words that haunted her. Her daddy would disappear. She wanted to say all of those things so bad it made her head pound and her throat ache.

Lanny Ray was confused and surprised at Angela's behavior and her crying. She'd hardly ever cried. He wondered how, after all this time, he hadn't realized that she felt that way about waiting for him on the nights he went out? She had never once said anything, had she? Was he just really not paying attention? He thought she was fine about it. In fact, he thought things with his daughter were great. They had made this fine trip together, and he still got to do a little drinkin' with the boys and meet up with his old friends. Angela always seemed so much older than she was, and he hadn't thought it necessary to worry about her. Well, now he didn't know what to do.

"Listen, I won't go tonight, Ang. Dry your tears. I didn't know you felt this way, you know." Was he angry? Maybe he was. Maybe he did need to get her on home earlier than planned. If Arlene knew about this, there would be hell to pay. He knew the wrath of Arlene.

Angela dried her tears as fast as she could, wiping them away with the backs of her hands. She hated to get emotional and cry in front of anybody. It left her feeling bewildered and out of control. She was usually so tough. She didn't ever want to cry anymore. She had already learned that it was better to keep most feelings to herself. She took a few deep breaths.

"I'm sorry," she said softly. She cleared her throat so she could speak up. "I don't know why I got so upset. I don't mind if you go out. Really. And I'll be just fine here. I know Red and Char and Billy are right there close."

"Naw," Lanny Ray said. He had lost all desire to go anywhere. "Why don't you go get Charlotte and the cards, and we'll sit outside here and play a few hands. I need to get some sleep pretty soon anyway. Really, Ang. I'd like to stay here and play some cards."

Angela finished wiping her wet face on her shirt sleeve and left their room to find Charlotte. Lanny Ray sat on the edge of the thin, lumpy mattress of the motel bed for several minutes, looking around the dreary room. She was right. It was a crappy motel room. He sure had some thinking to do. He didn't feel he was really a bad guy, but there was something inside of him telling him he wasn't doing a lot of things right, either. He let out a big sigh. Yep, he had a lot of thinking to do.

Chapter Eighteen

*I*nsistent pounding on the motel room door yanked Angela and Lanny Ray out of the deepest, much-needed sleep of their restless night. Lanny Ray peeked around the edge of the heavy window curtain by his bed and saw the glare of headlights from a car parked as close as it could get to the door of the motel room. If not for the sidewalk, the car's bumper would have reached the door.

Who the hell would do such a thing? Lanny Ray wondered.

"Garrett, its Deputy Beale. Meet me at the coffee shop across the street. I'll be waiting. Bring your friend, Red."

Lanny Ray lay back on his bed. God, what a jerk the guy was. If this wasn't all about Toby, no way would he cooperate with him anymore. Toby? Where the heck was Toby? Lanny dressed and went to knock softly on the door of Red's room. Red opened the door a crack and squinted out at Lanny Ray, who told him about Beale coming to say they had to go across the street to talk to him. Red yawned big and said he would be right along.

Lanny Ray made his way across the wide street, pushing his unruly hair back and resetting his hat. A night of worry about Angela left him feeling tired and headachy. He could have used another hour or two of sleep. He pushed the door open into the café and blinked against the bright light. Beale sat in a big horseshoe-shaped booth. He could barely sit comfortably within the confined space where the table crowded his great belly. He watched Lanny Ray walk past the counter and sit down across from him. It was too early for many customers to be in yet. The waitress came right over with a menu and a big lipsticked smile. She looked fresh for so early in the morning and greeted Lanny Ray with obvious interest.

"What can I get you this morning, suga'?"

"Just coffee, please," Lanny said to her. "Red will be along in a minute," he said to Deputy Beale.

Beale nodded and didn't say a word, so Lanny Ray didn't speak any more, either. The waitress brought coffee and another smile. Lanny sipped gratefully. Red entered and made his way toward them.

"Morning," he said. "Deputy Beale, how are you this morning?"

"I'm good, Red, how about you?" He still had not spoken to Lanny Ray. It was apparent that Beale didn't care for Lanny any more than Lanny cared for him. Lanny Ray wondered how Red could be so nice to such a bastard, and so early in the morning.

"I heard you boys made your way to the local police station after I saw you yesterday. Talked to Robbie, did you?" Beale said.

"We did," Red answered. "Officer Glenn was just getting off shift, so he took a few minutes for us. Nice young man, Officer Glenn is."

Maybe Red had his own way of getting to big Beale. Lanny liked that.

"This morning, I am going to put out word to the surrounding counties that Toby Abel should be considered a missing person, so we therefore have to consider there may have been foul play. There's a group of folks from this county here, and a couple more, that can get organized to do some searching once we have an idea where to begin."

He looked at Lanny Ray. "I hear that after you left the rodeo in Milton, you stopped over at Josie and Rafael's place. That right?"

"Yes, I did. They're old friends of mine."

"So you know Rafael pretty good then?"

Lanny gave a short version of how he had come to know Josie and Rafael.

"I see. Somebody said there was a young cowboy there who could have been Toby. Know anything about that?" Beale said.

"No, I sure don't. I was there for a bit, and I never saw Toby. I'd a told you if I had," Lanny Ray said.

"Did you go in the cardroom at all that night?" Beale asked.

"I sat at a table over in the corner where they serve food. That's where I was the whole time I was there. Josie and Rafael visited with me there as much as they could. They were pretty busy all night."

"Uh-huh. You ever been in any bar fights yourself, Mr. Garrett? Got any good stories you share with the boys sometimes? A lot of men get a little temperamental after a few drinks. You one of them, Mr. Garrett?"

"I reckon right now my past is none of anybody's business. If you're askin' me if I was in a fight there at Josie's, the answer is no." Lanny Ray was tense with anger at Beale's accusation.

"I'm just wondering, did you ever have anything personal against Mr. Abel? Never argued over anything? Money, women, anything like that?"

"Again, the answer is no. What are you gettin' at here? Are you accusing me of something?"

"Well, seems kinda odd to me that both of you fellas were in the same establishment, and you insist you never even saw Mr. Abel. It's a little hard to believe, and I wonder why you might deny seeing him."

"I'm not denying anything. It's a big place," Lanny Ray said through his anger. "For you to even think I would have anything to do with Toby missing is crazy." The two men stared hard at one another for a moment.

"So you didn't sit up at the bar at all?"

"No, I didn't. It was too noisy to talk with my friends there. The band was playing that night," Lanny Ray said.

"Where was that girl of yours while you were in there visiting?" Beale said, putting a strong emphasis on *visiting*. A slight sarcasm had edged his words once again.

Lanny Ray hesitated. "She was waiting for me."

"Where?" Beale said.

"In our car."

"Alone?" Beale said, almost smirking now.

"No. She wasn't alone. She had a friend with her," Lanny Ray said.

"Really. Who might that be?" Now he sounded downright disbelieving.

"She's just a good friend of Angela's. They were playing card games and reading their books." Lanny felt his anger at Beale working its way up his spine again.

"My daughter was with her," Red spoke up.

Beale shifted his look to study Red for a few seconds. "How old is your daughter, Red?" he said.

"She's fifteen," Red said.

Beale looked a little disappointed. If the friend had been someone younger, he could probably make something of those two girls sitting out in a car alone.

"What about Toby? Did you hear anything else?" Lanny Ray wanted to get back to the subject of where Toby might be. "We were thinking maybe we would head back the way we came, see if we could maybe find him, or at least find out something about him." Those words were another mistake on Lanny Ray's part.

Deputy Beale sat back in the booth and puffed up his chest.

"Well, Mr. Garrett, I reckon that is what the law is for, and we know what needs to be done."

The radio MJ Beale wore on his belt crackled, and the men could hear a voice through the static.

"I have to take this. You boys hold on here a minute." Deputy Beale hefted himself out of the booth seat and headed for the door.

"Man, this guy is hard to abide." Lanny Ray rubbed his face with both hands and felt the stubble there. "I still think we ought to head back where we came from and see if we can come up with anything. Anything at all about Toby might help. I'd like to talk to Josie and Rafael myself."

"I think you're right. Let's get the kids going and head on back."

The men rose from the table and paid for their coffee. The waitress didn't smile at Lanny this time. She looked disappointed. When they stepped outside the café, Beale was hoisting himself out of the driver's seat of his car.

"I think I asked you boys to hold on a minute. I got some news if you want to hear it."

"What's that?" Red said.

"It ain't too good. Toby's pickup was found a while ago." He looked at Lanny Ray. "Your friend Rafael found it. It was about a mile or so from his place. Down in one of those desert washes. Guess he was out there searchin' in the dark. No sign of Toby. There are some belongings in the back. Suitcase, riggin', stuff like that."

Lanny Ray immediately turned and headed across the street.

"Let's get going," he said to Red. They didn't bother looking back at MJ Beale.

Even though they weren't sure what was ahead, both men felt a real sense of urgency about getting back to where they knew Toby had once been. They also felt an impending doom, and nothing was clear.

It was very quiet in Lanny Ray's car and Red's pickup as they all headed back along the road toward Josie and Rafael's place. The men were deep in thought. Both girls had their own frightening memories to deal with. Angela would rather do anything than go back to that parking lot. She had tried hard to push the recollections of that horrible night out of her mind. Now it was flooding back in vivid pictures. Unlike the first few days of reliving the parking lot scene in a dim, surreal way, now the pictures were alive in all their ugliness. She was going to have to work hard at acting as if nothing was wrong when they arrived at Josie's Place. And how was Char going to handle being back in the parking lot again? Would she break down? Would she tell Red or Billy what had happened there?

When they pulled into the dirt lot of Josie's Place, Angela was surprised and relieved to see how different it all looked in the daylight. The puddles had dried up, and there was no mud, just a hard-packed expanse of damp dirt filled with ruts. She was glad they parked in a different place than they had parked on that dark, wet night. But, in the light of day, it wasn't as bad as she expected it to be.

Josie came out of the front door of the long, low building right away and walked quickly to Lanny Ray's car. She was a pretty lady with long, black hair, pulled back in a silver barrette, and she wore a big smile. Her colorful skirt floated around her legs. Josie bubbled with welcoming hospitality. It was easy for Angela to see that she was a nice lady.

Josie and Rafael had run the bar, café, and cardroom for many years. They were still a young couple. The two had been together since they were practically kids. They had grown up together and had gone to school together until their education ended in the eighth grade. They were married when they were sixteen years old. No one disagreed with their decision. It had meant fewer mouths for their parents to feed.

Josie and Rafael had done whatever they could to support themselves, including working at the bar and café that was now called Josie's Place. When the business had come up for sale, they jumped at the opportunity to own it. With a small savings and help from a local bank loan, they were able to scrape up a down payment.

Anyone who knew them knew Josie was a gracious and friendly person who knew hard work was how people accomplished things in life. She liked people, and they liked her. Rafael, on the other hand, tended to be stubborn and surly at times. He was a moody man whose manner ran hot and cold. He ran the bar and the cardroom, and Josie did the cooking and serving, going out of her way to make her customers comfortable.

Rafael could manage to ignore a little bar tussle now and then, but if he thought for one minute that someone was trying to cheat him or swindle one of his regular customers out of something, his hot temper could blaze. He had chased patrons out for turning over dice or marking cards more than once. His dealers—there were two of them—had been instructed to signal either the bartender or Rafael himself if they had even a notion that someone was being dishonest. He had been known to get rid of cheaters or troublemakers with the homemade billy club he kept stashed behind the long bar.

Locals who knew him well and had witnessed some of Rafael's ire could laugh about those nights. As long as they weren't the ones on his wrong side, they could find humor in those situations. But newcomers who tried conning and got caught didn't find it so funny. They usually left with bumps or bruises or worse—and an order to never come back.

Some folks suspected maybe Rafael wasn't always good to Josie. That was mostly rumor, for Josie had never complained about how Rafael treated her. They worked well together after all those years, but she was known as the glue that held them, and their business, together. She was the one people were drawn to. It was her good-heartedness that showed when Red and Lanny Ray and their children drove into the parking lot.

"Lanny, you and your friend bring those children in here so I can feed them," she said. "They must be hungry for some lunch."

Rafael came then, and introductions were made all around. They all settled in the little café corner of the bar room, and Josie went to the kitchen to get lunch for them. The small area was separated from the rest of the large room by a squat, decorative split rail fence. Beautiful, colorful, handwoven blankets and a Mexican saddle, heavy with silver, adorned the little fence. Several small tables with bright tablecloths and green wine bottles with pretty colored candles invited people to sit and enjoy some of Josie's fine Mexican food. Even though Josie's Place was some distance from town, people were willing to make the drive. They could drink, dance, play some poker, and have a good meal all under one roof.

"So tell us what you found, Rafael," Lanny Ray said to his friend after everyone had pulled up a chair.

"Not so good, my friend. I found the pickup quite by accident. It was in a deep wash. Like a ravine. I almost drove into it myself." With wide eyes, he tapped his chest with his fingers. "That is when my lights saw the shine of the windshield on Toby's truck. I was afraid to walk down to see inside, but I finally did. All his things were there still. It did not look like when someone is robbed of their possessions. I found nothing on the ground. No tracks, no nothing. Too many days gone by." He shook his head sadly.

"They have searchers there now. Some walking, most horseback," Rafael said. "Maybe something will turn up."

In no time at all, the small tables were laden with food enough for twice as many people. Josie made numerous trips with heaped plates. Unfortunately, worry and anxiety had stolen most of their appetites. They ate what they could to be polite.

"It's okay, you bambinos," Josie said when she noticed their plates not being cleaned. "I know how you worry."

The urge to get out to where Toby's truck had been found made Lanny Ray fidgety, and he could hardly be still in his chair. They finally divided up and climbed into Red's and Rafael's pickups and headed out through the high desert. As the crow flies, Toby's truck was indeed only slightly more than a mile from Josie's place. The drive there seemed much farther. In some places, there were faded ruts from other pickups or jeeps that could be followed until lost in the sagebrush and coulees. Lanny Ray wondered why in the world so many people wanted to drive around out there. Exploring maybe, or hunting a lost cow or steer. But that seemed highly unlikely. He doubted there were any cattle nearby. There was no feed for them in that part of the desert. In fact, he didn't see a living thing, not even a rabbit.

Maybe kids came out to raise a little hell. Drink some beer. It was a long ways from town for that, though. Well, somebody had reason to be out there. The proof was in the tire tracks. And the trash.

They bumped past some discarded rubble scattered on the desert floor. Beer cans glinted in the hot sun. There were small piles of trash that had been burned, leaving only charred tin cans and tangles of wire. There was even a broken toilet bowl lying on its side. Pieces of porcelain were scattered about. Nearer the main road, bits of trash blown from littering passersby hung trapped in the stiff, prickly branches of the desert brush.

It felt like a long time until they finally topped a slight swell in the scrubby land and saw Toby's truck sitting cockeyed in the bottom of a ravine. Just seeing it sitting there gave Lanny Ray's heart a little lurch. They all stepped out of the pickups and stood looking silently, squinting in the white sunlight.

"Sad sight, ain't it?" Red stood with his hands on his hips, looking down into the ravine.

"Leaves me feeling kind of scared like," Lanny Ray said. "I just don't know how this could happen. Who in this world, Red, would want to cause harm to somebody like Toby?"

Red just shook his head. They walked slowly down the slope to Toby's truck. Some distance to their left, they could see two pickups with horse trailers parked where the ground was more level and not as scrubby with brush. There was no one around them, so Red and Lanny Ray assumed someone was out there looking for . . . well, for Toby they guessed. Or something to give them an idea of where he might be.

Lanny Ray looked back and saw the three kids sitting at the top of the slope. They sat in the red dirt and watched the men make their way to the abandoned truck. Angela and Charlotte sat close with arms linked, and Billy sat away, alone. What an awful thing for them to have to worry over, he thought. If he couldn't understand why this was happening to Toby, how could those kids understand it?

When they reached the truck, the men looked in the back bed first. Toby's things were still there. His old brown suitcase, his bronc saddle, some rusty baling wire, and a few odd tools.

The passenger side window was down a little more than halfway, and the wind wing on the driver's side was cranked all the way open.

Lanny Ray and Red took turns peering in through the window that was wound down. Not much to see. There was a shallow cardboard box with Lucky Lager Beer printed on the side of it on the passenger side floorboard, a thick tablet of writing paper and some stubby pencils lying in the bottom of it. The men could see some numbers written in columns on the top page of the notebook, but they looked blurred and faded from moisture. Toby's spurs were there, too, and his rope was on the seat, the coils poking out from under his jacket. Probably the same rope Toby had used to teach Angela how to swing a good loop. His chaps were draped over the truck seat.

Rafael said yes, this was how he had found it. Nothing had changed.

"Do you see, my friend, how the rain water came in the window and wet the seat and floor? There are stains there, no? It is dry now, I know. But you can see where it was very wet before. It has not rained since the night you came to visit Josie and me. It rained very hard that night, and then, whoosh, it was gone in the morning." He motioned to the east with his open hand. "No more after," Rafael said.

"So you think the truck was left here on the same night?" Red said.

"That is what makes sense for me," Rafael said.

Red and Lanny Ray leaned on the rail of the truck bed, and both became quiet and thoughtful.

Rafael turned and stared over the sagebrush on the far slope of the ravine. Heat waves jumped up and down on the horizon.

"Somebody was very mad at your friend. Maybe he was not so good a man as you think . . . maybe he was not so honest all the time. Maybe he cheats somebody that night." Cheating was obviously the worst thing a man could do, according to Rafael's way of thinking.

"I don't know, Rafael. I sure never knew Toby to be the kind of man to cheat. Hard to picture it," Lanny Ray said.

"I don't let nobody cheat in my place," Rafael said, pointing his thumb into his chest. "I take care of the problem real quick," Rafael said without looking at Lanny Ray. "I have a nice big club under my bar to remind people not to cheat in my cardroom."

When Rafael turned around to face the other two men, he had a smile that showed just a touch of something sinister. This was a part of Rafael Lanny Ray knew nothing about. An attitude he had never glimpsed. For an instant, he seemed a stranger.

"I guess we may as well let Rafael get back now. Nothing more to do here," Lanny Ray said.

They started back up the slope, picking their way through the sage. Angela watched her father wind his way up the hill. His head was down, and he walked as if he was wading through the heat waves and his boots weighed too heavy. Angela felt sad for him.

A drift of brick-colored dust arose and hung in the still air, just over the low hill, letting the men know a Jeep or pickup had nearly reached where the kids sat. They met up there at the same time. Two uniformed men got out of a Jeep and walked to the group of men and kids.

One of them said, "Y'all must be the friends of Toby's that came back from the rodeo. Deputy Beale called to say you would be here. We came out to check this truck again and make a note of what's inside and collect Mr. Abel's belongings. His family said they would be down as soon as they can, so we want to gather up his things for them. We don't even know if his truck will run or not yet. If not, we'll have to get somebody out here to pull it out of the ravine."

"Maybe y'all could come into our office later in case we need to ask you anything," the other deputy said. He gave them directions and headed down the slope to the forlorn-looking truck.

The men and kids climbed back in the pickups and drove slowly away through the desert. They would be put up for as long as they needed to be there in the small but welcoming rooms of Rafael and Josie's adobe home that sat behind the bar. They guessed there would be no reason to move on until all this about their friend Toby was cleared up.

Lanny Ray and Angela rode back with a silent and sullen Rafael.

CHAPTER NINETEEN

"*I*s that Olin's pickup?" Lanny Ray asked when they were in sight of Josie's Place.

"I think it is," Angela said. "Why would he be back here?"

"I don't know. I reckon he's worried about Toby, too. They weren't real good friends, but I guess he liked Toby okay. He just don't seem like the worryin' type to me," Lanny Ray said. Rafael remained silent.

Angela was disappointed to see Olin's pickup parked in the lot at Josie's. She would be happy if she never had to see him again. As Rafael drove closer, Angela started looking for Marie. She was there, sitting on the running board on the shaded side of the pickup. She watched Rafael's pickup pull up and stop.

Rafael touched the brim of his straw hat and nodded a greeting to Marie. Marie gave him a small forced smile and looked away. Lanny Ray stepped out of the cab.

"Where's your old man?" he said to Marie. "It's too hot to be sittin' out here."

"He's inside," was all Marie said.

"Well, come on with us and get a cool soda pop."

Marie didn't say anything to Lanny Ray or Angela, but she stood and walked with them toward the door of the bar. Rafael drove on around the big building to park his pickup.

"Did y'all come back to see about Toby, too?" Lanny Ray asked Marie.

"That's what Olin says," Marie said.

Angela thought that was a peculiar answer. It seemed to her Marie and Olin never said things like any nice, normal people would. There was always a tone of rudeness and sarcasm in Marie's way of talking that Angela couldn't get used to hearing.

"Looks like we're all going to miss out on some rodeos, doesn't it?" Angela gave a try at having a conversation with Marie.

"Don't matter much to me. I was about ready to take off for Phoenix, anyway. Might still," Marie said.

It was when Marie turned to speak to her that Angela saw the bruises around her left eye. They looked much the same as the ones Olin had left there before. Pity flooded Angela's heart. *Oh no, not again,* she thought. She kept glancing toward Lanny Ray as they walked to the door of the building, trying to signal him to notice Marie's face. He opened the door for the girls, and just as Marie passed by him, he saw what Angela had seen. He and Angela looked at one another, sharing the same silent thoughts.

When they entered the building, they saw Olin sitting on a stool at the bar, drinking a beer. He was the only one in the barroom of Josie's Place.

"Olin," Lanny Ray acknowledged him with a nod. It was hard to be polite to somebody who beat up on his own daughter. Lanny Ray's greeting nearly caught in his throat.

"Hey, Garrett," Olin said too loud. "Where you guys been? I came on back quick as I could to help see about ol' Toby." His words were too loud and slow, as if he'd maybe already had too many beers.

"Well, there ain't much to do, Olin. We drove out to take a look at his truck is all. His stuff is all there, and his family is coming after it as soon as they can. There are a couple of deputies out there getting his things so they'll be put away safe." Lanny Ray turned away toward the café tables.

Marie hesitated for a minute, as if she wasn't sure which way she should go. She surely didn't want to be near Olin, but she wasn't comfortable with the others, either. Lanny Ray gently laid a big hand on her shoulder and guided her back to the tables with Angela. They sat and waited for Josie to come out.

Red, Billy, and Charlotte came in and joined them. Olin swallowed his beer down and ambled over to sit with them.

"Howdy there, Olin. What are you doin' back in this neck of the woods?" Red asked.

"Same as you," Olin said. "I been wonderin' what happened to poor ol' Toby. Hear they got people out there in the desert looking for him. Maybe I'll go out later and see if I can give 'em a hand. More the merrier, right?"

"Ain't anything to be merry about, for God's sake. That's a hell of a way to put it." Lanny Ray couldn't contain his disgust. Besides, Olin would be lucky to find his way out to his truck if he had any more to drink.

And then they all turned to Charlotte as she spoke up with all her innocence and no tact.

"What in the world happened to you, Marie? You have a bruise on your face by your eye. Did you see Marie's bruise, Ang? Did you fall down, or did you have a fight with somebody? Does it hurt?"

Marie's eyes darted to meet Olin's and then quickly down at the tabletop.

"It's nothing. It don't hurt," she said. There was defiance in her voice. She wasn't going to let Olin know she was upset about the bruises on her face.

Billy reached to pat his sister on the arm, hoping she would get the signal to say no more. It didn't work.

"You had that bruise before. Didn't she have it before, Ang?" Charlotte said. Everyone at the table had become uncomfortable, and Angela had no idea how to answer Char in front of them all.

"She's just clumsy," Olin spoke up. "Ain't ya, girl?" His smile was more like a sneer. "Come on, Marie. We need to go find us a place to stay. Where y'all stayin'?" He looked at Lanny Ray.

"Here. My friends are putting us up," Lanny Ray said.

"Well, ain't that nice. I didn't know these folks was your good friends. You must know ol' Rafael pretty good then, huh?" Olin said.

"Pretty good." Lanny Ray wouldn't look at Olin.

Olin pushed his chair back with a loud scrape and put his hand on Marie's shoulder. She was still studying the tabletop.

"Come on, let's go." Then to Lanny Ray, he said, "I'll be back this evenin' to look for Toby."

The tension left the room with Olin. The little group sat and drank cold soda pops and talked about what might happen next. They all agreed that they were feeling useless in the investigation of Toby's disappearance.

Josie came and led them through the kitchen, out the back door of the bar, and into the cool rooms of the adobe house. The relief from the heat was immediate. She showed them where they would sleep—the girls in a tiny room with two tidy beds. Angela would bring her quilt in from Lanny Ray's car, just for comfort. It would feel nice in the coolness of the adobe. The men were in one bigger room. Billy got the army cot, and the men claimed the beds. There was another heavy wooden door at the end of a hallway that accessed the outdoors and gave the visitors a way in and out without disturbing Josie and Rafael. They would be very comfortable here, but they were all hoping they would not have to overstay the hospitality offered to them.

To the relief of all, Olin never returned that evening. Angela and Charlotte sat outdoors at dusk and talked in low voices.

"Ang, are you okay? I don't think so, Ang," Char said to her friend.

"Yeah, I am. It isn't so bad now. Sometimes that night seems like a long time ago. What about you, Char? Are you okay being here?"

"Ang, do you think that Olin was here that night? I mean, in the bar. Ang, do you think Marie was in the parking lot, too? Ang, what if Marie was in the parking lot, too?"

Oh no. What was Char saying? Does she think Marie saw something that night? A familiar uneasy feeling settled in Angela's stomach.

"Char, what are you thinking?" Angela was almost whispering. "We didn't see Olin's pickup that night. Even if Marie was out there, she wasn't close by us."

"We couldn't see anywhere, Ang. Remember how the windows looked?" Now Charlotte was whispering, too.

"Of course, I remember," Angela snapped.

"You're not whispering, Ang. I thought we were whispering," Char scolded.

Angela couldn't help but smile. No wishy-washy words from Char.

"Well, we don't even know if he was here that night. I'll try to find out tomorrow," Angela said.

"What are you girls whispering about out here in the dark?" Both Angela and Charlotte were startled by Billy's voice.

"Billy, you scared me and Ang," Char scolded her brother.

Billy laughed at his little prank. "So, what's the big secret?" he said.

The girls glanced at each other, which was a dead giveaway that there really was a secret, then they tried to deny it.

"Maybe we're talking about boys, huh, Ang?" Char said.

"Or about you, Billy," Angela teased.

Billy looked back and forth at the girls for a moment. Finally, he said, "I know you two are up to something, and you have been for a while. You act weird. You're both too quiet most of the time. 'Course, that's not really bad," he teased. "But you hardly ever spend time together like you used to, and you aren't giggling all the time. Angela, you avoid everybody and stick to Lanny Ray like glue, except when you go off somewhere by yourself. So what's goin' on, girls? Want to share your big secret?" Billy looked to them both and waited for an answer.

The girls' silence confirmed the answer. There was a secret. He had no idea how much both girls wanted to tell it. All of it. Telling would be sharing their burden, for sure.

Unexpected tears welled in Angela's eyes. She was too young to realize how all the trauma of that night had affected her. She had bottled up all the emotion and capped it tightly. She'd had to. She could hear the words again. She had been threatened.

Char put her hands up to her face, as if she could not bear to look at Angela's teary eyes.

"Tell him, Ang. Tell Billy the secret," she whispered through her fingers.

"What about my father, Char? Remember what the man said." Angela wiped at her eyes with the back of her hand.

"What man?" Billy said. He was beginning to understand that something serious was going on. It wasn't just silly girl stuff.

Angela took a deep breath, thought for a few seconds about where to begin, and then told Billy the story of the dreadful night in the parking lot, just around the building from where they sat as she spoke. In the beginning of the telling, her voice was breathy and trembling, as if she couldn't get enough air in her lungs. She envisioned every second of it and told exactly what had happened as accurately as the rerunning of a horror movie. As the story continued, her voice became stronger, but it was still low so no one else would overhear. It was, after all, a secret.

Enormous relief rushed over her as quickly as her words were released. Now there would be someone else to share the burden. Another person would know that something awful had happened. Something that was more than two young girls should have to bear alone.

Billy sat mute. He looked stricken. His jaw twitched, and he couldn't look at Angela's face as she finished her story.

"See, Billy, you can't ever tell anyone about this. No one. The man from that night knows my dad, and he will do something to him if he finds out I told you. Promise me you won't say a single word. Promise me right now." Angela cried openly.

Billy was already torn. What if the man that Angela saw being dragged away was dead and nobody knew who beat him up bad enough to kill him? Shouldn't the deputies or cops know? And besides, his own sister had been in the car that night. Even if the girls were convinced that the man didn't know Char was there, it was still an awful experience for her. She should be able to talk to her own father about it. Billy also wondered how Red would feel about it all. He sure wouldn't like this secret being kept from him.

He finally said, "It's okay. I won't tell anybody, for now. But Ang, are you sure you can't tell your dad, or our dad, or maybe a deputy? Are you positive you don't know the man's voice?"

"I've thought about it a million times, Billy, a million times. I thought about it so much that sometimes I'm not sure if I remember the voice the same way or not. At first, I thought it was *how* he said things that seemed familiar to me, not his voice. It was so gruff and vicious. He was breathing like a person who had run a hundred miles, and he smelled repulsive. Like he was rotting inside."

"He sounded like a bear, Billy. Like a big bear. Growly, like he had a sore throat." Tears were still sliding down Char's face.

They sat long enough for the girls to quit crying and let the tears dry up. Angela felt a deep tiredness overtake her. She was uncomfortable having the darkness all around her as night came on. She said she wanted to go in to bed. They all stood and walked to the big wooden door. Billy opened it, and the girls went down the hallway and into their room without another word.

Angela didn't always say prayers before sleep, but she did that night.

"Please, God, don't let Billy tell anyone the secret. And please, please watch over my father."

Chapter Twenty

Angela woke with a lighter heart the next morning. Telling Billy about her dark memories had eased her constant fear of saying the wrong thing in his presence. Speaking aloud about her secret had given her immense relief.

Red and Lanny Ray had to leave Josie's to meet with the deputies who had been out at Toby's truck the day before. They would drive in to town to the sheriff's office and planned to be back in a couple of hours. The girls and Billy didn't want to go along this time, and they asked to stay with Josie. With promises of not being a bother, they were allowed to stay behind.

Josie was delighted to have their company. She gave the girls little jobs in the kitchen to help her get ready for the day. There was endless cooking and cleaning up to do. As it turned out, Charlotte had done more cooking and cleaning in her home than Angela had ever done in hers. Char easily fell right into being a big help to Josie. Angela had her responsibilities at home, and Arlene often left her a list of chores for after school, but she usually rushed through them and escaped to the outdoors the minute her work was done.

It was fun, though, to work in Josie's kitchen for a while. The girls watched how Josie prepared the food she was famous for and learned from her. Angela thought about how fun, and surprising, it would be to cook up some Mexican food for her mom after she got home. Home.

Imagining herself in the kitchen with her mother caused Angela to feel such a deep homesickness she stopped what she was doing. It seemed like such a long time ago that she had crawled into Lanny Ray's big car and rode down Main Street and out of Jewel. She'd been giddy with the excitement of the unknown then. Now, for a moment, she thought about her comfortable bedroom and all her own things there. For an instant, the desire to be home was so strong a lump formed in her throat, and she had to swallow it away. She thought about the river park and the big swing and the crooked merry-go-round. She wondered what Joseph was doing and if he was having a good summer.

She longed for home. When she and Lanny Ray got home, there would be no more problems. Being home with Arlene would be safe. Angela wouldn't have to worry anymore. Maybe she could take the Greyhound bus home, like Lanny Ray had mentioned a while back. No, she couldn't do it now. She should stay with her father until she knew the man wouldn't do something bad to him.

"Angela," Josie was saying, "where did you go? You're a daydreamer, pretty girl. Bring me that big pot there on the table."

As soon as she had the chance to leave politely, Angela stepped out of the kitchen through the back door and walked around the big building. As she rounded the corner of the building, she saw a pickup bouncing over the ruts toward the bar. It was Olin's. Angela watched the front of the old pickup come toward her and then pull up and park only a few feet away from where she stood as if her boots were stuck to the ground. She wanted to turn and run back inside, but she seemed to have lost the spontaneity to do that. Olin's window was down, and he leaned out over his arm. He sat in the cab and looked at Angela for a minute before he opened the door and stepped out. Angela looked away. Marie got out of the passenger side, walked around the back of the pickup, and leaned against the back fender.

"Where's ol' Garrett?" Olin asked Angela.

"He and Red went to talk to the deputies. They'll be back pretty soon now," Angela said. "Hi, Marie," she added.

135

"Hey, Angela. Where's your dummy friend? She's not taggin' along behind you." Marie leaned as if to peer around Angela.

"Marie, don't talk about her so mean," Olin said to his daughter. "She can't help it if she's slow thinkin'."

Angela squirmed with her own cowardice. She wanted to speak up in Char's defense but was afraid to speak at all. She knew she wasn't supposed to hate anyone. Arlene wouldn't even tolerate the word being used. She couldn't help it now. She wished Olin and Marie would just go away and leave everybody alone. Why were they such mean people?

Olin turned and looked out across the parking lot, as if studying it. Then he looked down and scraped the heel of his boot into the hard-baked ground.

"I bet this lot is a real mess when they get some rain around here." He looked directly at Angela. "What do ya think, missy? Bet it gets pretty messy out here. You know, I believe it was rainin' that night you were here with your daddy, wasn't it? All wet and muddy."

Marie was still standing back by the pickup, her arms crossed in front of her. She was looking at Angela, too. Waiting?

What did Olin just say? "Here with your daddy . . . your daddy." A tiny, hot poker touched the pit of Angela's stomach. Her breath caught in her throat. "Your daddy," Olin had said. It had a tiny little bit of a drawl, some kind of accent, so slight you would hardly even notice it. That was it! The sound she had heard in the man's words on that night right here in this parking lot. "Your daddy will disappear."

Angela turned away sharply and hurried, almost running, back around the building. She went quickly through the big door of the adobe, down the hall, and entered the room she shared with Charlotte. She was thankful Char was not there. She lay down on the bed and buried her face in her mom's quilt. She closed her eyes. She needed to think. She had to be careful. Was it Olin out there in the mud and rain that night? Could it be possible? The voice hadn't sounded like Olin's. Had it? No, that man's voice was deeper and gruffer. Char had said, "Like a bear." But he said those words the same. Exactly the same.

She begged off joining the others for the rest of the day. When Lanny Ray returned, she told him through the closed door that she had a stomachache. It wasn't really a fib. Her stomach did feel bad. As she lay on the little bed through the afternoon, she would doze from time to time under the comfort of her mother's quilt, but each time she woke, she would think of Olin's voice again. By that night, she had made the decision that she would say no more about what had happened until she was home in Jewel. They would all be safe there, and she would tell Lanny Ray and Arlene exactly what had happened and what she had seen in Josie's parking lot. If they got mad at her for keeping the secret from them, well, she would just have to pay the price. At least she would be home, and Lanny Ray would be far from the man who had threatened to hurt him. She was already wishing she hadn't told Billy anything. Her fear was creeping back to haunt her again.

The following morning brought the deputies back out to Josie's. They had come to drive Toby's pickup out of the ravine. It had started up okay, and if they needed a tug to get it out of the soft ground, they could do it with the Jeep. They told Lanny Ray and Red that the searchers were all done. They had found nothing of interest in all the miles they had covered. If Toby's body or any evidence of foul play was out there, they sure couldn't find it.

One of the deputies asked if Rafael was around. He said they had a few questions for him. Red had seen Rafael drive out earlier and hadn't seen him since. The deputy asked that the men tell Rafael they wanted to speak to him. They said sure they would, as soon as he returned.

Toby's family was expected to be in town the next morning. The deputies wished they had more to tell them. They were well aware that until folks really knew what happened to their loved ones who disappeared they forever carried hope in their heart that the missing person would turn up somewhere, someday. Once in a while it would happen. Maybe a fella had just got fed up with his job or his woman, or maybe he had committed some kind of crime, and he would just take off to the unknown. Some of those people turned up months or even years later. For now, though, no one believed that was the case with Toby. He wasn't the type to just up and leave.

Red and Lanny Ray agreed they would stay at Josie's one more night and talk to Toby's family before they headed out. It would be the kind and decent thing to do. Now was the time Lanny Ray had to decide just where he was going when they left Josie's for the last time. He could go one direction, eventually catching up with the circuit he had intended to follow, or he could go the other way, head home, and pick up one or two rodeos on the way before he got home to Jewel. He knew in his gut he should head to Jewel. He would miss out on a couple of big rodeos, but he would be getting Angela home a little sooner. Man, he hated to think about missing those rodeos. Payout was damn good, and he had never ridden better than he had this season. He would talk to Angela to see how she was feeling about getting home. He had a strong feeling she was ready to head on in, if she would admit it. She seemed tired, and her enthusiasm had really dipped. Part of it, he knew, was all this worry about poor Toby. It was wearing all of them down. He dreaded having to meet up with Toby's family in the morning. It would be a real tough go.

Later that day, Lanny Ray, Red, and Billy had gone off into the desert to look around again. They didn't hold much hope of finding anything, but it gave them something to do besides wait and worry. Char was in the cool adobe room. She had been dozing when Angela left her. The heat outside felt thick and heavy, but Angela went out anyway. It was hard to stay in the small room unless she was sleeping, and she was too restless for sleeping. She sat in a narrow strip of shade cast from the adobe and read a book. It was a real book, not a funny book. It had a green cover, and she liked how it felt to hold a hardcovered book and read the cream colored pages. She had found it in the little room she slept in and started reading it right away. It was about a girl and her horse, and Angela loved it from the first page. It was easy to get lost in the story. It took her far away to another place where there was no worry. She wanted to be the girl in the book. Angela was discovering another way to explore. She'd already decided she wouldn't be buying any more funny books.

Olin and Marie showed up back at Josie's place in the afternoon. Olin had already had too much to drink to be driving his old truck all the way from town. Staggering a little, he went inside and straight to the bar as soon he stepped out of his pickup. Marie followed him inside, but she sat at one of the little café tables to have something to eat. She was there when Angela came in the back door to get a cold drink. Marie spotted her and waved her to her table. It felt too awkward for Angela to avoid her, so she brought her soda pop over and sat down.

"I guess we'll be leaving out tomorrow," Angela said. "What about you guys? What are you going to do?"

"I don't know. Olin's too far gone on his damn binge to talk about it. I don't know what he's thinking. Like I said before, I might just hitch a ride to Phoenix," Marie said.

"You've been saying the same thing for weeks. I don't really believe you anymore," Angela said. She wished she hadn't sat at the table. She was weary of Marie and her deviousness.

Marie stared at Angela for a moment, and then a wicked smile twisted her mouth.

"Well, aren't you a little smartmouth today?" she said. "You know, you are about the most ignorant person I have ever known. You're almost as big a hick as your retarded friend, and you should talk real nice to me, Miss Angela. I know some things you would sure like to know. Would solve a lot of problems around here if I told what I know." She rolled her eyes around, indicating the room.

Angela leaned forward, crossing her arms on the table. She looked square and steady into Marie's eyes. Marie attempted to look back but leaned away slightly in her chair.

"Marie," Angela spoke in a low steady voice, "I know you have had bad things happen to you in your life, and my dad says you can't help how you act. I think you could help it some if you wanted to. But, for

139

some reason, you like to be mean. You say you hate your father, but you act just the same as him."

They still looked intently at each other, but Marie was listening.

"My friend Charlotte is a hundred times a better person than you. She's smarter, too. You won't get the best of Char and me, Marie, so you might as well leave us alone."

Angela wasn't finished yet, but Marie got up and left the table.

"Good riddance," Angela said aloud. She took a deep breath and exhaled long and slow. She felt real good about speaking up for her friend Char.

Angela sat alone for a long while, drinking her soda and thinking about what Marie had said. She "knew some things" Angela would like to know. Now what the heck did that mean? What things?

"Well, if it ain't little Aaangil-la sittin' here all by herself." Angela's spine prickled and her stomach contracted into that familiar knot of unease again.

Olin pulled out a chair and supported his swaying height with his big hands on the back of it. He reeked of stale sweat and alcohol. He sat clumsily and leaned toward Angela, showing his ugly teeth in a leering grin.

"We should have us a little talk, don't you reckon?" Olin said.

Angela recoiled from Olin's sour breath. She turned her face away so she didn't have to look at him, glancing toward the door to Josie's kitchen. She needed somebody to come through it right then. Anybody.

"No, Olin. I have to go. My dad will be back real soon. I can't talk to you right now." Angela scooted her chair back and stood to leave.

Olin put a big heavy hand on her shoulder and forced her back down onto the chair. Angela instantly felt numb with fear of him. She didn't try to stand again.

"I know you don't like me and my daughter much. Some folks just think they're a lot better than others." Saliva gathered at one corner of Olin's mouth, and his words slurred. Angela felt spittle sprinkle her cheek and reached to quickly wipe it away. Her hand trembled.

Olin attempted to look Angela in the face, but his eyes were squinty and unfocused.

"You and me, we know the same things, don't we Aaangil-la? We have ourselves a little bitty secret." He giggled, a drunken man's attempt at laughter. "And your daddy's good friend, Rafael . . . he knows a secret, too, don't he?"

Angela didn't think about what she did then, she just did it. She jumped up and bolted for the door. She ran as fast as she could across the floor and flung the back door wide open, running all the way to the door into the adobe. She didn't know that she didn't need to run at all. Olin was so slow in his drunken state, he had to work at just standing upright.

She burst into the little bedroom and shoved the door closed behind her. Charlotte was awake and looking at a book. She was startled by Angela's entrance.

"Ang, what happened?" Charlotte stood up quickly in her own anxiety. She grabbed Angela's arm. "What happened to you, Ang? You're too white. Oh God, Ang. You're so scared."

They both sat down on Angela's bed. Angela's entire body was shaking. She was short of breath.

"Oh, Char. I'm so dumb. How could I be so dumb? It was Olin who beat up that man in the parking lot. Now I know it for sure. And he knows I do. Charlotte, what if that poor man was Toby?" Angela was rocking herself back and forth on the bed. She grabbed on to the corner of her quilt and pulled it up to her face. "It could have been Toby. I couldn't see, Char." She sobbed, "I couldn't see clear enough." Her words were muffled through the quilt.

"I have to tell Billy. Billy might know what to do." She couldn't think clearly enough to say any more.

Charlotte sat close and was quiet for a few minutes. Finally, she said, "Billy will help us, Ang. He will." She patted Angela's back, trying to comfort her friend.

Angela lay down on the little bed, drawing her knees up tight, and when she became calmer, she tried making sense of things. Olin had not come right out and said what the secret was they shared. Maybe he had been testing her, just to learn if she really did think it was him in the parking lot that night. And Marie . . . that must have been the secret she was talking about, too. She probably knew what Olin had done. Maybe Marie had been testing Angela as far back as the day at the rodeo when she asked her if she had seen Toby. Marie might even have known then that Toby was dead. She was probably even in the parking lot that night. Oh God, she knew it was Toby! Poor Toby. It was horrifying for Angela to realize that she had listened to Olin hurt Toby so bad . . . had listened to Olin killing him.

But why did Olin mention Rafael? What could he have to do with anything? Was he there that night, too? She was getting all mixed up and couldn't think about it.

She was afraid to leave the little room, so she and Char stayed put and waited to hear Billy and the men come into the hallway. Angela was even afraid to have the door stand open. It seemed like such a long time passed before she finally heard the heavy door at the end of the hallway being opened and closed.

"Ang, they're here. Billy is here, Ang," Char said. "I'll get Billy, okay?"

"Okay, good, Char. Ask Billy to walk outside with us." Charlotte went through the bedroom door to get her brother. When they were outside together, they sat down on a small patch of scraggly grass.

"What's up? You girls got another secret?" He looked at both girls. *Uh oh, that's exactly what this is,* he thought. *Another secret.*

Angela told Billy everything that first Marie, and then Olin, had said.

"I was so scared, Billy. I have never been so scared in my life. Olin is mean and crazy. He put his hand on me and wouldn't let me leave."

"Angela, you have to tell. It can't be a secret anymore. I wish we'd figured this out last week. It all seems easy to see now. Toby's family will be here tomorrow, and they need to know what you saw and heard. It's their right."

"No! It's my right to keep my dad from being hurt or killed, too, Billy," Angela said. "And if *you* tell, it will be your fault if something happens to him."

"But Ang, if your dad knew about Olin, then he could tell the deputies, and they would protect him until they put Olin in jail," Billy reasoned.

"What if Olin hides? Or what if he does something to my dad before the deputies get him? Please don't make me tell. I won't. I won't do it."

"Okay, okay. We'll wait until tomorrow morning. But we have to do something, Angela. We can't just act like nothing happened." Billy looked pale and worried.

"Yes, we can. I'll tell my dad when we get home. I promise. I'll tell him and my mom everything. He'll be safe from Olin in Jewel. Olin and Marie will go home, too. Maybe the deputies can get Olin there."

Billy gave up. He would wait until morning to decide what to do. They went back inside the cool adobe together. He left the girls in their room and closed their door. They stayed there until Lanny Ray came to get them for supper.

Lanny Ray watched the girls closely through supper. *Now what,* he wondered. He couldn't ever figure these kids out. Girls. They were either laughing about nothing, or they were quiet and moody. He had found it didn't do much good to ask what was wrong. They mostly said, "nothing," and that was about it. *Must be their age,* he thought.

Olin and Marie were nowhere to be seen. Josie said they had left when she told Olin he shouldn't have more beer. He'd left in a drunken huff, staggering out the door with Marie right behind him. She'd seen Marie driving the old pickup out of the lot.

Marie? Driving? They were all astounded.

"Are you sure, Josie?" Red asked. "In all this time, we've never seen Marie drive. We didn't know she knew how to drive."

"I'm sure. I know because I thought it was good that Olin did not drive. He was too drunk. He was already very drunk when he and Marie came here today." Josie squinched her nose in distaste.

Billy caught on quickly. A piece of the puzzle. So that would have been how Olin could leave Toby's pickup in the desert that night in the pouring rain. Marie could have driven Olin's truck well enough to follow him out into the desert, meaning Olin and Marie had maybe taken Toby with them in Olin's truck. Then what did they do with Toby? He glanced at Angela. He wondered if she had caught on.

Like Angela, Billy wondered what Rafael could possibly have to do with this whole thing? Why would Olin say that Rafael knew about a secret, too? What a mess this is, Billy thought. He hated to break a promise to Angela, but he may have to talk to his dad. He never kept much of anything from his dad.

CHAPTER TWENTY-ONE

When Angela opened her eyes the next morning, she was immediately jolted to wakefulness by more emotions than she could grasp. The first was fear because she immediately recalled the horror of Olin. The next was actually relief, and then a joyful relief. She and Lanny Ray were leaving today. She felt an excitement like she hadn't felt in a long time. It gave her comfort to think about her and Lanny Ray heading down the road in the big car. She lay still, closing her eyes and picturing them rolling down the road. She would enjoy the passing scenery again, and they would sing to their favorite music.

She arose and laid her suitcase on the bed to finish her packing. Maybe at the next town she would ask for a new book. A real one, with lots of pages and a good long story. She could hardly get ready to leave fast enough.

She tried not to show her disappointment when Lanny Ray came by and tapped on the bedroom door. His words meant a delay in their leaving.

"Come on to breakfast, girls. We need to thank Josie and Rafael for all they have done for us. See you over there pretty quick."

"It's okay, Ang," Char said when she saw the look on Angela's face. "I'm sad to leave today, anyway. I don't know if we will be going the same way as you and Lanny Ray. Do you know, Ang?"

Angela stopped what she was doing and became very still. Oh no. She had assumed Red and Lanny Ray would be traveling together, as usual. But maybe this would be the last day she would see Char. And Billy.

"Oh, Char. Maybe we'll still be going together, like always."

"I think we're going home now, Ang. My dad said we would probably go home now. You're going home, too, right, Ang?"

"Yeah, soon. Soon we are. I don't know if we're going the long way to catch up with the circuit or the shorter way home." Angela's joy was fading fast. The girls finished up their packing in silence and headed to breakfast arm in arm.

They were the last to get to the little tables in the café corner. Everybody was there, including Josie and Rafael. Josie was up, bustling around the tables, moving plates of food around, and making sure everyone was waited on. Rafael, who sat next to Billy, had his arms crossed and looked sullen. He didn't greet the girls, but Red and Lanny Ray made remarks about girls being last to the table. They teased them about women always being late. Billy said they were primping. Rafael still said nothing.

They ate and made small talk until they knew it was time to leave. Then they all stood and hugged Josie tight and thanked her over and over for all she had done for them the last few days. She shooed them away and pretended she wasn't teary-eyed.

Rafael kept his distance, then moved toward the door to walk out with them. It was already hot outside, and the sunlight was blinding. The kids stood awkwardly around the big car and Red's pickup. It wasn't time for them to say any goodbye to each other yet. They still had to go to the sheriff's office before they actually got on the road. Nevertheless, there was a solemn feeling hanging in the air.

Lanny Ray and Red held their hands out to Rafael. He shook Red's hand first and then Lanny Ray's.

"By the way, I got a call early this morning. It came from the sheriff. The deputy wants to talk to me about Toby. Would you happen to know why, my friend?"

"That's right. We were supposed to pass the message on to you, Rafael. Maybe it's just because you were the one to find Toby's truck. Maybe they just have some questions about that. Don't know what else it could be," Lanny Ray said.

"You remember I was in the bar all night with you, right, my friend? We were working, Josie and me. You remember I was there the whole time?" Rafael said. He peered intently at Lanny Ray.

"Yeah, you were there. Sure. It was a real busy night for you and Josie. I know that," Lanny Ray said.

Rafael's dark eyes looked into Lanny Ray's.

"Yes, I was there all the time. Josie knows." He motioned to Josie with his hand.

Lanny Ray was baffled by Rafael's behavior and his insistence on convincing him to agree. Of course he was there most of the time on the night Lanny Ray visited. But Lanny Ray couldn't account for what his friend was doing every minute. Rafael and Josie had come and gone to the table where Lanny Ray sat whenever they found the time. They had a lot of customers to wait on. The bar was busy, and so was the cardroom. The band had played up on their platform, and the small dance floor had been packed with couples. It was a big, noisy building with a lot going on.

Well, whatever was going on with Rafael didn't have anything to do with Lanny Ray. He was anxious to get going. He thanked his friend again and headed for town.

The two-lane road leading them back to town heaved and dipped through dry desert, which wasn't very scenic. Lanny Ray tried to tune in a radio station, but there was no signal. Angela didn't mind. She was enjoying the light, free feeling of riding in the big car again. It was an easy feeling. She was happy to be going somewhere, anywhere.

After a few miles of quiet, Lanny Ray said, "I think when we finish up here today we should head over the mountains and take the short way to Jewel. It will still take a while, you know. There are two rodeos I can enter between here and home. How's that sound to you?"

"Sounds fine to me. But you'll lose out on the end of the regular circuit," Angela said. *And this will be my last day with Char and Billy,* she thought.

"Yeah, that's okay. It's just the tail end. We've had a rough week, and thinking about heading home sounds pretty good to me. Even if you don't want to admit it, I bet it does to you, too."

"What about Toby?" Angela looked at Lanny Ray. "How will we know about him?"

"Well, Ang. I don't think there's much more we can do about Toby. It's awful, but we can't stay here forever, and I don't know what we would do if we could stay. It'll be hard enough to talk to his family today," Lanny Ray said.

Angela remembered what Billy had said about Toby's family having a right to know the secret she had told him. She pushed the thought away.

They had traveled five or six miles on the two-lane road, with Red and the kids close behind. On a long, slow curve, they could see several cars pulled over and the flashing lights of a patrol car up ahead. Angela sat up, hoping it wasn't a bad wreck.

"No sense in you lookin'. We'll just get through it and go on," Lanny Ray said.

He slowed for safety as they neared the area where the cars were parked on the narrow shoulder of the road. There was more than one patrol car. In fact, there were three deputy's cars and a pickup parked close in line. Lanny Ray and Angela could see several people standing off the edge of the road on the right-hand side. There was a sloping bank from the roadbed down to the desert floor. Some of the deputies were looking down into a wash that took storm water through a culvert under the road. Several yards away, there were some people standing in the scraggly sagebrush. They were clustered together and watching the deputies. Angela could see that they were Indian. There were two kids with them. In the far distance behind them, there was a tiny community of small stucco houses.

When a deputy saw that it was Lanny Ray in the car, he waved for him to pull over and motioned to the front of the line of parked cars. Lanny Ray abided, though he would rather have traveled on. Red pulled over in front of him.

"I don't see a wreck," Angela said with relief.

"Stay put. I'll go see what's going on," Lanny Ray said.

He and Red both walked back past the patrol cars. A deputy climbed up the slope to meet them.

"What's going on?" Red asked.

"It ain't good. Those little Indian kids were playin' down here and found a man dead. They ran off back to their house, scared to death. They told their uncle what they saw, and he had to drive into town to let us know. There's no phones here." He squinted out toward the houses on the desert. "It's bad. Poor fella's been here for a while and, you know, with the heat and all . . . and the animals. Poor little kids probably won't ever forget seein' this."

Lanny Ray was listening, but he was feeling lightheaded, and there was a kind of squealing noise in his ears. His breath came ragged.

"Is it Toby Abel?" he managed to ask.

"Well, that's what we're thinkin'. I really hate to ask, man, but do you think one of you could take a look and see if you can tell us if it's Toby or not? Man, I really hate askin'." The deputy looked down at the ground.

Lanny Ray and Red looked at each other and then both gave a small nod. Red said, "Yeah, okay. We'll both go take a look."

Lanny Ray went first, and both men made their way down the embankment and lower toward the culvert. What they saw was pure horror, no doubt about it. Toby was a mess. He had been out there way too long. He was fully clothed, but the material of his shirt and pants was tattered and shredded—and very dirty, as if they had been in the soggy mud of the culvert and then dried up in the desert heat. His once boyish, handsome face was stretched tight over his cheekbones and forehead. His features were mostly gone—eyes and nose—but it was Toby. Red and Lanny Ray couldn't speak, but Red put his hand on Lanny Ray's shoulder, and they turned away to climb back to the road. Lanny Ray saw Toby's black felt hat lying close to the mouth of the culvert. It was caked with dirt, and the brim was bent, but it still looked like Toby's hat.

"Maybe somebody could pick that hat up and keep it for Toby's family. Maybe clean it up a little bit." Lanny Ray said.

"We'll do it, for sure," was all the deputy answered.

Red and Lanny Ray leaned against the nearest patrol car. They were silent. So now they knew where Toby was. Poor guy. Poor guy. How could this happen to him? Who could do such a thing?

When the deputy approached again, Red asked, "Do you know how Toby died? Was he shot?"

"Well, we don't know yet. The coroner is on his way out. Kind of hard to tell with the poor guy in such bad shape, but from what we can see now, it don't look like he was shot. Looks more like he was beat."

"Oh, my Lord," Lanny Ray said.

"Should we go on in to your office? That's where we were headed just now. We were supposed to meet up with Toby's ma and sister," Red said.

The deputy said they should go on ahead and just wait until they knew the family had been told. Somebody would let them know if they needed to go on inside.

Lanny Ray and Red walked slowly back to their kids. They found all three of them leaning on the hood of the big car. Their faces paled when they saw their fathers walking toward them. They knew by the men's stricken expressions that something bad had happened.

Lanny Ray took Angela's small hand in his big one and said, "Ang, they found Toby, honey. It's real bad. He's been gone for a while. Some poor little boys found him."

Angela and Charlotte both threw their hands up to their faces and burst into sobs. Billy turned and leaned over the fender with his face on his arms, and the tears came. The men stood helpless with their hands on their kids' backs and waited. Neither of them knew what to do to help them. Eventually, they were all wrapped in somebody's strong arms and stayed that way until the sobs quieted.

The men had no way of knowing that all three kids were thinking about what they suspected had happened to Toby.

"We have to go on into town now. So let's get in and give ourselves a chance to calm down a little. I know it's all just too much of a shock," Red said.

In silence, they all went back to their places in the car and pickup. Lanny Ray got behind the wheel and sat for a moment before he started the car and pulled out onto the road. Angela stared out of the side window, and the tears poured down her face. She felt like the breath had been taken right out of her. She didn't even see the desert scenes going by her window. All she saw were images of a beaten man in a dark, muddy parking lot.

She said, "Did you see him? Did you see Toby back there?"

"Yeah, I did."

"Did he have on his red-and-blue plaid shirt? The one with the hole in the elbow?" she asked, needing more proof that it was Toby back there.

Lanny Ray looked over at her. Poor Angela. Death was strange to her. This was real hard on her.

"You know, I think he did, Ang. Yeah, I'm sure he did." She didn't need to know the shirt was just a rag, clinging to a moldering body.

Angela nodded her head slightly.

By the time they drove into the parking lot of the sheriff's office, they were all a bit calmer, but the tears still ran down the kids' cheeks, and their eyes were red and swollen.

Lanny Ray left the car to talk to Red. They stood in the shade of the office building. The heat was sweltering.

"What are you thinking might have happened?" Red asked Lanny Ray.

"Man, I don't know. It would take a real bastard to do this to Toby. Toby wouldn't hurt nobody." Lanny Ray shook his head. "I sure hate having to face his family."

"Maybe it will help 'em to know how much everybody liked Toby," Red said.

"Not everybody."

CHAPTER TWENTY-TWO

The three patrol cars, the coroner's wagon, and two more pickups rolled into the sheriff's office parking lot. It was a sad sight to Red, Lanny Ray, and their kids. It had the air of a funeral procession.

The coroner stepped out of his van and spoke for a few minutes to the deputies, then got back in and drove out of the lot, no doubt headed for the local mortuary. The deputies and the Indian family all went through the front door of the office. Almost at once, another car pulled into the lot. Lanny Ray spotted the Utah plates first. He looked to Red but didn't say anything. Three of the big car doors swung open at the same time, and three people got out of the car. There was a middle-aged man who had been behind the wheel, an older woman from the passenger side, and a younger woman from the backseat. One needed no imagination to know that the women were related to Toby. Same stoutness, same smooth round faces, same coloring. Kinfolk, obviously. The man let them walk ahead, and they, too, went inside the office.

Time passed slowly. The sad men and their children sat or stood silently in the shade of the high wall. They were all lost in their own thoughts. Angela suffered the most. She knew now it was just a matter of time until she would have to tell her long story. Billy had been right. She wasn't going to get to wait until she was at home in Jewel. She wasn't going to have Arlene to help her through all this. She felt lightheaded with the heat and the worry.

Lanny Ray saw that Angela wasn't holding up too good. Her face was ashen. He felt a sense of protectiveness for her that he had never felt before. He smoothed her hair back from her sweaty forehead with his big hand. It wasn't a normal kind of gesture for him to offer her. Not even when she was a little thing. He wasn't good at showing his feelings that way. Right now, though, all he wanted to do was help her feel better.

"I'll be back in a minute," Lanny Ray said. "I'm going to see how long we need to be out here." He returned almost immediately. "They said we should come on in now. It's cool in there. You'll feel better," he said to Angela.

She stood from where she had been sitting against the building. Even though she was only a child, she knew something ominous was about to happen. She had no control over any of it anymore. She reached to take her father's hand as they went through the door.

It was very cool inside. That alone helped them all feel somewhat better. There was a water cooler in one corner of the front lobby and a tube of tiny paper cups attached to the wall next to it. The kids went straight to it and took turns drinking cup after cup. Then they sat on stiff-backed chairs along the opposite wall and looked around the room. There were many pictures of men in police uniform, and on one long corkboard, there were mug shots of wanted criminals. To Angela, they all had a look in common, even though their features and hair, or lack of it, were all different. It was a certain expression they wore. A vacant look in their eyes. Like Olin's.

A man came into the lobby from the hallway and said Lanny Ray and Red should come on back with him. The kids could wait there.

When they had filed off down the hallway, Char spoke to Angela.

"Are you going to tell now, Ang?"

"Yeah, I am."

"I should have told my dad, Ang," Charlotte said. "He might be mad at me, Ang."

"I'll tell him for you, Char. I'll tell him why I made you keep the secret. Maybe he won't be so mad when he knows why we couldn't tell. He wouldn't want anybody to hurt my dad."

"Maybe we can all be together when you have to tell," Billy said.

The same man who had led Lanny Ray and Red down the hall appeared again and said the kids should come on with him now. They all stood and trailed after him with heads down and shoulders slumped. He opened a door and motioned them inside. The small room seemed too full of people. There were two rows of tables set end to end, with several chairs behind each one. More pictures of men in uniform hung on the walls, and an American flag stood in one corner. Chairs were being shuffled around so the kids could sit down.

When Angela sat and looked around, she saw two women sitting close together with their arms linked and a man next to them. The women looked sad and haggard. Their faces were very pale, and their eyes red-rimmed. They both had handkerchiefs in one hand. Angela met Lanny Ray's eyes and then looked away. A deputy stood and spoke in a quiet voice.

"Kids, this here is Toby's mother and sister, and this is their good friend who brought them here from their home in Utah. Mary," he said to the older woman, Toby's mother, "and Nan," he motioned with a nod to Toby's sister, "these here are these two fellas' kids. This is Angela, and this is Charlotte, and this handsome boy here is Billy."

The women smiled weak smiles to be polite and wiped at their eyes. The kids sat completely still, not sure what was expected of them. After a pause, the deputy spoke again.

"Mary and Nan, these kids were friends of Toby's, too. Their fathers have told us how they got to know Toby pretty good these past couple of months."

"I'm glad you were friends with our Toby," Mary said. "He told me a little about you all when he called me on the phone." She spoke as if her voice didn't want to leave her mouth. Like she didn't have the energy to push it out into the room.

"Toby was real nice to me, ma'am. He always treated me like a grown-up. He didn't act like I was just some kid," Billy said, and tears ran again.

Charlotte put a hand on Billy's arm. "Don't cry, Billy. You were a real, real good friend for Toby."

"Toby taught me how to rope," Angela said, "and then he gave me a rope to keep for my own to use when I get home. He was always nice to us and treated us good."

Toby's sister, Nan, said, "Thank you all for talking to us. You are such good kids, and Toby was lucky to know you." She cried hard then. The man with them offered a hand to each of them and helped them up and out of the door of the little room.

One of the deputies said, "You fellas think of anything else to tell us?"

"Wish we could," Lanny Ray said.

"I do. I mean, I have something to say." Angela's voice was hardly more than a whisper.

Everyone in the room stared at her.

"What do you want to say, Angela?" one of the deputies said.

"I saw something. I saw something that happened at Josie's. On the night my dad visited there. When we . . . I was out in our car." She spoke brokenly, as if the words kept catching in her throat. The men sat back down. Char and Billy looked at the floor.

"There was a fight by our car. Men were yelling at each other, and they kept bumping into the back of the car. When I looked, I saw one man dragging another man in the mud."

Red stood back up. "Charlotte, is this the same night you were with Angela?"

Char nodded.

Billy said, "Wait, Dad. Let Angela tell all of it." Red shot Billy a look of disbelief and sat back down.

Angela told all of it. Just like the first time she had told Billy. She told it word for word. Action after action. She was careful to leave nothing out. It seemed like a long story to her. Like it would never end.

The men hung on every word and were silent. All the questions would come later. Angela looked around the room as she spoke. She didn't want to look at anyone's face. No tears came until she had to tell about the threat to hurt Lanny Ray, and then they flooded down her cheeks, and her voice weakened.

Tears welled in Lanny Ray's eyes. His mind could hardly grasp what Angela and poor Char had endured that night. He felt sick. And sorry. And so damn guilty. He stood and went to Angela, pulled her up, and wrapped his big arms around her little body.

"I'm sorry. I am so sorry," he said over and over.

Finally, Char spoke. "That man never knew I was in the big car," she said to Red. "He only thought it was Ang. Ang made me stay on the floor so I would be okay, didn't you, Ang? I couldn't tell you because the man said he would make Lanny Ray disappear. I heard him say it."

Red buried his face in his hands. Charlotte had kept this horror story to herself all of these days and nights. She was stronger and braver than he ever would have imagined.

"Billy said we should tell, but he knew we couldn't." Charlotte felt a need to defend her brother's silence.

One of the deputies had been writing on a tablet while Angela told her story. When everyone became calmer again, the questions started. The man who had led them from the lobby brought in cold soda pops for everyone and asked if they needed anything else. All three kids said no thank you.

Some of the same questions were asked over and over, only in different ways. The girls were asked about a time frame, but they weren't very good at explaining timing. When Angela thought something lasted a short time on that night, Charlotte would say it seemed like a long time. It was difficult for the deputies to make the time sequences fit the story at first. Questioning kids was not the same as questioning adults. They went over Angela's story for another hour.

Then Angela shocked them all again, so much so that they stared open-mouthed at her as she spoke. They were stunned into silence. No one moved a muscle as she told them her suspicions about Olin. This was even harder for her to tell in a way that made sense. She had to repeat so many of the things that Olin and Marie had said to her since the fight that night, all the things that had made her suspect it had been Olin in the parking lot.

Angela told them she didn't know for sure it was Olin fighting that night. It was a feeling she had. It was his talk about knowing a secret and the way he had said the words about her father. She talked about how she had always been afraid of Olin anyway, and how her fear was worse after he hurt Marie at the motel.

One of the deputies tapped Lanny Ray lightly on his shoulder and motioned to the door. Lanny Ray squeezed Angela's hand and followed the deputy out.

"I need to ask you a couple of things about your daughter, if you wouldn't mind."

"Sure, I guess." Lanny Ray looked pale and tired.

"Would you say Angela is usually a pretty honest kid?" The deputy saw a dark flash in Lanny Ray's eyes. "Even the best kids fib sometimes. They can make a story a lot bigger than it really is. Does she like to tell stories?"

Lanny gathered his temper and his thoughts for a minute.

"There's some things you should know about Angela. She isn't much like other kids her age. Her mother always says she was born with an old soul. She's way too grown up sometimes. It seems to her mother and me that Angela knew right from wrong since she was a tiny little thing. No, she don't make up stories. I can tell you that everything she's said would be the truth. She only kept all this to herself to protect me. 'Least, that's how she felt." Lanny Ray's voice cracked, and the corners of his mouth turned down.

"Do any of you know where this Olin is now? We need to find him."

"I don't know. I don't even know where he'd go from here unless he planned to catch up with the circuit again. In that case, he would be headed on up the road."

The deputy took a description of Olin's pickup, Olin himself, and Marie, and went to make some calls.

Lanny Ray returned to the room where Angela and the others were sitting quietly. They appeared to have finished talking about Olin.

"Do you know how long we will need to be here?" Lanny Ray asked the remaining deputy. "We really wanted to get on over the mountain this evening. Be nice if we can get on our way soon."

The deputy was as unlike MJ Beale as could possibly be. He was worried about the kids and understood Lanny Ray wanted to get going toward his hometown. He was a nice man who wanted to help out.

"Let's see what we can find out in the next hour or so about this Olin guy. Why don't you folks all go get something to eat and come on back here. By then we should know something, one way or another."

"Will Toby's folks be taking him on home?" Red asked.

"Yeah. He'll most likely go home on the train. Soon as the coroner releases the body, the family will all go on home," the deputy said. "I sure hope we'll be able to have some answers for them soon. We'll keep in touch every day till we figure out what happened to their boy."

Red, Lanny Ray, and the kids walked a short ways to a café to try to eat something. They were changed people who walked that half a block. Not one of them would ever be the same again. Lanny Ray feared Angela might never again be the brave, independent girl she was. It would be a different kid who returned to Jewel. For the time being, he couldn't think about how he would explain all of this to Arlene.

Lanny Ray wondered what it was within himself that made him selfish and irresponsible. How did he deserve a daughter willing to endure the memory of such horror just to protect him?

CHAPTER TWENTY-THREE

*T*he afternoon dragged on until it was apparent Lanny Ray and Angela wouldn't be leaving town that day. When they returned to the sheriff's office after lunch, they had to sit and wait again. They were exhausted. Especially Angela. She felt numb. She thought she should feel better. The story was out. No more secrets to keep.

She was relieved, though, that Red didn't seem angry at her or his kids for not telling him what had happened sooner. He seemed sad and tired, like the rest of them, but not angry. Angela knew that would help Charlotte and Billy feel better about keeping her secret from him all those days.

The deputies came to tell them that, so far, there was no information from surrounding counties about Olin. Nothing. They would keep trying. They also said they'd had an interesting conversation with Rafael.

"Any reason you know of that he would be nervous about telling us what he remembers from the night you were at Josie's Place?" one of the deputies asked. Lanny Ray remembered at once how Rafael had tried to get him to agree to his own account of where he was on that night.

"Well, I don't know if you could say he was nervous, but he mentioned I should remember he was with me there most of the time, or at least that I would know where he was," Lanny Ray said. "He was kind of peculiar about the whole thing."

"Did you know where he was all night?"

"You know, most of the time I did, but I can't say for sure how long it was between times he came back to sit with me. They were real busy out there that night, so he came and went. Him and Josie both," Lanny Ray said.

"Did he talk to you about the morning he found Toby's truck in the desert?" the deputy asked.

"Not really. He said his headlights caught the windshield on Toby's truck, and that was when he found it," Lanny Ray said.

"Yeah. We were thinking about that. We thought it odd—with Toby's truck sittin' down in that ravine and facing the direction it was—that Rafael's lights would shine on the windshield," the deputy said.

Lanny Ray thought for a minute. "Yeah, you're right. But you know, he did say something about how he almost drove into that ravine himself."

"Well, folks, we hate for you to have to stay around another night, but it looks like you need to. We're going to try to talk to the card dealer and a couple of the men who were in the cardroom that night. We'll start first thing in the morning so maybe we can get you out of here."

Their disappointment at not being able to leave town made them feel even more dejected. They headed to a motel that was recommended to them and once again rented rooms. It was stifling inside, so Lanny Ray and Angela sat on a bench outside, beneath a nice shade tree. Neither of them said anything for a while. Both of them, no doubt, thinking what a mess everything turned out to be.

"Angela, I'm sorry things have turned out like they have," Lanny Ray said. "I wanted this to be a good trip for you, and for me, too. A special time, you know. I'm truly sorry I left you out there in the parking lot that night. I sure wouldn't have if I'd ever dreamed something like this could happen."

"I know. It's okay. I mean, it's all awful, but it isn't your fault. I wish I could have just ran and told you right then what happened. I was too afraid. The man said such mean things, and I believed him."

"Ang, do you really think it was Olin out there that night?"

Angela sighed deeply. She was so weary of the story.

"Sometimes I'm almost sure, and then other times I'm not. I wish I would have watched him more when I peeked through the window. I was afraid he would see me."

Lanny Ray gave her shoulder a gentle pat. "Well, I promise we'll be out of this place tomorrow. I think we're both homesick now. It's time to head to Jewel."

The next morning, they all waited around impatiently. They had awakened early, had some breakfast, and then sat outside and waited to hear from a deputy. There was no rodeo talk or friendly teasing. There was only the tension of waiting. When the sheriff's car pulled into the motel parking lot, they all scrambled to their feet.

"Y'all can stay put," he said. "My partner will be along in a minute, and we can do our talking right here."

Indeed, his partner came right along, and they all sat on benches and outdoor chairs to talk. Nerves grew taut again. Angela sat near Lanny Ray.

"We spoke to a few people this morning," the deputy said. "The card dealer was reluctant to talk to us, at first. I think he's afraid he'll lose his job. It ain't much, but it's a job, and he makes pretty good tips when the cards are right. He finally admitted he remembers there was a player who fit Toby's description, and he knows for sure Olin was there. He says Olin was the one who started an argument. He says he was just about to signal Rafael to get Olin out of there. Says he was drunk and causing problems with all the players at the table. Olin had said the other guy, who the dealer thinks was Toby, cheated him. The dealer says he's sure there was no cheatin' going on, or he would have known."

The first deputy spoke. "We talked to one of the regular card players who was there that night. He agrees with the dealer. Says that Rafael came in the cardroom and told Olin he was going to have to leave. Olin didn't put up too much fuss about it but insisted Toby had cheated in the game. The player says Toby just got up and left of his own accord.

Says he said something about not wanting to get involved in a mess with Olin."

The other deputy spoke again. "So here's what we understand at this point. Toby went out first. Olin and Rafael had a conversation by the door. Next thing anybody knows, they were both gone, too. Since there were people waitin' for seats at the table, the dealer was busy and didn't pay any more attention to the situation. But now we know that all three of the men were outside at the same time. That puts Rafael out there, but we don't know why or for how long.

"We still have no word about Olin and his daughter. We'll be talking to Rafael again. We know now that he hasn't told us everything he should. We've decided, though, that we can't just keep you folks waiting around here till we learn more. We know you need to get on your way, but you're going to have to stay in touch with our office and let us know where you will be in case we need to talk to you again. Eventually, we will, you know." The deputy looked at Lanny Ray. "Fact is, there may come a day when you and your daughter might have to come back here. When we figure all this out, and when it goes to a court of law, your testimony will be required. Whoever killed Toby needs to go to prison."

Lanny Ray nodded his head, but no one said anything. The relief Angela felt at the news of being able to head on home nearly made her cry again. Charlotte, who had said nothing nearly all morning, went to Angela and put her arms around her.

"It will be better now, Ang. You get to go home," Char said.

Angela turned to Red with a questioning look. He pulled his hat off and ran his hand through his curly red hair. His words came slow.

"Well, little Ang," he said, "I hate to say it, but we will be headin' back the other way, I reckon. Katie is doin' a bit better at home, and she needs to see the kids. And they miss her like heck, too."

Tears slid down both girls' cheeks, and they hugged each other tight. Billy waited his turn and then hugged Angela, too.

They all walked slowly to their rooms to gather their belongings. Angela took her time, placing things exactly where she wanted them. This could be a much longer ride. She knew Lanny Ray's driving habits well by now. He would most likely want to drive through the night. She wanted her things all in order. She wanted them just like she had them when this long adventure began.

They all ate their last meal together early in the evening. Red and Lanny Ray talked about how the girls could visit each other. Maybe ride a bus to each other's hometown during a school break. Meanwhile, they could write letters. Angela was thrilled to think about someone coming to Jewel to visit her.

Char noticed how quiet Billy was and took the opportunity to tease him.

"You can write letters to Angela, too, Billy. You can, Billy. And on the back, you can write SWAK. That means 'sealed with a kiss,' Billy."

"I know what it means, Charlotte." Billy's ears turned red, and he couldn't look at anyone, especially Angela.

Lanny Ray and Angela drove out of the motel parking lot first. They all waved to each other until the big car drove out of sight. Angela sat back in her seat and let the hot wind blow on her face. She had the same giddy feeling she'd had when they drove out of Jewel that early morning that seemed so long ago. Lanny Ray looked peaceful, too. With his elbow resting on the window ledge and one big hand on the steering wheel, they headed out on the road.

CHAPTER TWENTY-FOUR

*T*hey traveled for miles, with the sun sliding down the sky behind them. It was a time of year when evenings stayed long, and the sun hung in the western sky for hours. Angela watched the range of mountains in front of them grow closer, but it seemed to take forever before any details showed in their blueness. When the canyons and ridges became clearer, Angela felt excited about the change of scenery. These were real mountains, high and rugged. She could see where the outline was of the huge stands of tall pine trees that grew along the ridges and spread down into deep shadowed canyons.

Lanny Ray pointed up ahead to where their road left the high desert floor and began its ascent into the range. Angela followed it with her eyes until it faded away into the distance. She was enjoying life again. She felt lighthearted—and safe.

Even though they were on the sunny side of the mountains, the air grew cooler as soon as they climbed in elevation. It wasn't long until the clean scent of pine blew on the wind that came through Angela's window. She breathed deeply to take it in. The road zigzagged and meandered as it made its way higher. The shadows grew longer and longer as the sun sank behind them. Then the dark came quickly in the depths of the twisting turns of the narrow road. Angela's eyes grew heavy with the drowsiness of relaxation. When they came to a turnout area, Lanny Ray pulled over and told her she should crawl in the back and get comfortable. They still had a long way to go.

Angela leaned into the corner of the backseat and pulled her quilt up against the cool breeze. She watched through the side window as the pine forest's shadows grew darker.

Lanny Ray, who was intent on driving the twisting road, noticed in his rearview mirror that there was another car behind them and began to watch for another pullout so he could let it go on by. He didn't want to drive fast on an unfamiliar, winding road in the dark. The car had come up in a hurry, and the driver most likely wanted to go around Lanny Ray's car so he could speed on. *Probably a local driver who knows the road well*, Lanny Ray thought. On a wide outside curve, Lanny Ray could see in his mirror that it was a pickup traveling behind him. Its driver had begun to annoy him a bit. He was following too close for such an unsafe road. Well, he would just have to wait until Lanny Ray could get out of his way.

Lanny Ray continued to glance often in his rearview mirror. The pickup would come closer and then back off for a bit. After that happened several times, Lanny Ray fumed.

"Dammit, buddy," he said aloud, "what do you want me to do here anyway?"

Lanny Ray did speed up just slightly, but he refused to go any faster. They were climbing higher into the mountains, and the road grew even narrower. Lanny Ray's window was still down, but the air had a night chill. He was rolling the window up when the pickup came up so close to the left rear fender of his car it caused Lanny Ray to grip the steering wheel with both hands. What the heck was going on with that guy? Was he drunk?

Again the pickup backed off. Lanny Ray glanced quickly at the backseat. Angela looked to be sound asleep. It crossed his mind to try to wake her, though he wasn't sure why he should. No, the son-of-a-gun behind them would only scare her.

The pickup moved up again. This time it moved up alongside the big car's left rear fender and stayed right next to it for some time. The pickup's headlights glared in the side mirror. Lanny Ray could see in his own headlights that there was just no place else he could go to get out of the way. The two vehicles kept swooping around one mountain curve after another. If someone should come from the opposite way, they would surely crash into the pickup. Lanny wondered if he should just begin to brake slowly until he could stop. He could do much better face-to-face with whoever the maniac was than to try to battle it out with his car.

It was too late for that idea. Just as Lanny Ray slowed, the pickup moved up again. This time, the driver jerked the pickup toward the car, causing its front bumper and fender to hit the left fender of the car. There was a thud of impact and the screech of metal on metal. Angela woke with a start and a scream in her throat. She sat straight up, but before she could call out to Lanny Ray, the pickup maneuvered into position and ran into the car again. Angela's small body was bounced across the seat, and her head struck against the side window. Lanny Ray continued to brake and held tight to the steering wheel.

"Lay down, Angela! Now! Lay flat down on the seat and find something to hold on to!"

He had slowed a bit and was feeling more in control when the pickup moved up and this time slammed into the car hard. Lanny Ray tried to steer in the direction the car skidded, but it seemed to have a mind of its own. Here it came again, and this time Lanny Ray had a flash of premonition that this was the one to send them off the road. He was suddenly sure that this was not just an angry driver. This was someone bent on killing. Olin was driving that pickup truck, and he was probably way past drunk.

"Hold on, Angela! Hold on tight!" he yelled.

When the pickup hit this time, it didn't back off. The driver kept fender to fender until Lanny Ray's car spun around and was facing the high rocky bank on the opposite side of the road. The big car slammed into the bank, head-on, with such force that it was propelled backward. The pickup rammed into the driver's door. The front of the car spun away. The noise was deafening, and the stench of burnt rubber was immediate and sickening. Lanny Ray could do nothing. He no longer had a hold on the steering wheel. His body had been thrown to the side, and his grip on the wheel torn away. He couldn't see anything anymore. At least nothing that made any sense. All he knew was that the pickup had hit the car for the last time and then continued to push it sideways until it left the road. His body was flung around the inside of the car as it plunged down the mountainside.

Angela's short, shrill scream had filled the car the first time the pickup hit them, but she didn't make another sound. She tried. It just wouldn't come, or maybe she just couldn't hear herself. She gripped both the armrest and the edge of the backseat. She held on until the second or third hit and then was flung so hard she lost her hold. After that, her little body bounced from seat to seat and floor to ceiling. She heard, rather than felt, her head slam against the side window again. Then she couldn't see or hear anything for a time.

Neither Lanny Ray nor Angela knew when the car stopped moving. Lanny Ray was unconscious. His long body lay cramped and wedged beneath the collapsed steering column and dashboard.

Angela lay squeezed behind the front seat, with the backseat folded over her. She was awake, but she had no idea where she was or why. Her mind struggled for what seemed an eternity to make sense of something. Anything. No matter how hard she tried, nothing came to her. She was too tired to think. She closed her eyes to rest.

When she became aware again, she noticed an acrid odor. What was that? Smelled like burning rubber and . . . what . . . grease maybe. Hot grease. Oil? That was it. Why was she here? She made a move to turn over. No. Can't do that. She went back to sleep.

She awoke again. Why was she so darn cold? Where was her quilt? Lanny Ray should roll the windows up. She heard herself ask him to please roll up the window. It was too cold, her voice said. She trembled all over. Sometimes she would feel herself jerk violently with a spasm that ran through her body. She sure wished she could just turn over. Noises. What the heck was that? Creaking and ticking. Was it a clock? No. It was loud, though. She couldn't know it was the metal of the car, settling in the coolness.

Her father! Where was Lanny Ray? Little flashes of reality snuck into her thoughts. Oh! They'd been in an accident! That's right. Now she remembered. And then it was gone again for a time.

"Dad! Dad!" she yelled. "Lanny Ray!" She could barely hear herself. She was yelling as loud as she could.

Lanny Ray moaned, long and low. He could hear her, but he couldn't speak. He could only make some awful noise. He moaned again.

Suddenly, Angela's eyes flew wide open. She remembered. They had crashed off the side of the road. Wasn't there another car? Where did it go? Did it wreck, too? She heard her father moaning. He had to be close. She tried to call him again, louder this time. Inside her head, she sounded like she was screaming. He answered with only another moan.

Angela wondered if she might die. Well, maybe not, since she was able to think. Maybe you don't die while you're thinking. She prayed to God that her dad didn't die, either. She wondered if he could think, too.

CHAPTER TWENTY-FIVE

$\mathcal{T}$he big car was wedged in its place by pine saplings and boulders, clinging to the steep hillside by its front wheels and pointing up toward the road it had plunged from. Its passengers were unaware that they were both drifting in and out of consciousness at different times. They both tried to speak, and sometimes were successful, but their voices were weak. When a bit of clarity roused one or the other of them, he or she would desperately try to piece together what had happened.

Angela felt no pain, but she was so cold her teeth chattered. To her, it was a muffled sound, from somewhere other than herself. Her left arm and hand were free to move, but her right arm was beneath her body and wouldn't budge. She tried to reach around her to make sense of why she wasn't able to get up or even turn herself over. Her hand touched familiar things. She felt pages of a book and the small plastic box she kept her pencils in. On the third try, her fingers touched the softness of her quilt. She grasped it the best she could, and with all the strength she could muster, she gave it a sharp tug. It came to her, bringing a comfort that made her begin to weep. It was then she called for her mother.

Lanny Ray could hear his daughter calling, "Mama, Maaama." She sounded sad and scared.

"Don't cry, Ang. I'm here," he would say over and over. But he couldn't figure out yet where "here" was, exactly.

Lanny Ray also shook uncontrollably. He had excruciating pain somewhere on the right side of his body. If he turned his head slightly to the left, he could look up through the glassless windshield opening. Every time he would drift off into blackness and then wake again, he would remember something more about what had happened. At some point, he recalled the car being pushed over the edge of the road by another vehicle, but then he questioned the reality of that.

He wondered how far from the road they were. What if no one saw them! He panted as panic overtook him. If he could get up, he would try to find the road. He knew he had to get Angela out of the car soon. What if she was bleeding bad or getting too cold?

An inch, or less, at a time, Lanny Ray willed himself to move. The pain in his side was agonizing. Every move he made caused broken glass to fall from one place to another, stinging and stabbing at his skin. The car groaned and quivered.

In spite of feeling icy cold, he would break out in a sweat when he tried to move for too long at a time. He had to reposition himself so slowly it took what felt like eons to make progress. He eventually found his bearings enough to know he had to somehow move upward, up where he thought he could see stars. That was the only escape from the car he could concentrate on. It was not completely unlike bronc riding. Focus, he kept telling himself, focus on what you are doing. Don't think about anything else. Not even for one second. First he had to pull himself from under the steering wheel. The work sapped his strength so severely that he would drift off into darkness and sleep, again and again. He had no way to know how long those dark times lasted. Could have been hours.

He spoke to Angela when he rested. Sometimes he rambled on senselessly and sometimes reassuringly. It made him feel better to talk to her, even if she didn't often answer him.

After what seemed like a hundred nights had passed, he stood on whatever footholds his boots could find and thrust the upper half of his body through the frame of the missing windshield. Glass shards tore through the flesh of his chest and belly. By then, he was aware of the fact that he could not use his right shoulder, arm, or hand. For whatever reason, his pain had lessened to at least tolerable. Using his trembling left arm, he struggled for leverage until he pulled himself out of the car and let his body roll off the cold metal and onto the ground. He heard the sound of the air leaving his body when he landed hard on the ground. Finally, finally he could begin crawling toward the road above him.

Angela knew her father was moving about in the front of the car by the jiggle of the car and the creaking sounds. Each time she felt glass fall against her skin, she would close her eyes as tight as she could. When she felt the car move, it would frighten her more, and she would cry out. When she could hear Lanny Ray's voice, even if she couldn't understand what he said, it was a comfort to her, like her mother's quilt.

Lanny Ray lay motionless on the cold ground. His breath was raspy and labored. His fingers made a claw in the loose dirt and grass left in the path of the skidding undercarriage of the car. In his mind he begged God that if he was going to die someone would come to save Angela.

Angela had given up on trying to move. She had accepted the fact that the backseat had her pinned to the floorboard, and she only exhausted herself trying to squirm from beneath it. She gripped an edge of the quilt in her left hand and thought about Lanny Ray and Arlene and Jewel. She had quit shivering.

CHAPTER TWENTY-SIX

*M*arie scribbled on the scrap of paper with a stubby, yellow pencil. Her hand shook so hard she couldn't make her letters be still. There was no eraser on the pencil, it having been wore away long ago by someone else's mistakes, so she turned the paper over, took a long breath, and tried again. Hurry . . . she had to hurry before he came back. "We saw a accident on the mountain road. Bad one." She folded the already small piece of paper several times and clenched it in her fist.

She left the pickup and rushed around the back of the gas station to find the restrooms. She stepped into the women's and stood stock still in the dark. When she heard the squeak of the men's room door open and close, she hurried back out and around to the front of the building. Good. Olin was not at the gas pump. She whispered to herself, "Please let it be him in the men's bathroom." She stepped inside the office door. Nobody was there. She was nearly choked with panic. Where was the damn attendant? She would just have to leave the note. She unfolded the piece of paper and laid it on the desk. She turned away, then turned back again and smoothed the paper out, carefully sliding it to the center of the old desk. She ran to the pickup and clambered back in as fast as she could and was in her place when Olin came around the corner, got behind the wheel, and drove away from the gas pumps.

When the phone rang, the attendant hustled through the door from the work bay to answer it, wiping his hands on a greasy, red rag.

He hoped it was his girlfriend. She always called him when she was leaving work.

"Shell station. Derek speaking," he said. It was her. "Hi, baby. Okay, drive careful. See ya later."

When he saw the note, he was puzzled. Where'd it come from? He read the words and then read them again. He sat down in the chair behind the desk. What the heck . . . ?

Maybe he should call over to Dora at the police department. Oh hell, now he was going to have to stay around the station and wait until one of the cops came to see about the damn note.

Maybe he wouldn't call. Stupid note didn't make much sense anyway. He didn't even know where it came from. That grubby lookin' old guy in the pickup was the only customer he'd had in almost an hour. And the girl with him.

No, Derek was a responsible young man. He picked up the phone and told the operator he wanted the police department. Dora answered, listened, and said she'd have Eldon stop by.

Chapter Twenty-Seven

𝒯he inside of the car lit up with an eerie glow. Hello? Why was somebody saying hello? Was she dreaming again? No, it was real. The voices were clear. Angela could hear most of what they said. ". . . some help up here. I'm going down to check this guy out, then we'll check the car."

Tears of sheer relief rolled down Angela's face. Help was coming.

Lanny Ray raised himself as far as he could on his left forearm. He tried to look upward toward the voices. Pain struck again. And the deepest darkness.

It took a long time to get Lanny Ray, and then Angela, up to the road. Lanny Ray could be hauled up on the backboard with enough strong men. He was only a few yards down from the road's edge. He had made it that far, in spite of his injuries. But it took time and planning to get Angela out of the car. The rescue entailed ropes and chains to stabilize the car. They were all fortunate that the car had not slid farther down the steep slope. It was high and centered on a good-sized boulder, but the saplings holding it in place were spindly. Men had to get inside the unstable car with Angela and unbolt and dismantle part of the backseat. Dangerous for all involved, and awkward, it was slow work. She still faded in and out of reality, but when she was aware, she talked to the men and tried to be brave. Her rescuers breathed a sigh of relief when she was free of her confines and on the stretcher. She was light to carry, but it was difficult to get good footing in the loose dirt. A ripple of relief passed through the officers and rescuers when Angela's stretcher was given over to the hands that would put her into the ambulance.

Reality continued to come and go for Angela. Time was distorted far beyond any understanding. It was midmorning when Angela could make sense of what had happened. When she asked about Lanny Ray, she was told he was resting, and he would be fine. That was reassuring enough to ease her worry for the time being.

They had been taken to the small community hospital and placed in rooms across the hall from one another. X-rays were taken, and they both endured the poking and prodding of thorough examinations. By afternoon, it was confirmed that there were no life-threatening injuries to either one of them, but there were horrific bruises and deep lacerations, and Lanny Ray had broken bones. His shoulder was badly wrenched, and he had several broken ribs and a broken collarbone. The cuts, contusions, and swelling made his body painful all over.

The biggest concern for Angela was where she had hit her head against the window. She had a large swelling behind her temple and a severe concussion and had to be monitored carefully. The side of her face and the area around her eye were a garish purple color. Her head ached badly, in spite of the medication they gave her. When she was awake, she longed to slide back into the darkness where she didn't feel anything, but the nurses woke her often, speaking to her in soft voices.

The police and a detective they had yet to meet waited for the chance to speak to Lanny Ray and Angela. The detective assigned to their case was Adam Glover. Detective Glover had jurisdiction over two counties. Intelligent and having a businesslike manner, he would waste no words when he got the opportunity to speak with Lanny Ray.

On the second day, Lanny Ray related as much as he could to the detective. Try as he might, he wasn't very helpful.

"I couldn't tell what color the pickup was. The glare of the headlights in my mirror, and then just trying to drive on the narrow road, kept me from seeing much of anything. I just yelled for Angela to lay down on the seat, and that was about it."

"It's obvious this was no accident. Someone was out to harm you. Do you know who it might be?" the detective asked.

"Detective, we left a whole lotta trouble behind us on the other side of the mountains. You probably already know there are a lot of unanswered questions about what happened to my friend, Toby. And I'm sure you know about the two men being questioned about it all. I can only think that what happened to Angela and me has something to do with that. There's just nothing else it could be."

Detective Glover asked Lanny Ray to relate as much information as he could about what had happened the previous few days. It seemed like a very long and complicated story, and the telling of it all exhausted Lanny Ray. Eventually, he began to lose his voice.

Detective Glover then went straight to Angela's hospital bed and pulled up a chair. He explained who he was and asked a few questions, and her own version of all that had happened to her in the past few weeks came out with stilted words and tears. She did the best she could. Glover took pages of notes as Angela spoke. He seldom looked up. His expression remained serious. One time he excused himself and left the room for several minutes to let Angela close her eyes and rest. When he returned, he reminded her of where she had left her story and encouraged her to continue.

Because he already knew some of the facts about the Toby Abel homicide, Detective Glover was aware that Olin had not been found and questioned as of yet. Also, the deputies who wanted to speak with Rafael again had not done so because he, too, seemed to have disappeared. A "Be On the Lookout" had been put out on both men.

The next morning, Angela was carefully placed in a wheelchair and rolled into her father's room. They were both shocked speechless when they first saw each other.

"Little heavy on the purple eye shadow there, Ang," Lanny Ray finally said in a voice rough with emotion. Angela managed a crooked smile.

"Are you going to be okay?"

"Yeah, I will. Sooner than you think, sissy."

"Does Mom know what happened?"

"No. But I'll call her this morning."

"How are we going to get home? Will we get our stuff from the car?"

"I'll figure out something. Try not to worry, okay? I asked the police if they would get as many of our things as they could out of the car. They drug it up the slope yesterday. They will, Ang. They really want to help out."

CHAPTER TWENTY-EIGHT

"*N*orma! Oh God, Norma," Arlene shouted into the phone. "They've been in a horrible accident. I have to go there, and I don't think my damn car will make it. I know it's a whole lot to ask, but can I borrow your car? I have to go there. They're in the hospital, and Lanny Ray is all broken up, and poor little Angela's scared to death." Arlene was on the verge of hysteria and talking fast.

"Arlene, slow down. Start over. Where are they?" Norma said.

"Some little town east of Milton, after you come over the mountain. I forget right now. But I have to go see Angela, and I need to leave right now." Arlene was too frantic to make very much sense.

"Arlene, you can't just drive there all alone. It will take a couple of days. Stay by the phone. I'll call you right back." Norma hung up.

Arlene raced around the house from room to room. Angela had their only suitcase with her. Oh well, a box would do. She was throwing some clothes into a cardboard box when Norma called back.

"Okay, this is what we'll do. I have somebody to work mornings for me, and my neighbor will keep her eye on my kids. As long as they remember to feed Willy and don't burn the house down, I can leave 'em for a few days. I'll be over as soon as I can, and we'll get on the road. We'll take turns at drivin', and we'll be there fast as a cat scats."

"Oh God, Norma. How will I ever thank you for bein' such a good friend?" Arlene was crying.

"I'll figure out something," Norma said and hung up.

Norma drove the first leg. Arlene was too upset to drive. She talked up a storm for miles out of sheer nervousness. It seemed to Norma that Arlene, given enough time, could manage to blame herself for every bad thing that happened on Earth. She came up with about a half dozen ways to blame herself for Angela being hurt in a car accident.

"Why in God's name did I let her go with him? What is the matter with me? I thought I was a good mother, but now look what I've done." The regret kept coming.

Attempting to change the subject, and also because she was being snoopy, Norma asked about Arlene's relationship with Grady.

"He's a nice man, Grady is. But I probably won't be seein' him anymore. I just don't want to be involved with another man when Angela gets back home. You know how I feel about that, Norma." Arlene was teary-eyed again at her own mention of Angela.

"That's plain crazy talk. Here's this nice, good-lookin' man, wantin' to be with you, and you lettin' your daughter keep you apart. You don't even know but what Angela might really take a likin' to Grady. I bet he would be a good step-daddy." Norma gave Arlene a sideways look.

"Oh, hush. I ain't marryin' nobody, and Ang won't have a step-daddy. We do fine, the two of us, without a man in the house. Besides, how would Lanny Ray feel about me and Angela havin' another man around?"

Norma could almost feel smoke come out of her ears.

"I can't believe you just said that. I could run this car right off the road. After all this time and all the shenanigans that man has played on you, and you still worry about his feelings. Please say you don't mean that."

Arlene gazed out the side window and didn't answer for a while.

"I don't expect you—or anybody else for that matter—to understand. Lanny Ray was the love of my life, Norma. There won't ever be nobody take his place, you know? I know better than anybody what a rascal he is, but there's just something between us that never really goes away.

That don't mean I want to be with him the way it was. I don't want to fight and argue and all that." Arlene let out a big sigh and shook her head. "It wouldn't be very fair to be with a nice man like Grady when I feel like I do."

Norma couldn't stay mad at her friend. She concentrated on the road and didn't try to make any more conversation. She wondered how long it would be before word of this trip hit the gossip fan in Jewel.

Not long. By midmorning the next day, the third round of gossip involving the Garrett family was on the wing.

Poor, poor Arlene. Angela had nearly been killed in a car wreck. And Lanny Ray was broken up so bad he might never recover.

Fuzzy said Arlene would never get over this one as long as she lived. Lanny Ray had been determined to make her life a living hell, and now he'd done it.

Linc harrumphed and slid away to his end of the bench. No way would Lanny Ray Garrett hurt his little daughter on purpose. It had to be somebody else's fault. Arlene never should have let Angela go in the first place.

Everyone agreed on how nice it was that Norma was such a good friend to Arlene. No one seemed to remember back when Norma herself was the subject of gossip—back when her no-good old man went off and left her with those poor little kids. That was one of the good things about the people of Jewel. Their memory for gossip nearly always proved inadequate. In with the new, out with the old.

CHAPTER TWENTY-NINE

*J*osie was a mess. Rafael hadn't been home for two nights. The sheriff's deputies had been by the day before asking for him. She knew they didn't believe her when she said she didn't know where he was, but they quit asking when she started to cry.

Rafael had come back from town the day Toby was found and told her what had happened. Josie had seen a little fire in his eyes when he said the deputies questioned him as if he'd had something to do with Toby's murder.

"I told them I didn't know anything about what went on the night that Toby fellow went missing. We were very busy that night, you remember, Josie? I told them I was here working, and that you knew I was here the whole night. I told them they could ask you. You and Lanny Ray both know I was right here," he motioned around the barroom, "all that night."

Josie was quiet with thought for a moment. "Oh sure, Rafael. It was very busy. We ran ourselves ragged to keep up." She was thoughtful again. "Maybe only one time I lost track of you."

"What are you talking about, lost track of me? You know I was right here." He spoke harshly and pointed at the spot where he stood.

"Rafael," Josie looked at him questioningly, "I did not see you for some time after you had to go to the cardroom. Remember? I think there was some trouble there."

Rafael wrapped his fingers around Josie's arm above her wrist and squeezed hard.

"Josie, if someone asks you about that night, you will tell them you saw me in here all night. You will not say you lost track of me. Do you understand?"

Josie tried to pull away, but Rafael held his grip and continued to look into her eyes. His own eyes had narrowed to slits, and his mouth was set in a hard line. He was scaring Josie.

"You're right, Rafael. I must have been mixed-up with another night." He let go of her, and she stepped back. "I need to do my work now." She left him then, her insides churning.

The next day, Olin showed up again. He sat at the bar and had a beer and talked with Rafael in a low voice for a while. Josie steered clear of them. She was still upset about Rafael's behavior toward her, and she wasn't comfortable around Olin. He made her skin prickle. She was relieved when she saw that he had finally left. *Good riddance to that man*, she thought. He was trouble, for sure.

Later that evening, a man who sometimes tended the bar on weekends came in and took over for Rafael. Rafael told Josie, without explaining, that he had to go to town, and the next thing she knew, he was gone. She had not seen him since.

Josie knew better than anyone about Rafael's temper. It had always been there. Even when they were young kids, when he would get mad, he would rant and throw or kick something. He tended to be sullen for periods of time, and Josie had learned not to provoke his temper. She knew he was a worrier, and she truly believed that he just wanted to take care of her and his business. She also knew she was important to Rafael. He loved her, and she loved him.

But this was different. He had been brooding about something. He was even rude to Lanny Ray and his daughter, and he barely acknowledged Lanny Ray's friends when they came back to see about their friend. And then, he had not been home in two nights. He had never stayed away from home like that before. Josie was aware, of course, that everyone was anxious and upset about the night Mr. Toby was killed. She couldn't help but remember that Rafael had left her to work alone for too long that night. She had been frantic with trying to keep up with cooking and serving when it was so busy. Her anger at Rafael had grown with every trip through the kitchen door, and she had searched for him to come and help out. When he finally came back, he didn't bother to apologize to her. In fact, he didn't even talk to her for the rest of the busy night. He just set to work, helping her and the bartender get caught up.

Now she had no idea where her husband was, and the police were looking for him. She had to admit to herself that it didn't look good for Rafael to act this way. Maybe he did know something about what happened to Toby and was afraid.

Josie wasn't too far from the truth. It was fear that had put Rafael on the path he chose to take the night he told Josie he had to go to town. Fear tore at his gut as he drove away from the bar. He knew the deputies suspected he was involved in Toby's murder. When he allowed himself to think about what could happen, a fire burned in the pit of his stomach, and he felt as if his head might explode. As that long night went by, he would slip back and forth between the grip of fear and his maddening anger. Sometimes he would have to pull his pickup off the road until he calmed himself enough to see through the blinding haze of rage.

His imagination ran with its own version of what might happen to him. He could be arrested and sent to prison. He would not let that happen. Rafael thought of running away from the whole mess. Leaving right then. But he had no idea where to go. He knew no place else. He had been here all of his life, and he had no idea what was beyond the radius of two or three hundred miles. He was as afraid to leave as he was to stay.

He wished he knew what Angela had seen and heard in the parking lot that night. If she hadn't already told the police she thought it was him she saw, then maybe he was safe. He thought how good it would be for him if Angela was not around to tell about anything at all. If she wasn't able to tell about that night, nobody would ever know what really happened.

Rafael was positive that no one knew he had gone back to the desert and collected Toby's body in the early morning hours before he reported finding the truck out there. He had decided that the body should not be found inside the truck. It should be separate, he reasoned, to make it harder to connect him to what had taken place that night. He had looked like a caring man by being the one to drive into the desert and come across Toby's pickup and like a good citizen when he reported his finding to the sheriff's department.

The truth was, Rafael had struggled for at least a half an hour to drag Toby out of his pickup and into his own that morning before calling the sheriff's office. There was no way he could lift him into the bed of his truck, so the horror of it was that Rafael had managed, a little at a time, to hoist Toby onto the passenger side seat of his own cab. He had laid him across the seat and then driven back to the main road and toward town until he came to the place where the desert downpours drained under the road through a culvert. He had thought through every step carefully and had taken time to brush away the marks he may have left on the ground around Toby's truck. He was careful again when he dragged and then pushed Toby's body over the steep bank above the culvert. He knew there was a chance that Toby might never be found there, and even if he ever was, who could know that Rafael had anything to do with his murder?

But on the night when Rafael drove and drove, with his demons chasing him and confusing him, he imagined all kinds of ways to protect his freedom. Rafael took the back roads of the desert through the dark, and in his exhausted state, he continued to imagine one scenario after another. Sometimes he would think he was being hunted and would try to find places where he could park his old pickup truck and be hidden. Then the next thing he knew, he was driving again. And thinking and thinking. At times, he'd begin to form ideas about how to get rid of Angela so she couldn't talk about that night again. He imagined shooting her or strangling her, and his fingers would grip the steering wheel until they were white. He would never be sent to prison without Angela around to testify that he was the killer. As long as she was able to say that she thought it was him out in the muddy parking lot, his freedom was at stake. He had to find Lanny Ray and Angela.

Clarity came and went for Rafael. When he was lucid, he could reason that all he had to do was say that Olin had killed Toby. But Olin could do the same. He could say Rafael was the killer. He and Marie could be witnesses against him. Angela may be the only one who knew the truth. And then his mind would snatch him back to the ugly darkness again.

CHAPTER THIRTY

$\mathcal{M}$arie had quit talking to Olin. There was no way she could escape from him, or she would have done so. She would need a ride to get away, and there wasn't a truck stop in Milton or anywhere else in this godforsaken county. She knew, though, that as soon as she was able, she would take off. She remembered what Angela had said to her about that. She didn't believe Marie would do it. Well, she would do it now.

Olin was drinking even more than usual. Whiskey, straight from the bottle. He warned Marie over and over in his drunkenness that she'd better keep quiet about everything. Everything meant anything she knew—or thought—since the night the fight had happened at Josie's Bar. She had tried to convince him, time after time, that she didn't really know what had happened. At least not the part where Toby ended up dying. She'd finally given up trying to convince him.

She had heard arguing voices across the lot that night, but she couldn't see the men. At first, she assumed it was two men in a usual bar fight. They fought over women at these places. She'd seen it a dozen times. More than once, she had witnessed a couple of men start out fighting over some woman and then end up shaking hands and going back inside. *Men are idiotic suckers for women*, she thought.

From where she had sat huddled in the pickup, she thought she'd heard at least two voices, maybe three. They carried on for a long time. She couldn't understand what they were saying. She was cold and didn't want to roll the window down and let the rain in. Marie had grown weary of seeing—or, in this case, hearing—the viciousness Olin subjected her to. She had closed her eyes and tried not to listen.

She was startled when she heard the metallic clang of the tailgate drop down behind her. The pickup jiggled a bit. She'd wiped away the fog from the back window and watched with disgust as Olin worked at putting something in the pickup bed. She wondered if maybe he had stolen something. He was struggling and lifting an object that seemed hard for him to grip. She could hear him breathing hard and grunting with exertion. Another man came out of the dark and helped Olin. Marie heard the tailgate slam shut.

Olin had yanked the driver side door open, and he'd given her orders.

"Drive this truck," he'd said. "Follow me out of here. I'll be in another truck, and I want you right behind me, understand?"

"Where are we going?" Marie asked. "What's going on?"

"Just get over here and start the truck. Do what I say."

Marie was scared then. She barely knew how to drive the old pickup and didn't know if she could even get it out of the muddy parking lot. She was shaking so hard she could hardly get the engine started. She ground the gears, trying to get it in reverse, and it died several times because she couldn't let the clutch out smoothly. Her leg kept jerking involuntarily. She was afraid she would flood the carburetor because she had to keep restarting the engine. Finally, she was turned around and could see Olin waving impatiently for her to follow him.

Was that Toby's truck? It sure looked like his. *Why are we doing this?* she wondered. Marie bumped along an old dirt road that seemed to be headed out into the desert. With the rain on the side windows, it was hard to tell what was around her. All she could see was the back of the other pickup, and that's when she became sure it was Toby's. She followed as close as she dared, afraid of being left behind. She couldn't tell if there was even a road most of the time. The pickup dragged the undercarriage over the sagebrush and bounced across gullies.

When Olin stopped, and he and his passenger quickly climbed out of the cab, they hurried to the back of Olin's pick up where he again dropped the tailgate. Marie leaned to watch through the window as they pulled the bulky cargo out. She saw what it was—a body, a dead person. Her stomach turned, and she had trouble breathing. She watched in horror as Olin and Rafael struggled to put the body in the cab of Toby's truck. They were soaking wet, and the body was covered with mud. Rafael tossed a dirty, misshapen cowboy hat haphazardly into the cab and slammed the door. Once they had accomplished that, the two men together gave the truck a hard push from behind and watched as it slowly rolled down into a ravine. It settled to a stop at an awkward angle.

They hurried back to Olin's truck, where Olin opened the door and shoved Marie across the seat. He and Rafael climbed in, and Olin quickly turned his pickup and headed back toward Josie's Place, driving fast and bumping and banging hard over the rough terrain.

Marie was too terrified to speak. She was cold and her stomach felt sick. Did her father or Rafael kill that person? Olin was mean, but was he a killer, too? She buried her face in her coat collar. God, what she would give to be back in Phoenix.

"Let me out by the back of the building," Rafael said. "I have to get out of these clothes. Hurry up. I've been gone too long. Josie will wonder what's going on. What am I supposed to tell her?"

"I don't care what you tell her, as long as you don't mention my name. I find out you told anybody anything, I'll lay this whole thing on you," Olin said.

"Ha, my friend, I could do the same, no? We're both in this now. Maybe you should worry more about your girl here, Mr. Olin."

"Don't worry about her. She knows better than to say anything. She knows what happens if she doesn't do what I tell her."

As soon as they slowed, Rafael jumped out of the truck and hurried around the back of the building to the adobe house. Olin pulled back out of the parking lot and headed down the main road.

"Was that Toby?" Marie's voice was weak, and she hadn't been able to look at Olin. She just stared out through the windshield.

He didn't even hesitate or attempt to make something up.

"Yep, that was Toby. It was an accident, Marie. He wasn't supposed to die, but he did. He shouldn't have cheated in the first place, and none of this woulda happened. People like me and ol' Rafael back there, we can't abide by cheatin' a man out of his money."

Marie had been dumbfounded at Olin's words. She was afraid to ask him which one of them had killed Toby. She already hated her father because of who he was—and how he was—and now he might even be a murderer. What if somebody had seen them? She hoped someone had. For a brief moment, she experienced a sense of calming relief to think that someone else could tell what they saw, and Olin would go to prison.

CHAPTER THIRTY-ONE

Olin had got on the road and headed over the mountains to the east soon after he heard that Toby had been found in the culvert. He hoped that if the deputies were looking for him they would naturally think he had gone in the opposite direction to catch up with the rodeo circuit or toward Phoenix. Olin didn't like to think of his actions as running away—that would be almost like admitting guilt and cowardliness. No, it was more like avoidance. As usual, he didn't volunteer any information about his plans to Marie. Actually, he didn't have much of a plan until one formed as they crossed over the high mountain road. As he rounded the curves in the narrow road, he imagined what would happen if a car went over the edge where the road seemed to cling to the sides of the mountains. Twice he pulled to the side and got out of the cab to look around. In some places, it was a long way to the bottom of the canyon. He looked down to the tops of the mature trees and saw saplings struggling to grow on the steep mountainside. It was easy for him to imagine a car crashing down the mountainside.

When Olin and Marie rolled down through the foothills on the east side of the range, he found an out-of-the-way place to stay in the first small town they came to. It was a crummy, rundown motel that sat back from the main road. It looked dark and dirty beneath low-hanging trees. Olin was tired and needed a drink and some sleep. Once in the motel room, he drank and ranted about how unjust his life was until he finally passed out. The next day, he announced to Marie that they were going back the way they had come. Back over the same mountain road. When Marie dared to ask why, Olin told her he'd changed his mind and decided to try to catch up with rodeoin'. Maybe get in on the last two or three. Marie never knew if he was telling her the truth or not. He had become more sullen and mean-mouthed than he'd ever been.

Marie had grown so weary of her crazy life, she hardly asked any questions anymore. She was so sick and tired of riding in Olin's old truck. She would rather be back in the house in Phoenix with her drunken mother. As bad as it was there, at least she could sleep in the same bed for a while. It had even crossed her mind that a foster home might be better than living like this. Here she was, traveling back over the same mountains they had just driven over the evening before, and she didn't even really know why. If Olin kept drinking, he wouldn't be able to ride in a rodeo, even if they got to one.

Olin pulled into a gas station about twenty miles before the city limit sign of Milton. The attendant there filled the truck's tank, and Olin and Marie went inside the adjoining store to buy sodas. When they exited into the heat of the bright sunshine, Marie stopped when she noticed a pickup sitting just around the corner of the building. Only the front end could be seen, but it looked familiar.

"Is that Rafael?" she said.

"Looks like his pickup, don't it?" Olin said. "Go get in the truck. I'll see if it's his."

Olin, who was hardened to most any bad thing one could think of, was taken aback when he saw Rafael sitting behind the wheel of the truck. In fact, he had to look close to be sure it was Rafael. The usually neat and handsome man was a wreck. He didn't react at all when he turned and saw Olin peering at him through the open side window. His black hair, always shiny and groomed, was a matted, oily mess. His brown eyes were dull and sunken, dark circles surrounding them. Black stubble grew across his upper lip and around his jaw line.

"Rafael?" Olin said. "What the hell you doin', man? You're lookin' pretty bad."

Olin was unnerved by Rafael's long stare. When he finally spoke, his voice was rough and raspy. His eyes took on a wide, wild look.

"Olin, they're hunting for me. I'm going to prison for murder. I don't know what to do."

"Who's huntin' you? The sheriffs? They ain't going to send you to prison, Rafael. They can't prove nothin', you know," Olin said.

"Where's Lanny Ray and Angela? I have to find them. If Angela can't talk, nobody will know what happened to Toby." Rafael's eyes welled up with tears. "We have to save ourselves, Olin." A hoarse sob came from Rafael's throat.

Olin was bewildered for a minute. It slowly dawned on him that Rafael was no longer confident that laying the blame for Toby's death on Olin would save his own neck. He was literally going crazy with the thoughts of prison life. Olin's malicious mind formed ideas.

"I agree with you, Rafael. If we could find those two, we could eliminate any prospect of that little gal testifyin' against you at a trial. It shouldn't be hard to find 'em. They had to head one way or another. My guess would be that ol' Lanny Ray is hightailin' it home. You sit tight right here, and let me see what I can find out. Try to relax a little bit." Olin walked around the station to his own truck. This was perfect. Rafael had become so crazy with worry that he seemed confused about just what had taken place at Josie's that night.

"I need you to do something," Olin said to Marie while he dug deep in his pocket. "Go to the phone and call the Milton sheriff's office. Say you're a friend of the Garretts from Jewel, and you want to know if they're on their way home yet. Just say you thought maybe they could help you out. Talk natural. Tell 'em you're Angela's friend, and you're worried about her gettin' home."

"I don't want to do that, Olin. They'll know I'm lyin'," Marie said.

"How they gonna know? A good liar like you can do it easy. If they ask too many questions, just hang up. Can't hurt nothin'."

Marie had been given an order, and she knew it would do no good to argue. She looked up the number, dropped coins in the slot, and made the call.

"Sheriff's department, how can I help you?"

"My name is Sue Smith. I'm a friend of Angela Garrett. I was wondering if you could tell me where Angela might be, you know, how I can get in touch with her."

"Who'd you say this is? Where you callin' from?" the deputy asked.

"My name's Sue. I live in Jewel, and I'm askin' about Angela Garrett." Marie's voice wavered a little bit.

"May I ask what your concern is with Angela?"

Marie was speechless for a second. She hadn't thought about being asked that.

"Well, I know her mother. She said I could call and see if they left yet." Maybe that would work.

"Just a minute," the deputy said. He came back on. "Yeah, well, I guess they're headed home, as far as we know. She and her dad were headed over the mountain this evenin'. Least that's what they said, I guess. They were all packin' up to go a little while ago."

"Okay, thanks." Marie quickly hung up. She told Olin what the deputy had said.

Olin went back to Rafael's truck. He didn't appear to have moved at all. He was staring straight ahead again, still looking oddly bewildered.

"I might have an idea for ya, Rafael. If you can find a place to wait and watch for Lanny Ray's Olds, you might be able to tail him right over the mountains there. There's some pretty steep drop-offs up there. Be easy for some poor guy to miscalculate and run off the edge. Know what I mean?" Olin smiled a broken-toothed, wicked smile.

It slowly dawned on Rafael what Olin was saying. Could he kill someone? Maybe, if it meant keeping his freedom and going back to Josie to live his life. He said nothing more to Olin, started his pickup, and drove off.

Rafael knew exactly where he could wait for Lanny Ray's big car. He backed his old truck into the hidden space under the low branches of a stand of gnarled old pepper trees on the south side of the main road. Many years before, they had been planted to provide a tiny spot of shade for the small adobe house that was now only a pile of mud and debris. Even though he sat in the shade with his windows down, there was a sheen of sweat on his face. He was pumped so full of adrenalin, he could hardly sit still. His hands trembled, and he had to force himself to breathe slowly. He needed to think clearly to pull this off. He had to have a plan.

It was getting dusky in the flatlands of desert, but the sun was still bright up on the high mountain range. If they came by in the next half hour or so, it would be dark when they got up toward the top of the mountain road.

Not far away, Olin and Marie also waited for Lanny Ray and Angela to drive by on the main road. They were some distance away, parked on a dirt road that appeared to lead to a little cluster of Indian houses far out in the sagebrush. Even if Lanny Ray or Angela happened to see their old truck, it was doubtful they would recognize it. The area was full of old pickups that the Indians drove, and theirs looked like all the rest.

Chapter Thirty-Two

*A*bout that same time, Lanny Ray had been pointing out the mountain road to Angela as they headed east on the highway. They had unknowingly driven first past Olin and Marie, and then, a few miles farther on, past Rafael.

Gauging the distance at which they should follow, and the time it would take to catch up when necessary, was risky for the followers. It did help that Lanny Ray drove slowly as the road rose into the mountains. Since Olin had recently been over the road and had already developed his own sinister thoughts and vague plans about what could happen there, it was an easier drive for him than it was for Rafael, who was struggling to keep himself together. The winding, narrow curves were fresh in Olin's mind. But on this trip, he had to judge how far he should stay from Rafael.

Rafael knew the road well. He had been over it many times in his life. When he was younger, the route had been even more treacherous. It had been improved some over the years and was a smoother, easier drive now. The little town on the far side of the mountains was as far east as Rafael had ever been. He'd had relatives there a long time ago and had always looked forward to traveling over the cool, beautiful mountains to visit, but this time the trip was much different. The problem with the drive now was his frenzied nerves and his growing paranoia. No matter how he tried to calm himself, he could hardly gain control of his thoughts. He saw very little to his right or left. He was trying to stay focused upon a plan.

Once confident that he knew what to do, he hoped his old pickup was up to the task. Rafael visualized an idea that could work, as long as Lanny Ray didn't drive his car too fast. There was no way he would be able to overtake the big car if Lanny Ray ran away from him.

When the mountains finally stood in the dark, and Lanny Ray had pulled over to let Angela settle into the backseat, Rafael's headlights caught the glowing red spots of a car's taillights on a curve ahead of him. It didn't occur to him that it may not be Lanny Ray's car. In his fixated mind, he assumed it was. As his anxiety increased, he sped up faster, his foot pushing down on the accelerator. The distance between the big car and the old pickup closed.

This is it, Rafael thought. *I'll do this, and then everything will be back to normal again.* No more worry. No more thinking about going to prison. No more wondering if the words of a young, stupid girl would send him away. He could almost feel the relief that would come to him when this night was over.

It was not because Rafael was especially smart about what took place during a car wreck, or because he was an expert driver, that things happened as they did. In the dark plans in his mind, he had thought he would run into the big car once or maybe twice, sending it veering off of the road and down the steep mountainside. But it wasn't as easy as that. He tried bumping into the car several times, but it wouldn't leave the road. When it dawned on Rafael that his plan wasn't working as he had imagined, he accelerated and steered the old pickup toward Lanny Ray's car. He could no longer think clearly about where he should try to hit the car—he just drove into it again and again until he literally pushed the car over the edge. Only by chance did he avoid following Lanny Ray and Angela into the dark abyss. His foot had found the brake pedal in time.

When he came to a stop, he sat for a time and stared out into the nothingness where his headlights eventually faded away into darkness.

He started to get out of his pickup to look over the edge. As he gripped the door handle, panic started to crawl up from the pit of his stomach, and he thought he might vomit. For a reason he didn't know, he backed up his pickup, turned, and headed back down the mountain the way he had come. Rafael did not see the other pickup truck parked in the dark with lights off and engine killed. He could see only the blur of the road in his own headlights. Tears were streaming down his face.

It wasn't until pinpoints of light from houses down on the desert floor could be seen that he wondered if he should have gone the opposite way. He hadn't thought about what he would do when he had accomplished his mission. He could only see himself at home with Josie. Where else could he go? He stopped in the road, not bothering to pull over. The tiny lights below swam in his tears.

"Oh, my Josie. What have I done?" Rafael said aloud. "I can't come home now," he whispered. "The devil, he has taken my soul. Pray for me, Josie."

When Olin knew that Rafael was on his way down the mountain, he started up his truck and drove to where Lanny Ray's car had left the road. He got out of the cab and walked to the place where the red dirt had been plowed by the car as it was pushed over. He couldn't see much, but he could see the light of the stars glinting on the metal of the car. He turned and called to Marie, motioning for her to shut off the truck. When she complied, he stood perfectly still, straining to listen for any sounds from below him. He could hear the creak and groan of the car settling, but no human noises reached him. The stench of burned rubber was heavy in the air. He reached down and picked up a dirt clod and gave it an underhand toss down the mountainside. He heard the sound it made when it hit the metal of the car. He stood very still, head cocked to one side, offering his good ear. Nothing human came back to him.

Marie sat in the cab and watched Olin standing in the dark with his back to her. *How easy it would be*, she thought. If the truck was running, she could shove Olin right off the edge, just like Rafael did to

Lanny's car. She pictured him flying out into the space of darkness and not landing for a long time. The world would be a cleaner, purer place without Olin in it.

"Couldn't hear a thing down there," he said matter-of-factly when he climbed back in the driver's seat. He pulled back onto the road and headed east. "I'm tired. We're going to stay in that motel in the town at the bottom of this damn mountain again."

Marie didn't speak at all. She was frantic with the thought that Lanny Ray or Angela might be alive in that car. If they were, and no one found them soon, they would probably die there. She knew that, as soon as she could, she would be running away from Olin, but she couldn't wait until then to tell somebody about the accident.

As Olin pulled into a gas station, she decided she would take a chance at leaving a note for the attendant. As soon as Olin left the truck to talk to the young man pumping gas, she looked on the floor for a pencil and scrap of paper.

Chapter Thirty-Three

$\mathcal{A}$rlene and Norma spent hours on end at the hospital. They would sit for a time with Angela and then check on Lanny Ray across the hall. Even Norma ran short of things to say. Doing nearly nothing exhausted them both. They walked the short hallways, drank endless cups of coffee, and ate as little food as possible in the drab cafeteria. Angela was allowed to be up and walking slow, careful steps, as long as she didn't tire herself too much. When Arlene and Norma weren't with her, she sat in a chair near Lanny Ray's bed and read while he slept.

Arlene tried to temper her nagging resentment at feeling a responsibility for Lanny Ray's well-being. She wanted to spend her strength and energy on Angela. Besides that, probably none of them would be there if he hadn't gotten into some mess to begin with. If he hadn't been in such bad shape, she would have really given him a fit. She and Norma knew only that Lanny Ray's car had been forced off the mountain road.

"Lord, Norma. Who in the world would want to hurt a child like that? Even if somebody was out to get Lanny Ray, what kind of monster would hurt Angela?"

"We need the whole story, sweetie. I think Mr. Detective Glover needs to share his information with us . . . or you, I should say. I love the strong, silent type, but not right now," Norma said.

They were all relieved when the doctor said that Angela could leave the hospital. He peered through his bifocals and shook a fat finger in Arlene's face when he laid down the rules for Angela's care. Arlene could take her to their motel and make her comfortable there for the time being. Lanny Ray would have to stay. Once again, Arlene felt put upon. What could she do? She couldn't just go off and leave Angela's father stranded. She had to have a serious talk with Norma about how long she was willing to stay.

"The only other idea I can come up with is for you and Angela to go on home and for me to try to get Lanny Ray on the bus when they release him. I don't see how he can do all that by himself, in his condition," Arlene said.

"I can't leave you here to ride a bus home with a crippled man, Arlene. And there must be stuff they salvaged from his car that has to be got home somehow. No, I'll stay a couple more days and see what happens. My kids are okay, and the house is in one piece, so I'm willing to stay on for now," Norma said

"How can I ever thank you, Norma?" Arlene's eyes welled with tears.

"I told you I'd think of something," Norma said.

When the moment finally came, Angela wasn't as happy to leave the hospital as Arlene and Norma thought she would be. She was too worried about leaving Lanny Ray there by himself.

"It's only for a couple of days, Angela. And I'll be checking in on him. He won't really be by himself." Arlene tried to soothe Angela's worry.

When she finally gave in to it, Angela thought it wonderful to be out of the hospital. The first thing she wanted to do was sit on the little grassy place at the motel. Norma threw a blanket down for her to sit on in the shade of a scrubby tree, and Angela took a nap there in the fresh air. When it became too hot out, she went into the room to cool off. She felt better already.

Arlene and Norma fussed over her. They brought her chocolate malts with extra cherries from the hamburger place down the street and bought a deck of cards so they could play games when she felt up to it. Angela's heart was full to bursting with love for her mother and Norma. She felt safe and cared for. She was too quiet, though, and tired because closing her eyes meant seeing the scenes of recent days all over again. They would play like a haywire movie, beginning all the way back on the night Olin had hurt Marie in that motel, and then skip to the night she and Charlotte had witnessed that horrible thing in Josie's parking lot. And there were newer pictures to deal with—those of someone pushing Lanny Ray's big car over the edge of the mountain road. She fought sleep so she wouldn't have to see those things again.

Midmorning, the day after Angela was released, a policeman came by the motel and left off a cardboard box of things that the tow company owner had picked out of the rubble of Lanny Ray's wrecked car. Laid over the top of the cardboard box was the quilt that had been such a comfort to Angela so many times. It was filthy dirty and tattered on one corner. When Arlene carried the box and quilt into the room, Angela gathered the edge of it in her hand, and tears flooded down her cheeks. She had thought she'd never see it again, so to have it laid there in front of her was like being reunited with a loved one.

Norma and Arlene soaked the quilt in Ivory soap in the bathtub, gently washed it by hand, and when it was rinsed, they took it out to dry in the sun. They repaired it the best they could with tiny careful stitches, and when they presented it back to Angela, they all had both tears and happy smiles.

That night, as Angela lay next to her mother and Norma lay quiet in her bed, Angela started talking. She spoke in a soft but steady voice. The room was dark. The cooler made a humming sound. At first, Angela only had in mind to tell Arlene and Norma about all the times the quilt had been such a comfort to her. She started with telling about how it felt good to snuggle with when she and Lanny Ray were traveling in the car and how, in spite of the heat, she took it into most of the motel rooms, just to have it nearby. Arlene and Norma lay still and quiet while they listened to Angela's small voice.

And then, to her own surprise, Angela told them everything, even the bad things. She told them all about Olin and how she didn't like him from that very first day she saw him. She described Marie and her obnoxious behavior. She told what happened the night Olin hit Marie that night in the motel room. As she talked on, she came to the night that she and Charlotte were in Josie's parking lot. She almost stopped there. She was quiet for a few moments, thinking about how her mother would feel when she heard everything that happened, but she decided to tell it all. It seemed to be something she couldn't help but do anyway. So she continued and didn't stop until she told them about being carried up the hill to the ambulance when Lanny Ray's big car was pushed off the road.

Over in her own bed, Norma held back sobs. She didn't want to make all of this harder than it already was for Angela or for her friend Arlene. Tears ran down and soaked her pillow.

Arlene's eyes were still dry. She felt numb. She held Angela's hand in hers and murmured soothing words to her over and over again. She wanted to be a comfort to her when what she was feeling was a rage building like a fire inside of her. And a hatred. A hatred for each and every person her daughter had just spoken about. Out of all of those people, why did someone not help Angela? Not take care of her, for God's sake? Were they all blind or crazy?

Red was a sensible man, wasn't he? Why hadn't he helped Angela? True, Angela said he didn't know the secret until much later. But hadn't he noticed any difference in Charlotte's behavior? Arlene wanted to sit up and scream into the night, "Why didn't somebody see?"

And those people . . . Josie and Rafael. Maybe Josie didn't know about anything, and it sounded as if the kids had liked her, but Rafael sounded creepy and intimidating to Arlene. He may even have been involved with Toby's beating that night.

When she finally allowed herself to think of Lanny Ray, she felt a pain like the slice of a knife through her heart. How on earth could he let all this happen to their daughter? He was there with her, for God's sake. He spent every single day with her and never noticed that she was in trouble? That was hard for her to fathom because, as a mother, Arlene could tell in a minute if Angela was tired or hungry or didn't feel well. Parents just knew those things about their kids. How in the hell could he not know she had been through this nightmare? Once again, Lanny Ray had failed as a father, only this time it was much more serious. Their daughter had been changed forever.

CHAPTER THIRTY-FOUR

*E*arly the next morning, while Angela slept, Norma and Arlene sat outside the motel room with paper cups of bad coffee from the pot in the little motel lobby. The women were tired and red-eyed. Norma smoked her first cigarette of the day. They spoke in soft voices, not only so they didn't disturb Angela, but also because the subject matter commanded a kind of reverence. All the raw emotion that haunted them through the night left them drained and exhausted. Angela told them her story as though she were an adult. They were in awe of how wise and courageous she had been.

"Sweetie, I think the first thing you'll need to do is try to get all that hatred out of your system." Norma spoke quietly to Arlene. "Don't get me wrong. I can't blame you one bit for feelin' like you do, but I think you should just hate all those people as hard as you can and get it over with, and then just go on and do what you need to. Know what I mean, sweetie? You can't dwell on 'em. And I ain't going to stick up for them, but maybe some of those folks really didn't know all the goin's on. There's been a lot of secrets and unsaid things, Arlene."

"I know. I'm still trying to put all the pieces together." Arlene put her hands to her face and rubbed her eyes with the pads of her fingers. "I guess some are still missing. In the night, it even occurred to me that Lanny Ray doesn't even know all the things Angela told us. I had to quit being so mad, or I might of gone to the hospital and killed him off.

205

I don't know why he didn't protect her better, Norma. He should have sent her home when that sick S.O.B., Olin, beat up his own daughter. Lord, what a pair they are, huh? How do people get to be like that?"

"Everybody's got a story behind 'em. Probably one of his parents knocked him around when he was a kid." Norma paused a minute, then went on. "I noticed that Angela holds no real bad feelings against that Marie. That's real mature of her, you know? Marie was so nasty to Angela, but she seemed to be able to handle her okay. I guess she felt kinda sorry for her, don't you think?"

"Yeah, that would be about right. You know how Angela takes up for stray animals and needy people. She has a good heart that way."

"She's going to be all right. You know she will. She's a smart child and strong. She's ahead of her time, you know. One more thing, then I'll shut my mouth." Arlene rolled her eyes at that. Norma ignored it. "It won't do you no good to try to turn her against her daddy by blamin' him for all this. She'll only resent the holy heck out of you if you do that. She adores that man, and that ain't ever going to change. You are the one that's going to have to live with it, or around it."

Arlene sometimes wondered if Norma was a mind reader. What she said was the absolute truth. Arlene was already thinking how she could get some vengeance on Lanny Ray by keeping Angela away from him. She'd convinced herself she had that right. She was going to have to clear her mind of that way of thinking. All she wanted to do was get her girl home, and she would have left at that very minute if she could have. Arlene was determined to talk with Lanny Ray and the doctor and then make a plan to head home. It was what they all needed.

When Angela was up and they were about ready to go and get something to eat, they decided to first dig through the box of things that came out of the big car. They put it on one of the beds and all sat around it. Angela took things out one at a time. There were pens and pencils and funny books. Lots of those. Her hairbrush and some barrettes. There was even a buck and a half in loose change. They all commented on the tow company's honesty. Angela found her little pink plastic box and discovered it still had her mother's tube of pale-pink lipstick in it. It had melted into a tube-shaped glob. It could have been like that since the first hot day of her trip.

"Angela Garrett. You took that lipstick? I couldn't for the life of me figure out where that went. Shame on you." Arlene was more than surprised, not only that Angela had taken it, but that she would even want it at all.

"I'm sorry. I shouldn't have taken it. I thought I might want to put some on when we were on the trip. I forgot all about it. But I am going to be thirteen, remember?" Arlene snatched the tube up and tossed it in the garbage can.

"Oh, I remember all right. That means only three more years and you can wear lipstick." They all laughed a little at that and dug into the box again. The rest was mostly papers, either receipts of Lanny Ray's or pictures and things that Angela had drawn or written on her tablet. Arlene ran her hand around the bottom of the box and felt in the corners for anything they missed. Her hand came back with an object between her fingers.

"What's this?" she said.

"Oh, that's an old snap from a shirt. I forgot all about that," Angela said. She took it from her mother's fingers and held it in her palm. She told about how Lanny Ray had found it on the ground at Josie's when he came back to the car that night. "It was shining in the light, and he thought it was a jewel. It was just this old snap. Must have been tore off of some man's shirt. Funny where things turn up, isn't it?" Angela dropped it back in the box.

"Wait a minute," Arlene said. "Let me see that again." She held the snap and turned it over in her palm. "This isn't old. It isn't rusted or corroded. It was torn clean out of the material. Odd that it was just layin' there in the mud like that." She laid the snap back in the bottom of the box, and they replaced the rest of the items.

When they got to the hospital, Angela hurried to her father's room, and Arlene went to find his doctor.

"Tomorrow or the next day," he answered when Arlene asked when Lanny Ray could leave the hospital. "He has some serious injuries. His spleen is badly bruised, and two of his wounds need to be carefully tended to prevent any infection. His pain and discomfort should begin to wane now."

"Dr. Blaine can take care of him once we get him home. He's a good doctor and has known Lanny Ray all his life." Arlene was trying for only one more day there, instead of two.

"We'll see," is all the doctor would say.

Arlene wasn't looking forward to seeing Lanny Ray. It would be hard to keep quiet about Angela telling her story until she could be alone with him. She put a smile on her face and entered his room. He was sitting up and talking with Angela and Norma. Like Angela, he was still badly bruised and battered. There were stitches on the right side of his forehead that tracked up into his hairline and more around his chin. His right eye was opened wider than it had been, but he still appeared to be squinting through it. But his old smile was back. He had said something to make Angela and Norma laugh as Arlene entered the room.

"Well, look at you this morning, all bright and funny," Arlene said. "Doc says you might be leaving tomorrow or the next day."

"Yeah, I guess we need to talk about that, don't we? Norma says if I can be comfortable enough to ride that far in her car, she'll get me back to Jewel. How you feel about that, Arlene?"

What could she say? There was Angela's little face looking at her, waiting for her answer. How about if she said no, it wasn't okay? He would just have to drag himself on a Greyhound bus and ride it for three days without using the bathroom. How about that, Mr. Rodeo Man?

But she said, "Well, sure. We just all need to get back home. Norma here has been so good to take the time for all this."

Norma took Angela's hand and suggested the two of them go get something for all of them to drink from the cafeteria down the hall. She gave Arlene a look that said *here's your chance*, and they left the room hand in hand. Arlene sat in the chair near the bed and looked, without speaking, at Lanny Ray for a long time.

"What, Arlene?" he said.

"Angela told us a long, long story last night. She talked nonstop for nearly two hours. She said things that made my blood run cold. I don't think she could have left anything much out. She described things that happened as clear as could be. Norma and I felt like we lived through some things with her. It was horrible, Lanny Ray. I was mad enough to commit murder, and that's not a joke. I can't describe how I felt when I listened to her story." Arlene spoke steady and stayed dry-eyed. No crying.

"What were you thinking about, Lanny Ray? How could you not know that Angela was suffering so with what she saw and heard?"

Lanny Ray adjusted himself in his hospital bed. He took a deep breath and let it out slowly.

"I don't know. I don't know why I didn't notice what was happening. She never let on, Arlene. Not one time. She and Charlotte and Billy shared things between them, and they all kept everything they knew to themselves. Even Charlotte. She was true to her word to the very end."

He put his head back on the pillow and looked at the ceiling.

"Everybody had secrets. The kids, Rafael, Olin, and Marie. All of them knew things they couldn't or wouldn't tell. Right up to now, Arlene. We still don't know who pushed us off the mountain road. Don't you think I want to know who did that to us? To Angela? Besides Red, I probably have known the least about all that went on of everybody."

"But didn't she ever act different? Couldn't you see anything in her eyes or in the way she talked? There must have been some sign that she was suffering."

"Maybe there was some things, but how the hell was I to know? I thought that mood changes were just normal for Angela's age. She and Charlotte would be laughing one minute and then quiet the next. She never said one single thing that made me think something so bad had happened. I swear that to you, Arlene." Lanny Ray strained to sit more upright, and the cords of his neck bulged. He gave in and let himself lie back.

"She kept all that to herself to protect you, you know." Arlene's words were bitter.

"I know that now. But I didn't know it until the day Toby's body was found and I heard her tell it in the sheriff's office." Lanny Ray was getting tired and was feeling defenseless. What more could he say?

After a minute, he spoke again. "I know I didn't do things just right. I shouldn't have left Angela alone in the car to wait on me those times. And I know she was getting sick of staying in cheap motel rooms. I should have paid more attention. That's true. But I want to tell you, Arlene, we had a lot of fun together. She loves rodeo. She watched every single one of my rides. She and Char and Billy would cheer and clap like the devil when Red or I rode. We sang every country song there ever was with the radio. She would snuggle down and watch the stars go by out the back window, and she was happy as could be. It wasn't all bad, Arlene. Angela is wise and special. She isn't like other kids."

There was a quiet knock on the open door.

"Excuse me. May I come in?" It was Detective Glover. "I wanted to let you know what has happened and see if there was anything else you could tell me."

Chapter Thirty-Five

$\mathcal{R}$afael had been found. He was dead. His old pickup had left the twisting road about halfway down the mountain to the desert floor. It had gone over the edge from a turn-out area. It was not likely that it happened as an accident. There would have been ample time to stop the truck after it left the narrow pavement and long before it reached the drop-off. That had not been the case. In fact, the tracks told that it had been driven off the edge at a right angle to the paved road, which meant the pickup had to be steered in that direction. It had also been propelled all the way across the wide turnout to gather enough speed to send it far out over the deep canyon below. The pickup had cleared a stand of young evergreens and landed just beyond. It rested, nose down, on an outcropping of rock. Rafael had been ejected through the windshield.

A local man, who drove the road almost daily, had pulled over to relieve himself and saw the tire tracks that led to nowhere. He had told the deputy who answered the phone at the station that he had been scared to look over the edge, but when he finally did, he was sure no one could have survived such a wreck. He could see where the pickup rested, but that was about all. It was too far down the steep mountainside.

At the time the deputies responded, the same men who had rescued Lanny Ray and Angela were being sent up the mountain road. This

211

time, their job was much more difficult. It was a precarious situation, and it took great care and a lot of time to get to the pickup. It was fairly demolished, and they had to search for Rafael's body. It was determined that he had died on impact. It was not a rescue mission at all—it was a recovery mission. It took hours to raise Rafael back up to the road. An investigation of the wreck was done, but it was apparent to everyone there that a suicide had taken place. His truck would be left there to rust away. Rodents would appreciate the warm place to burrow in for the winter.

The county coroner, who seldom had to be called out twice in such a short time, said that Rafael had been down in the canyon at least four or five days. That would mean his crash, and death, could have happened near the time of Lanny Ray's and Angela's accident.

A deputy was sent to give poor Josie the news. Josie had locked the front door to the bar the day before and had been sitting alone in her adobe house, waiting. She was waiting for the bad news she knew was to come. Something very bad had happened to Rafael, or he would have come home.

When she heard a knock on the door, she did not move. She just sat. Her arms and legs felt heavy and drained of life. Her hands were clasped in her lap. There was another soft knock. She couldn't stand, so she summoned just enough breath to say, "Come in." The deputy slowly pushed the door partway open and spoke her name. His own face was slack with sorrow for her, and he had to look away from her direct gaze. He nodded, and she nodded back. She knew Rafael was gone.

At the hospital, Detective Glover told Lanny Ray and Arlene that Rafael was dead by suicide. Lanny Ray thought of Josie first. Such a good woman to have to endure such a horrible thing. There had been a part of Rafael that he had never known existed.

"So we're still looking for Olin and Marie Wheaton," Detective Glover said. "If we are ever going to get to the bottom of the murder of Mr. Abel, those two are going to have to come clean." He spoke directly to Arlene. "We have no way to know what Olin may do. I doubt if he would try anything here in town, but you should be careful to keep Angela close. I don't mean to scare you. Just keep your eyes open, that's all."

Arlene told Detective Glover about the story Angela had told the night before.

"She didn't see who killed that young man, but she believes that Olin was there because of the way he's acted ever since that night. By now, she's said everything she knows to say about it all."

"It won't be easy to put Olin there where the girls heard the fight without some sort of proof, and if there are no witnesses to his being there, I'm afraid it will be hard to come by. We'll keep on it. Something, or someone, may still turn up." Detective Glover tried to be reassuring.

"I know it's a small thing and probably doesn't mean anything, but there's something we found this morning. We have the box of all the belongings that were salvaged out of Lanny Ray's car when they drug it up the mountain. I found a pearl shirt snap from a blue shirt in that box. Angela said her father found it by the car that night in the mud." She glanced at Lanny Ray. "She said he thought it was a jewel of some sort when he saw it shining there."

"I remember that. I gave it to Angela, and we kind of laughed about it," Lanny Ray said. "But who knows how long it mighta laid there."

"I don't think it had been there too long. There's no rust around the metal part, and the pearl part of the snap is still smooth and shiny. I could see that the material it came from was blue," Arlene said.

"Where's the snap now? Did you keep it?" Detective Glover asked.

"It's back in the box where we came across it."

"Well, it's not likely it means anything, but hang on to it if you still have it," the detective said.

Chapter Thirty-Six

Olin was as down and out as he had ever been. He had holed up in a motel room in a small motor court for days. He pulled his old pickup into the garage designated for the room he had rented, and once he entered the room, all he did was drink whiskey and sleep. And rant at Marie. He was unshaven and smelled like old sweat and sour whiskey. Each time he woke, he would start in on Marie. He reminded her how no-good she was and how much like her mother she was turning out to be. He would ramble on about how unfair his life was. He deserved better, he said. Why was his life so hard? He told Marie she better not leave the motel room. He was going to be the one to decide what they should do next. He would do that as soon as he got a little more rest, he told her. Nobody was going to get the best of ol' Olin anymore, no-sir-ree, he said.

Every time he slipped into a drunken sleep, Marie would go outside and sit by the motel door. She couldn't bear to stay in the same room with him for too long of a time. She fantasized about smothering him with his pillow while he slept. She made up a whole scenario about packing some things, killing Olin, and then taking off in the pickup. She would go toward New Mexico. She had always heard about how the law couldn't get you after you crossed over the state line. She knew she wouldn't really do that, but it gave her a sense of revenge to dream it all up. Her head ached all the time, partly from lack of any nourishing food and partly from the stress of trying to figure out what she should do. She knew she could just walk off and go to the police, but if she did that, what was going to happen to her? Would she go to juvenile hall? A county orphanage or foster home? She knew the authorities were not going to put her on a bus and send her on her merry way. It was way too small a town to try to hitch a ride. Everybody would know in five minutes. She knew how small towns were about any good gossip. She would just have to keep biding her time until they got someplace where she could get away. Olin couldn't stay in that place forever.

Marie had no money, and it did no good to ask for it. She had asked for enough to wash and dry some clothes, but Olin had even refused that. Truth was, he didn't have much money left. Motels and bars and whiskey by the bottle had just about ate up any winnings he had. He was used to living on nearly nothing. As long as he could buy a drink and gas for his old pickup, he was okay.

Finally, he managed to go through an entire morning without a drink. After waking the second or third time that day, he told Marie to pack up their stuff. They were leaving. She didn't bother to ask where they were going. He wouldn't have answered her. She found something clean to wear and put their things in the pickup. She moved quickly, anxious to get going. Olin splashed his grizzled face with water and made an attempt at combing his greasy hair. He was shaky and gray as ash. He squinted against the bright light when he stepped outside the room.

"You drive," he told Marie.

She stopped in her tracks. He had never told her to drive inside any town limits. In fact, the last time she had driven was the night she had to follow Olin and Rafael out into the desert. She hoped she wouldn't have to drive back over that windy mountain road where Lanny Ray and Angela were pushed over the edge.

Marie sat up very straight and drove down the street toward the end of town. When she noticed the gas gauge needle was almost on empty, she panicked. Now they would have to stop at a station. As they approached the Shell station at the end of the main street, she informed Olin that they were low on gas. She jumped with a start when Olin slammed his fist into the pickup's door.

"Pull in here. Tell 'em to fill it up, and don't talk to nobody. Just pay up with this and get the hell out of here." He handed her some crumpled bills from his shirt pocket. She smoothed them with a trembling hand and counted and did as she was told. She was stunned when she saw the attendant approach the pickup. It was the same young man who had been here when she left the note. She slowly rolled her window down.

"Fill it?" he asked.

"Yes," she said. "Please."

"Let me get those windows, and I'll check under the hood for you," the attendant said.

"Oh, no, don't do that. I mean, it's fine, really," Marie said.

"Okay, then. You folks must be in a hurry. Where y'all headed today?"

"We're just passing through," Marie said.

"Yeah? I'd swear I saw you here before. Wasn't that you here just a few nights ago?"

"Nope. Wasn't us," Marie answered. She handed him the money and rolled her window back up to let him know they were finished.

"Dora," Derek said a few minutes later, "I think you need to let somebody know, that same old man and that girl were in here just now. You know, the ones from the other evenin'. She's driving the old pickup. He's in there, and he looks like hell."

"Oh, my gracious. I'll tell Eldon right away. They're lookin' for that man. You stay clear of him, hear me?" Dora hung up before Derek could say any more.

Marie had carefully pulled out of the gas station and back onto the main road. To her dismay, Olin told her to head over the mountain road once again. Maybe they were going home. It would be too late to catch up with the rodeo, wouldn't it?

Her fingers gripped the steering wheel until they ached. She had to sit bolt upright to see clearly and still work the pedals. Her back and neck hurt from the strain and tension. She thought of stopping right there and just jumping out and running away. Just run and think of what to do later. She glanced over at Olin. He sat staring ahead, glassy-eyed.

When Marie heard the siren, she wasn't sure how long it had been whining behind her. She only knew that suddenly it was near, and she didn't know what she was supposed to do. She stretched her neck to see in the cracked rearview mirror. Not far behind, there were flashing red lights. Olin turned to look out of the back window.

"Keep goin," he said to Marie. "Don't stop this truck, understand?"

Marie nodded that she did.

The police car moved up at a fast pace. Marie stayed at the same speed and continued on around the long, slow curves in the road. When the police car was close enough, Eldon spoke over the PA radio. His order was for the driver to pull to the right of the road and come to a full stop. Olin told Marie to keep driving. Eldon gave the order again.

When Marie slowed, Olin cursed at her, flung his arm across the seat, and hit her hard in the face with the back of his hand. He moved across the seat, reached across her, and grasped the pickup door handle. When he was finally able to push the door open, he shoved Marie hard toward the opening and the pavement below. She held on with all her might with one hand on the steering wheel, while Olin struggled to keep the pickup going. As he worked the clutch and gas pedal, the old truck coughed and died. When it rolled to a stop, Marie let go of her grip and fell to the pavement. She scrambled up and ran, but she didn't try to run away. She ran straight to the police car. Eldon had rolled to a stop by then. He was shouting for backup over his radio. Staying to help Marie, he watched as Olin drove away. He wouldn't make it far. There were now two sheriff's cars coming from the other direction.

Eldon put an arm across Marie's shaking shoulders and helped her sit on the backseat of his police car. He gave her his handkerchief for her bloody lip and tried to assure her that everything was going to be okay now. She wasn't so sure of that. She wasn't sure of anything.

Olin only made it a few more miles up the road when he met the first sheriff's car. The deputy had parked across both narrow lanes of the road. There was no use to try to get by him. There was nowhere to go. Olin stopped and sat still behind the wheel. After the second deputy arrived at the scene, Olin was ordered to step out of his truck. He refused by doing nothing. Intent on watching the deputies, Olin was oblivious to what was behind him and was jolted by Eldon's voice.

"Olin, open your driver door, then put your hands where we can see them and step out of the truck. Do not turn, just step out," Eldon said with authority.

Olin sat stock still, and Eldon was about to speak again when, finally, the fugitive did as ordered. Much to Eldon's and the deputies' surprise, he didn't resist being cuffed. He didn't say a word.

In less than an hour, they were all back at the small town police department. Dora kindly whisked a shaken Marie away to help her wash up and to apply first aid to her sore and swollen lip.

There were two jail cells in the back corner of the small block building. They were only used as holding cells for people brought in for petty crimes or drunk driving. Most of the time, the lawbreakers in the small town were allowed to leave with friends or family members who came to bail them out. Olin was probably the worst criminal who had ever been housed in one of the cells. Eldon had the pleasure of locking the door to the cell where Olin sat on the low cot against one wall. He showed little expression and still had not spoken, except to acknowledge his rights.

Besides being held as a suspect in Toby Abel's death, there were plenty of other charges against Olin. Endangering a minor and evading arrest were the two most blatant ones. Paperwork had to be done, and then Olin would be transported back to Milton. He never inquired about Marie.

Because of the lateness of the afternoon, it was decided that Olin would be kept in a cell overnight, and Marie could go home with Dora. Someone from the night shift would sit at Dora's to be sure Marie didn't attempt to leave. They need not have worried about that. Marie was so exhausted she could not have left if she wanted to. She was happy to have a bowl of soup and a hot bath at Dora's home and then slept the night through on Dora's lumpy, old hide-a-bed. Just before falling asleep, she shared with Dora the fact that she was worried about what would happen to her now. Dora sympathized but said she thought nothing could be as bad as the life she had been living.

"Maybe this will all turn out to be the best thing to happen to you," Dora said.

"Maybe," Marie answered.

CHAPTER THIRTY-SEVEN

The next morning, Olin and Marie were taken to Milton in separate cars. Olin knew he was going to have to answer questions about Toby, and he used his time to get his thoughts all together. And Marie knew someone was going to be making a decision about what was to happen to her. Her future would be in someone else's hands, as usual.

Detective Glover was waiting for them when they arrived in Milton. Olin was brought in handcuffed, and Marie was again taken to a different room. Detective Glover stepped into the room where Olin sat at a table with a metal top. Olin's right hand was cuffed to an iron ring bolted to the corner of the table. It stated on his paperwork that he was a possible flight risk and should be considered dangerous. The department would take no chances. The detective stood for several minutes, just looking at Olin. He seemed to be studying him. He took in everything about him, from his poor hygiene to his soiled clothing. It was difficult to determine any real expression in the small, dark, deep-set eyes.

Olin would not be intimidated. He wore the slightest smirk that never left his face. Detective Glover introduced himself and took a seat across the table. As was his way, he made no small talk. He told Olin who he was and asked pointed questions about where Olin had been at different times on the night of Toby's disappearance and listened to the short answers Olin reluctantly offered. Most of what he heard he already knew from other witness reports or deputies. His hope now was to pin down the timeline to make the facts he had come together. His job was proving extremely difficult.

Next he asked Olin bluntly what Rafael had to do with Toby's death. For the first time, he saw a slight change of expression on Olin's face. The detective knew he had given Olin an out, someone to blame.

"Now you're on the right track, Detective. That's who you should be talkin' to. He's the weasel that took Abel outside from the cardroom that night. He was burnin' mad, Rafael was. He has a real thing about cheatin' you know."

"It's my understanding that you were the accuser, Wheaton. You were the one who was mad at Mr. Abel, and you went outside also. Isn't that right?" Glover said.

"I left then. I picked up my money off the table and left. All I did was go out to my ol' pickup and drive back to the motel. What happened after that, I got no idea. It's Rafael you want, not me."

"Well, Mr. Wheaton, I'm afraid we won't be talking to Rafael."

"Why the hell not?" Olin studied Glover's face.

"Because he's dead," Glover said.

Olin looked disbelieving, as if he thought Glover was trying to trick him. When Glover didn't waver, Olin dropped his head. He didn't even ask what happened to Rafael. He didn't care. All he knew was that he was in serious trouble.

"I have a few more questions," Glover said. "Were you ever near Lanny Ray Garrett's car in the parking lot that night? Did you see or speak to anyone near there? You do know Mr. Garrett's car, right?"

"Yeah, I know his big, fancy car. But I didn't even know ol' Garrett was around that night. I never saw him or his car."

When the detective came to the subject of Marie, Olin laughed out loud.

"If you think you can believe anything she says about me, you're crazy. She might say anything. She hates me and wants to see me in prison or dead. Hell, she's a better liar than I am." He laughed at that, showing his mouthful of terrible teeth. He was one of the most disgusting men Glover had ever dealt with, and there had been plenty. The detective made a few short notes in his book, determined to figure out the timeline of the night Toby died. He was going to have to talk with Marie next.

Detective Glover stepped out into the hallway and stood looking over his notes, preparing to talk with Marie. A deputy led Olin from the room to put him in a cell. As the deputy and his prisoner moved past Glover, the detective saw something that stunned him. Olin's filthy, stained shirt was worn thin, and his sloppy shirttail hung down on the right side of his tarnished belt buckle. The facing and the bottom snap were ripped away. Gone. The rest of the snaps were white pearl-colored snaps. The shirt was faded blue chambray.

"Hey, Olin. What happened to your shirt there? Looks like you got your shirttail caught where it don't belong," Glover said.

Olin glanced down at his filthy shirt and walked on by.

Detective Glover got on the phone. First he tried the motel where Arlene was registered and then placed a call to the hospital. When Arlene finally came on the line, he asked her exactly what Angela had said about her father finding that shirt snap in the mud on the night Toby disappeared. Arlene repeated the story.

"I want you to get that snap and put it in an envelope and keep it in a safe place until I can get it from you," Glover told Arlene.

"Why? What's going on?" Arlene could hear a touch of excitement in Glover's voice.

"I just had a talk with Olin here in Milton. He's been arrested and is being held here. The shirt he is wearing is missing a snap like the one Lanny Ray picked up beside his car. It isn't much, but it might at least put him right there by Lanny Ray's car that night."

Arlene wanted to run down the hall to tell the others the news. Of all things, maybe one shirt snap was going to be a helpful clue to Olin's actions.

"So far, he denies doing or knowing anything," Glover said. "He was ready to put the blame on Rafael. He was pretty shocked when I told him Rafael was dead. I think he's thought all along that he could shift the blame, at least enough to keep from being charged with outright homicide. He made the mistake of denying that he was even near Lanny Ray's car. If the snap is a match, and I'm sure it will be, then that is the first proven lie."

Arlene had to hold herself back from running down the hospital corridor to Lanny Ray's room. She was almost breathless when she repeated the conversation to him and Norma and Angela. They spoke at one time. It took a moment for them to calm down.

"It was him. I just know it was Olin," Angela said. "I still can't say I actually saw him that night, but I knew it had to be him. I wonder if Marie really has known this whole time that her father killed poor Toby. That's why she was saying she knew secrets. If she saw him do it, maybe she'll tell now." Angela grew silent. Her chin quivered. "It must have been awful for her if she saw her own father beat Toby so bad he died."

"I wonder what they'll do with Marie now," Lanny Ray said. "I don't think she has a home to go to, does she Ang?"

"Not unless they let her go to her mother's house. The county was going to take her away from there before she came to be with Olin," Angela said.

Norma stood. "Come on, you guys. Let's go get that precious snap and put it in a safe place. What a crazy thing that is . . . a snap, for heaven's sake."

CHAPTER THIRTY-EIGHT

*B*ack in Milton, Detective Glover stood with his hand on the doorknob, preparing to enter the room where Marie sat alone. This would be difficult, he knew. Marie was a tough one for sure, but she was still a kid and had been through a lot. He would be as kind as he could. But she had to come forth with all she knew.

Marie hardly looked up when he and the deputy who stood outside the door entered the room. She looked tired, but showed little emotion. He asked her if she wanted anything. A soda or drink of water? She shook her head no.

"Marie, you know it's time now to tell us everything you know about what has happened," Glover said.

"You know that he tried to push me out of the truck out on that road? My father would have killed me to save himself."

"I'm sorry, Marie. I really am. Your father is an awful, vile person, Marie, but that isn't your fault. You can't help the things he's done," the detective said kindly.

"I didn't see him kill Toby," Marie volunteered suddenly "Bbut I know he did. I think Rafael was there, too, but I could tell the way Olin acted that he was the one who actually killed him."

"Are you ready to tell the story about that night, Marie?" Glover asked.

"I want to know what's going to happen to me now. I don't have any place to go. I don't want to live in a orphanage. Or with some family I don't know."

"We will figure that out as soon as we can. Maybe the authorities can talk with your mother and see what's going on there. But first we need to hear what you know, okay?"

Marie nodded her head, and Detective Glover excused himself to get someone to sit in with them while Marie told her story. He returned with a woman who worked at the front desk. She carried a steno pad and pen. She smiled a friendly smile at Marie and quietly took a chair. When they were all seated, Glover began speaking.

"Marie, what we would like for you to do, if you can, is to start from when Olin first decided to drive out to Josie's Place, okay?"

"Olin hardly ever tells me where we're going. I just go along, or sometimes stay in the motel room. That night was no different. When we got there it was raining pretty hard. I was mad. I mean, there ain't nothin' out there. No town or nothin'. All I could do was sit in that crappy pickup in the rain. The radio wouldn't even work out there. I slept for a little while. Then I heard like an argument. You know, men hollerin' and stuff. I couldn't see them. They were across the lot a ways." Marie went on to tell the story as she remembered. She told it all. She told about Olin trying to get Toby's body into the bed of the truck. She told how scared she was when she had to drive into the desert in the rain. She repeated what Rafael had said as they drove back to the bar. Because it had become so ingrained in Marie to show no emotion, she hardly changed expression throughout the story. The stenographer wrote diligently, and both men listened calmly. When Marie seemed to have reached the end of her telling, the deputy left to get her a soda. Glover thanked the woman who took the notes, and she excused herself and left the room.

"Marie, I'm going to make some phone calls now and see what I can find out about where you will be going. Please try not to worry. These things work out, you know.

Thank you, Marie, for your honesty. We appreciate it." Glover left to make the calls.

Certainly it took time and much patience, but Detective Glover, with help from the secretary, was finally able to speak with someone at Child Services in Phoenix about the case of Marie and her mother. It was finally decided, after hearing her story, that Marie could be returned to her mother's home for a probationary period. They would have to go before a judge who would set the probation rules. There would be many strict rules and regulations to abide by if Marie were to be able to remain there.

The detective found Marie in the little lounge room, resting on an old leather sofa. She sat up when he entered the room. "Well?" she said.

"You're going home to your mother's, Marie. You will be transported there. On-duty deputies will drive you from their county lines and deliver you home. We don't want to put you on a bus all alone. You'll be there before you know it. Please promise me that you will do the right things. I would like to see you stay in school. You have a strong independent streak. You need an education so you don't have to depend on someone else to take care of you."

"I'm going to honestly try. I am. Do I have to see Olin before I go?" she asked

"No. It's up to you, but no, you don't have to. We will tell him where you're going," Glover said.

"Oh, that don't matter. He won't care none. He was going to kill me out on the road, remember?"

"You don't have to worry about him anymore. Just take care of yourself, and maybe you can even help your mother out some."

"Maybe," Marie said.

Chapter Thirty-Nine

"Arlene, all this stuff just won't fit in here, sweetie," Norma said.

"It has to," Arlene said.

"It won't," Norma said louder.

"Norma, it has to fit. There's nothing else we can leave behind." Arlene brushed her hair back out of her eyes with the back of her hand. Her face was shiny with perspiration.

"Really? How about this beat-up ol' bronc saddle?" Norma said.

Arlene turned to look at Norma. She was jokin', wasn't she? Leave Lanny Ray's saddle? That would be the day.

They had spent the morning rearranging and trying to fit everything into the trunk of Norma's car. They had accumulated two suitcases and several boxes of Lanny Ray's and Angela's things, and now they were trying to squeeze the saddle in, too.

"He ain't ever going to use that saddle again, you know. His rodeoin' days are over. He'll be gimpin' around the rest of his life." Norma limped in a small circle to show how Lanny Ray would look.

Arlene and Angela couldn't help but laugh. Angela was sitting in a chair, watching the two women load their things into the trunk. It was already warm out, and the exertion wasn't helping. Norma flopped down on the lawn in a shady spot and lit a cigarette.

"It's going to be a long ol' trip home, I'll tell you that. We'll put the two sickly people in the back, and you and me will sit up front, Arlene. How's that?"

227

"Sounds good to me. We could tie Lanny Ray and his saddle to the roof of the car," Arlene said.

"Mom! Shame on you," Angela said.

It was indeed going to be a long trip home. It took more than a little while to get Lanny Ray in the backseat and in a position that didn't cause him severe pain somewhere in his body. Finally, he was settled into the corner of the backseat with his legs cockeyed so Angela could have the other corner of the seat. It would work for a while.

Arlene had handed off the shirt snap to Detective Glover the night before. He said there may come a time when Lanny Ray—or more likely, Angela—would be asked to be a witness in court if Olin's case went to trial. They would just have to wait and see what happened.

The detective had given Angela a little hug and told her she was the most courageous girl he had ever known. Angela had blushed with the compliment.

Angela had asked what would happen to Marie. When the detective explained what the agreement was, Angela spoke right up for Marie.

"She'll do fine. I know she will. There isn't anybody as strong and brave as Marie. She can do whatever she puts her mind to." Arlene and Norma both laughed. Angela didn't realize she could be talking about herself.

Once out on the road, the atmosphere in Norma's car was carefree. They, no doubt, were all thinking of home—of Jewel. With the windows down and the radio on, Arlene felt an overwhelming thankfulness for having her daughter sitting behind her, singing her heart out with the radio. She didn't care to make a big deal of it, but she was also glad that Lanny Ray was there. He had his head back against the seat with his eyes closed, and he looked peaceful. Maybe his pain had eased up.

They all did their best to stay in a good traveling mood and not get grumpy about the discomfort of all of them in the car. They stopped frequently to let Lanny Ray try to get comfortable and to get ice cream cones to cheer everybody up. Lanny Ray was generous with the money he had left in his wallet. Unfortunately, it was about to run out. All the motels, meals, and gas had taken their toll on his winnings. He had paid a large amount to the hospital and still owed more.

For a while, he grew melancholy in his own thoughts. He knew this was most likely his last rodeo run. He could be happy, in spite of everything else, that it was by far the best riding season he had ever had. He had ridden like a champ. Maybe it was because it was to be his last, or maybe it was because his daughter had been there to see him do so well.

CHAPTER FORTY

Angela thought for several minutes that she was dreaming. She would let herself drift back into sleep so she could savor the warm and blissful feeling. When her eyes finally opened and her hand felt the quilt beside her, she realized she wasn't dreaming at all. She was in her own bed, at home in Jewel. She didn't budge an inch. She lay perfectly still and let the contentment wrap around her.

When she finally sat up, she looked all around her room. Everything had a fresh look about it. Even her pictures on the walls and her chest of drawers. Everything seemed bright and new. She felt as if she had been away forever. Years. Her heart about burst with the joy of being home.

She could hear noises in the kitchen. Familiar noises. She had even missed those. They meant that Arlene was in the kitchen doing the morning things she always did. Angela could smell her mother's coffee perking on the stove. She left her bed and walked slowly through the door to the kitchen. When Arlene looked up and saw her there, she broke into the biggest smile and went to hug her daughter close.

"What are you going to do on your first day home, sweetie? You need more rest, you know."

"I'm going to walk to the river," Angela declared without a second's thought.

"Oh, Ang. I don't know if you should do that. The doctor said you shouldn't overdo things for a week or two," Arlene said.

"I won't. It's just a walk," Angela said. "I won't stay long."

It was the most beautiful walk to the river that Angela had ever taken. She missed absolutely nothing as she walked along. She was dazzled by every bright new yard flower and heard the tune of every chirpy bird in the neighborhood fruit trees. The smell of other people's breakfasts cooking drifted from open windows. She waved to Mattie Breams as she walked past her where she tended her yard but kept walking so she wouldn't have to talk right then. The sun was warm on her still bruised face. The bruises were an ugly shade of yellow-green by now, but the swelling was gone. Her right side still felt stiff and achy. But her head no longer hurt, and she felt wonderful, in spite of a little soreness.

She carefully climbed to the platform on the big slide at the river park. She perched there like a regal bird and took measure of her surroundings, as if to be sure all was still in its place. She let herself drift with the flow of the river's slow current and felt her body relax.

She thought of her father and wondered how he was doing. She remembered how it felt when they had driven into town and left Lanny Ray at his father's old house. Norma and Arlene had helped him to the door and carried his things up the walk to the porch. She and Lanny Ray had hugged a long, tight hug until he said he would see her soon and let go. It still seemed to Angela like he should have come with her and her mother to the little house on Opal Street. But he would be staying over there for the time being, and his sister, Rose, was coming to town to help him for a while. Angela could visit him whenever she wanted, as long as Arlene said it was okay.

Angela thought of Charlotte then. She hoped she was okay. Maybe Arlene would let her call Char on the phone soon. Maybe Charlotte really could come to Jewel to visit someday. And Billy . . . she had to admit she would sure like to see Billy again.

At home, Arlene answered the phone to hear her friend Norma's gusty voice on the line.

"How's our girl this morning?"

"Good as gold. She already went for a walk to the river. I didn't have the heart to say no," Arlene said.

"It's the best thing for her. Like medicine, you know? Lordy, is it ever good to be home. Well, I'm not actually home right now. I'm at the café. Looks like everything is all right around here. My kids even seemed happy to have me home, and the dogs alive, the café's still standin', so I guess we're okay."

"I have to go back to the Five and Dime tomorrow," Arlene said. "I sure will be glad when everybody gets through gossipin'. I bet the store will have more business tomorrow than it does on Christmas Eve. Every woman in town will need to run in and pick something up. I'll have to answer a million questions."

"Ha. You have no idea, hon. I been hidin' out in the kitchen as much as I can, but customers are flockin' in. Old Mrs. Lambert just charged right back here and stood over the grill with me. She was givin' me the third degree. She left when I asked her if she wanted a cookin' job." Norma laughed. "Gotta go, sweetie. Everybody in Jewel wants to eat breakfast out this morning."

"Norma, how in the world will I ever be able to pay you back for all you've done?"

"Oh, don't worry. I told you I would think of something." Norma hung up.

Epilogue

On the last day of August, 1958, Angela Jean Garrett turned thirteen years old. Arlene and Norma put together a birthday party for her down at the river park. Hot dogs, potato salad, and a three-layer chocolate cake with chocolate frosting were the fare of the day. There were fewer than twenty-five people there, most being adults. Norma's kids were there, of course, and Angela's best school friend, Joseph. There were a few other kids, but most were the younger children of Arlene and Norma's friends.

Arlene didn't invite her new friend, Grady. Angela had met him and liked him, but it was still just too awkward for Arlene. Grady had continued to pursue Arlene after she brought Angela home. She knew he liked her a lot. If Lanny Ray knew about Grady, and surely he must, he had yet to say anything. Arlene secretly hoped that Lanny Ray would be at least a little jealous.

It was a beautiful day under the shade of the big trees that grew along the Little Sweetwater River banks. Warm, but not so hot to be miserable. Both kids and adults splashed and cooled off in the tepid, shallow river water. The smallest kids played with the squirmy, black tadpoles that became entrapped in the long, brilliant-green moss that waved along the rocky edge of the water. Tiny frogs hopped for their lives. It was a pleasant and enjoyable day for everyone, except maybe Angela.

Being the center of attention made Angela uncomfortable. She avoided the rickety card table, overloaded with brightly wrapped gifts for her. She was embarrassed to open them in front of the partygoers. It wasn't that she behaved in an unfriendly way—she laughed and talked and played in the water—but she was feeling bashful. She was also beginning to be seriously worried.

She kept an eye out for one more guest to arrive. Lanny Ray was not there yet, and it was almost time to cut the birthday cake. As the minutes passed, she watched toward the dirt road that meandered down through a grove of cottonwoods to the park. More than once she noticed her mother was looking up there, too.

"Come on, Angela. Let's get this show on the road. I am dying' to know what all these presents are." That was Norma. She would be the one to give the party a kick in the pants. It was extremely hard for anyone to be in anything but a happy mood around Norma. She waved the cake spatula in the air and made the grand announcement to come and sing the birthday song.

Arlene stuck pink candles, thirteen of them, into the warm, gooey chocolate frosting and went in search of the matches. Angela gave in as graciously as she could. She mustered up a smile and stood at the end of the picnic table, waiting for everyone to gather and for Arlene to get the candles all lit up at the same time. With Norma leading, they all broke into an amusing rendition of "Happy Birthday." Just when Angela was about to inhale a long, deep gulp of air to blow the candles out, she glanced up and stopped in mid-breath. There stood Lanny Ray, leaning on a cane with his left hand and holding a little black-and-white dog in his right. The little dog wore a bright-red ribbon around its neck.

Lanny Ray had his big, charming smile on, and Angela heard Arlene behind her say, "Well, it's about darn time, Lanny Ray."

Lanny Ray hobbled to Angela and held the little dog out to her.

"Happy Birthday, Angela. Here, meet Tippy."

Angela was dumbfounded. Not a word would come. She took Tippy and hugged him to her, and he licked everywhere he could reach on her face. Everyone started laughing, and all the little kids crowded around to put a hand on the little dog. Angela's heart felt way too big for her chest, and tears of gratitude welled in her dark eyes. She finally had her own sweet dog.

Angela sought out her mother's face and was surprised, at first, to see a big smile and get a knowing nod. Then she understood. Her mom already knew about the little dog. She was in on the birthday surprise. Lanny Ray and then Arlene received the best hugs Angela could offer without squashing Tippy.

Finally, someone hollered about the cake being forgotten, and Angela blew out the few candles that were still flickering. Enormous hunks of chocolate cake were passed all around, and Angela asked Joseph if he would mind holding Tippy while she opened the rest of her gifts. Joseph accepted Tippy into his arms as if the little dog was precious and very breakable.

Eventually, the excitement died down, and people began to leave the park. Angela and Tippy walked along the river. He lapped the water and explored the rocky shore, poking his nose between rocks. When Angela moved away from the water, he followed on her heels.

Norma, Arlene, and Lanny Ray watched the thirteen-year-old girl and her dog move along the river.

"I just know this will help her heal," Arlene said. "She needs something to get that ache out of her little heart."

"She saw way too much. I will never forgive myself, you know. I hope I can make up for it. To her and you, too, Arlene."

"You folks have just got to quit kickin' this around. Just give her some time. That girl is going to end up bein' something great. You watch what I say," Norma said.

But Angela would have the memories for the rest of her life. The good and the ghastly. She would daydream about the girlish silliness of laughing with Charlotte, even as she grew older. She would also recoil from the horrific mind-picture of the silhouette of Olin in the big car's window on the night of poor Toby's murder.

All the rest of her memories from the summer of fifty-eight would ebb and flow, sometimes conjured, sometimes startlingly unexpected— all of them vital to the person she was then and the person she would come to be.

ACKNOWLEDGMENTS

This story, this book, began as a poem, and then developed into a short narrative that I wrote many years ago. Therefore, the list of people for whom I feel immense gratitude is a long one. Back in the days when I was falling in love with Cowboy and Western Poetry, my mentor, Virginia Bennett, who is an outstanding poet herself, made me believe that I had notions and reflections worth writing about. I honestly feel this book would not exist if not for her encouragement and example all that time ago.

Margo Metegrano—friend, master of CowboyPoetry.com, and true believer in *Summer of '58*—cheered me on, gave me boosts when I needed them, and never ever gave up on me. Ken and Betty Rodgers, first editors for both my poetry book, *Sometimes in the Lucias*, and *Summer,* convinced me that I had a good story to share and guided me from beginning to end.

I thank the readers of all the versions along the way, knowing that some might not have been the best reading material, but they read and responded politely anyway. I think friends Knute and Wendy Brekke were my very first readers, and I thank them for hanging in with me. Amy Hale Auker—poet, author and ranch woman—was one of the first to set eyes on a full manuscript (bless her heart) and still cheered me on. Thank you, Dave Stamey—friend, singer, and songwriter— who took time to read for me and whose input completely changed my book for the better. Thank you, Stephanie Davis, also an awesome singer, songwriter and fan of *Summer*, which she just happens to think should be made into a movie. Thank you, Jerry Dobrowski, my friend and website keeper, who was lucky to have read a recent, fixed-up manuscript and believed it was a great, original story. Rod Miller, Western and Cowboy poet and author of excellent stories and books, not only helped me with *my* book but also introduced me to Duke Pennell of Pen-L Publishing because he thought we were a good match.

Thank you to Duke and Kimberly Pennell, who stood by me and sent my book out into the world.

Thank you to my husband, Ron, who never seemed to doubt me and who bragged on my story, even before it became a book.

About the Author

Janice Gilbertson hails from the Santa Lucia Mountains in Western California where she lives with her husband and an assortment of critters. Only one or two crow-flown miles to the west lies the ranch where she was raised. Growing up in the '50s, a shy little girl with two older brothers, Janice learned how to entertain herself and developed a grand imagination. She was a conjurer of characters long before she began to put them on paper. Her love for all things Western, including the ranching lifestyle and eventually Cowboy and Western Poetry and story writing, have strongly influenced the story of the *Summer of '58*.

Dear Readers,
If you enjoyed this
book enough to review
it for Goodreads, B&N,
or Amazon.com, I'd
appreciate it!
Thanks, Janice

Find more great reads at
Pen-L.com

57658045R00151

Made in the USA
Charleston, SC
19 June 2016